THE FORGOTTEN

Demons, book 2

By Marina Simcoe

To my Captain

The Forgotten

Chapter 1

THEY WERE COMING FOR me.

I heard their footsteps down the corridor outside my cell. Closing my eyes for a moment, I inhaled deeply and prepared myself for what was to come.

The familiar dread hollowed my stomach. What was done to me in this place was wrong. All of it.

I had been abducted out of my bed and brought to this basement cell where they'd been keeping me ever since. At night, they took me to the large white room and locked me to an X-shaped cross. Then one of them—silent and impassive—touched my naked body, while thirteen others watched.

There was something dark and scorchingly dangerous in their stares that made my insides twist with terror at the same time as my body ached with desire building under the stranger's touch.

I couldn't accurately sort out my emotions in this place, but I was fairly certain that the shame I felt after each session on the cross had less to do with my exposing my naked body to the hungry stares of strangers and everything to do with my knowing that I shouldn't be enjoying it.

I hated them. They took my freedom and made me crave the shameful things they did to me.

With the sound of their footsteps approaching, anticipation filled me with tingling excitement. Immediately, a sharp stab of guilt for feeling this way triggered the usual disgust with myself.

I couldn't afford to risk losing myself to self-loathing, though. If I ever wanted to get out of here, I needed a sound mind and clear focus. Wasting my mental energy on self-pity would get me nowhere.

My abductors never hurt me physically. I got fed regularly. If I could keep my sanity intact, I reasoned, I could last here long enough to find a way to get out.

Because I diligently counted days, I knew that I'd been here for exactly five weeks and three days. Every one of those days was a mirror image of another—breakfast, lunch, sponge bath from a bucket of warm water, and a mind-blowing orgasm in front of *them* before dinner.

I was hardly ever able to come during sex before. Yet, here I was, writhing on that cross, burning with lust, coming on the vibrator in the stranger's hand every single time they took me to that room.

And now, I was looking forward to doing it all over again tonight.

How could I be enjoying any of this? I needed to get out of here before I'd completely succumbed to the depravity of this place.

As the sound of their footsteps moved closer, I wiped my sweaty palms on the sides of the dreary cotton dress they made me wear, and jumped to my feet.

Normally, there were three of them at night, wearing grey uniforms, their faces covered behind masks with only a pair of narrow slits for their eyes. Incredibly strong and coldly impassive, they acted more like automatons than people.

The group of thirteen in the white room never wore masks or uniforms. All male, without exception, they were young and stunningly attractive. The one in the middle normally had a loose robe on—the flowing material glaringly white against his dark skin. I'd caught him gesturing what appeared to be orders. By the way the rest of them obeyed, I figured he was the one in authority.

None of them showed any kind of emotion while watching me come. Frozen, motionless, they resembled beautiful statues, further confusing me about the actual purpose of it all.

One night, I managed a glance at them through the haze of arousal, right before an orgasm was ripped from me. I saw the thirteen pairs of eyes light up bright red. The glow flared and ebbed, terrifying me, then they lowered their eyelids and threw their heads back as if in a silent prayer.

I screamed as horror cut through the pleasure of my climax.

After that, they'd made me wear a velvet blindfold whenever I entered the white room, but the memory of the blood-red eyes in their eerily beautiful faces still kept me up at night. Later, I also noticed the eyes of the uniformed guards flash white-blue on more than one occasion. And by now, I had developed a strong suspicion that they were not really *people* at all.

The sound of their footsteps halted. The cell door slid open with a swishing noise, and two guards walked in.

Instead of a third uniformed guard, however, a man stepped into my cell.

My heart skipped in shock.

Wearing a charcoal grey suit and a navy-blue tie, he was average-looking, with neatly styled, receding blond hair.

"Miss Jones?" he asked, with a slight European accent.

German?

After five weeks of a surreal universe of concrete walls, grey armour suits, and bizarrely handsome men with hungry stares, the wool-suited figure of the man in my cell did not belong here. His sudden appearance was jarring.

My legs gave in from my astonishment, sending me back to the mattress.

"Who are you?"

"I'm Steffen Keller." He threw a nervous glance at the guards behind him. "Nice to meet you, Miss Jones."

"Kitty."

"Pardon me?"

"Everyone calls me Kitty, you may as well. You're not one of *them*," I stated the obvious. "What are you doing here? Did you come to take me home?"

He gave me no reason to believe he was on my side, but the fact that he looked different from the ones who imprisoned me made hope rise in me.

I jumped to my feet again, determined not to let him exit the cell without me.

"You will go home, Miss Jones. Eventually." He crossed his arms in front of him, and I noticed a grey file folder in his hands.

"When?"

"Technically, you're free as of this moment. However—"

"I'm free? As of right now?" I pushed past him to the door to test his claim. The guards moved towards each other to block my way. Their shoulder armour clanked together.

Frustrated, I slammed my fists in their chest plates. Neither of them moved an inch.

I spun on my heel to face the liar in the suit.

"They obviously haven't been informed about that." I flipped my thumb at the guards behind me and stretched up to my full height—all five feet and one half of an inch. The half of an inch was important if you had not that many to go around in the first place.

"Well. For one, it's a long way from here to your home in . . ." He glanced inside his folder quickly. "Seattle, in The United States. We will need some time to arrange for appropriate transportation for you."

"Where are we?"

"Canada. Yukon Territory."

That *was* a long way from home.

"I'm afraid you'll have to stay here for the time being."

"How long?"

"A few days, I imagine. It depends on the results of your assessment by the team of professionals. Our hosts here . . ." He gestured towards the guards.

"*Hosts?*" I nearly screamed. Just calling them that had to be criminal.

"Please, calm down." A note of steel warning in his voice forced me to pause.

Afraid he'd leave if I made a scene, I counted my breaths to stop my lashing out at him. The effort proved almost painful.

"Fine. Who are *they?*" I tipped my chin at the armour suits behind me. "And who are *you?*" It was becoming obvious Keller must be in some form of collusion with my abductors.

He inhaled deeply, rubbing his forehead.

"You have to excuse me, Miss . . . um, Kitty. This is the first time I've had to do something like this . . ."

"Like what? Setting a person free? Visiting a captive? Talking to a woman? You'll need to explain more than that." I crossed my arms, struggling to control the anger and anxiety rising in me again. "Why can't I leave right now?"

He shifted uneasily and rubbed some perspiration from his forehead, mumbling, "I told them it was best to wait," under his breath.

"Wait for what?"

"For the team to get here. With a bunch of professional counselors in tow. I'm not qualified to do this." He waved his hand in my direction, clear irritation in his expression. "Can I get a chair in here? Something to sit on?" he threw back to the guards by the door.

I noted, not without some surprise, that one of the guards immediately left the room, only to promptly return with a metal chair.

Keller sat, stretching his legs in front of him. "Your situation is not normal. Women taken by this particular group don't, usually, get to leave."

"You mean I was supposed to stay here forever?" I balled my hands into fists to prevent them from shaking as dread trembled through me.

"Things have changed." He waved me off. "Everyone is being released. All you'll have to do is to remain quiet about what happened to you here."

"Why would I?" I snapped. "Kidnapping and forceful confinement are serious crimes. So is sexual assault. Those responsible will have to be punished."

"You're not capable to bring any punishment on their heads, Kitty."

"The police—"

"—know nothing about *them* and never will. Trust me. The best thing in your situation is to stick with the plan of your release, get back to your life, and never speak about this place or the *creatures* who populate it."

Creatures?

"Why should I believe anything you're saying?"

"I hold an official position with the Priory of Grimien."

"Never heard of it."

"And you never would have, under normal circumstances. The Priory is a secret organization. It was created with a sole purpose to gain and keep control of the . . . um, individuals who took you."

"Well, you've been doing a poor job of controlling them then. How are they getting away with all of this?" My voice rose, as my patience thinned. "Who are they?"

He drew in a deep breath.

"They are . . . not from this world, Kitty."

"What?"

"Surely, you've noticed some unusual things about them during your time here."

"You mean besides them being perverts who like to watch?" I scoffed.

"Believe me, they can do far more harmful things than watching." His gaze shifted back to the guards again. "They've been part of our world for over a millennium, and they had wreaked havoc during their early centuries on Earth, before we found a reliable way to control them."

"Who are they?" I insisted.

"Demons." He leaned to me from his chair, his voice low. "In flesh and blood."

Was he out of his mind?

I shrunk back, all the way to the wall, worried for my own safety now, being one on one with a clearly insane man who seemed to honestly believe in demons.

'Surely, you've noticed some unusual things about them.'

Their eyes.

The blood-red glow I'd witnessed once. The flashing blue lights I'd noticed on more than one occasion. Could there be a more sane, *normal* explanation to that?

"You don't have to believe me, Kitty. Actually, it is irrelevant if you do or don't." Mister Keller leaned back in his chair. "All I want from you is your cooperation in keeping their existence a secret from the general population."

"Why would I do that?"

I definitely need to get to the closest police station as soon as I'm able, to let the proper authorities sort this mess out.

"Because, really, you don't have a choice. What good would it do for you to go public with your disclosure? No one would believe you. If you insist, you would be likely declared insane."

"There is plenty of evidence of their existence. This place—"

"Is a private property with no complaints against it. I guarantee you will never be able to obtain so much as a search warrant for it. The Priory would make sure of it."

"Why would any human organization cover up the crimes of these . . . *demons*?"

"This should not be of your concern. You will be provided a suitable compensation, appropriate counseling, and means to return to normal life as soon as possible. From this point on, our organization will guarantee your protection from the demons here."

"How?"

"The Priory agreed to go forward with a more agreeable alternative to our previous arrangement with them, which was suggested by their Councils. By the way, you wouldn't happen to have any particular affection for one of your guards?"

"What? God, no!"

"Good." He turned to leave. "I'll leave you rest then. Needless to say, there won't be any more . . . um, nightly sessions."

"Wait!" I jumped to my feet, spurred by a bout of panic. "I'm free—so I want to leave now."

"There is no suitable accommodation anywhere in the vicinity for you. You'll have to remain here for the time being—"

"No." I caught up with him at the door and got hold of his sleeve.

I was afraid that once the door closed behind him, it would be as if he'd never come here at all. Everything would go back to the way it was. Still essentially a prisoner, I had nothing but his empty promise of freedom at this point.

"They assured us that your mental state was sound enough to handle this news, Kitty. That you're stable." His voice sounded accusing. He became visibly more uncomfortable the longer I held on to his sleeve. "You are being released. It's good news, isn't it?" He tugged at his arm in an effort to pry the fabric from my clenching fingers.

"Do *they* know I'm free?" I gestured at the silent figures by the door.

"Absolutely. They'll leave with me, and no one will bother you tonight. Or any night, for that matter." He made another unsuccessful attempt to free his sleeve from my grip. "The door to your cell will remain unlocked. And you're free to move around the facility."

"I want to go outside." The sudden opportunity to see the open sky made my head spin. "Yes, I want to go for a walk."

"Now?"

"Right now."

"Um, I'm sure a quick walk outside could be arranged." Mister Keller threw a desperate look towards the guards as if asking them for assistance.

"I will inquire." The deep, rough voice came from inside one of the helmets so unexpectedly that I gasped in shock.

I had never heard them speak. Ever. Hearing one of them now had a similar effect to suddenly discovering that the walls could talk.

"There you go." Obvious relief spread over Keller's face. "I assure you, Kitty, as of this moment, you're simply a visitor here not a captive. A guest, if you will. You're free to move around as you please, order whatever food you like, we . . . *they* will do their best to accommodate you. And, as I said, there will be no more of what they call *feedings*."

"Feedings?"

"Er, the nightly sessions."

Why *feedings*? It made no sense. As far as I could tell, no one actually *ate* in the white room while I was there.

"Good night, Kitty." Mister Keller finally freed himself from me and stepped out of the cell.

"But—"

"Whatever questions you may still have will be answered by your counselors." He hurried down the hallway.

The door remained open for a few moments. I could run after him, grab him again, demand more answers, more proof. Deep inside, however, I understood that he wouldn't give me more information than he was prepared to give. The most likely result of my outburst would be me being subdued and locked up in my cell again.

'Stable.'

That's what they thought of me. All my efforts to retain my ability to think and analyze hinged on one thing—hoping to be free one day. I held on to it as to a lifeline, because I knew that once that hope was gone, my sanity would quickly follow.

If what Keller just told me was true, I might be closer to freedom now than I'd ever been. A meltdown now would only hinder my situation.

With a deep inhale, I closed my eyes, reining the panicky feeling under control. Then I heard the guard exit and the door swish shut, ruining my attempts to remain calm.

"Hey!" I rushed to the door and slammed my fists into the metal surface. "How about my walk!"

"I'll return shortly, with the appropriate clothing for you," a voice boomed from behind the door, then a pair of coffee-coloured eyes met mine through the barred window. "Wait here." Hearing his voice rendered me speechless. I still struggled with the idea of *them* actually communicating.

The sound of his retreating steps in the distance let my thoughts drift back to what I had just learned.

Demons.

Chill prickled my skin despite the warmth inside the cell.

Could that actually be true?

Chapter 2

WHEN THE DOOR CLOSED after Keller and the guards, I realized there was no usual click of the lock.

Was it true? The door was to be unlocked now?

I rushed to it and gripped the window bars with both hands. Feet planted firmly on the concrete floor, my whole body shook with strain as I struggled to slide the heavy metal door aside. It wouldn't budge, not by a millimeter. Now more than ever I really wished to be taller, bigger, stronger.

Huffing and puffing, I wrestled with the massive door long enough to hear the footsteps again. Then a gloved hand took hold of the bar right in front of my face.

The door slid open, smooth and swift, knocking me off balance. I would have fallen, had I not held on to the bars. A uniformed guard steadied me by grabbing my elbow as he walked in.

Demon?

I leaped away from him, yanking my arm out of his hand.

"Is it true?" I asked, keeping a safe distance from him. "Are you really a demon?"

"Yes." His voice sounded less raspy this time but still impassive. "Your walk has been approved. When would you like to go?"

I spotted a bundle of clothes and a pair of boots under his arm—grey flannel and what seemed to be a hooded winter jacket.

"How about right now?" I narrowed my eyes at him in challenge, but he nodded silently and handed the clothes to me, without arguing.

"Really?" I stared at the offering in his hands, still afraid to believe it wasn't some kind of a trap. "Just like that?"

He stared back at me, not much understanding in those dark eyes.

What exactly did *demon* mean?

The images that came to mind—someone red-skinned and winged, with horns, tail and goat hooves—didn't match with the tall figure in front of me dressed in some kind of modern armour.

There is no way that helmet could house horns, and the boots seemed to conceal a pair of normal human feet.

"Are you . . . You're not going to hurt me in any way, right?" I asked hesitantly, giving in to the urge to hear his reassurance. I'd made no move to accept the clothes from him yet.

"No." He walked around me and placed them on the mattress. "The sole purpose of my being here now is to assist you. If you've changed your mind about taking a walk tonight—" He went for the door.

"Wait." I stopped him on his way out, all concerns forgotten for now. "I'll go. I'll get dressed."

Hurriedly, I snatched a pair of grey underwear from the pile of clothes and put them on, feeling sudden appreciation for the familiar sense of security. I realized that wearing nothing but a loose, short dress all this time had made me feel exposed and therefore more vulnerable.

I threw a glance over my shoulder to make sure the guard hadn't left. As could've been expected he hadn't the decency to turn around to give me any privacy and just stood there, staring at me blankly. Carefully keeping my back to him, I ripped my dress over my head and put on the clothes he'd brought.

Getting properly dressed—even if just in a pair of long-sleeved pajamas, with socks, bra and underwear—brought back some feeling of normalcy.

"I'm ready," I announced, attempting to find a way to roll up the long sleeves of the winter jacket that was ridiculously big for me.

"Sorry, it was made for a man," came from inside the helmet, and I noticed he'd been watching my struggle with the sleeves. "We don't have a jacket in your size on the base."

"But you do have women's boots," I noted, shoving my feet into the winter boots that turned out to be only a size too big.

He just shrugged his armoured shoulders in reply and stepped aside, letting me exit.

For the first time ever, I walked out of the cell fully dressed and with only one guard to accompany me. And when we came to the turn in the corridor that would lead me to the white room on the left, he gently placed his hand on the small of my back to steer me to the right.

Up a set of concrete stairs, we entered a wide hallway with a solid metal door. Another armoured guard was positioned near it. He froze at the sight of us.

"We are going for a walk," my guard explained casually. Coming from him, the sentence sounded bizarre if not comical. I would have laughed had I not been this nervous.

The guard at the door just stood there staring through the slits of his helmet at us, in utter silence. It appeared to take him a moment to process the words, but finally he stirred.

"You can't take a *live* Source off the property, Handler." His voice sounded even more rough and raspy than my guy's. Obviously, they weren't used to talking much.

A live source? What did it mean?

"I have permission. We'll stay within the fence," my companion replied.

The guard at the entrance paused again, as if needing some time to absorb what he had just heard. Finally, he nodded.

"I will notify the Soldier at the gate that you're outside." He opened the door then pushed a button to make the barred gate slide open, too.

Bars, locks, gates, and guards—all of this befitted a high-security prison. Was I really soon to be released? How much could I really trust Keller on that, with his shifty eyes?

We stepped outside, and a wave of fresh air washed over my face, bringing all my thoughts to a halt. Immediately lightheaded, I blindly grasped at the arm of the guard at my side, forgetting who or *what* he was for a moment.

The sun had already set behind the horizon, but the sky was still the light-grey of twilight. A pleasant breeze moved the air. It was a little cool out here, but the weather definitely didn't warrant a winter jacket.

"What date is it?" I asked the guard.

"September," came the reply with a slight delay.

"Date?" I specified.

The pause stretched longer this time.

"I—I'm not sure."

"You're not sure?" I turned to face him, my eyebrow cocked in disbelief. "You don't know what the date is today?"

He silently shook his head.

The breeze stirred the flyaway hair around my face, and I inhaled deeply, savoring the fresh smell of wet earth. It must have rained. I glanced up just in time to notice the white-blue lights blink through the slits of his helmet.

"What is that? The thing you all do with your eyes?" I let go of his arm and stepped away from him to put some distance between us. "I've seen you do it before."

"Me?"

It was a good question. I couldn't be sure that the lights I'd seen earlier flashed in the eyes of this particular guard. Actually, I wasn't even sure if I'd seen this one before today at all.

"This is my first day of being assigned to you," he continued.

"One of you, then. Some of you I mean. Why do your eyes light up like that?"

"It happens when we feed."

"Feed?" I frowned.

"I use your positive emotions as nourishment," he explained evenly. "Your joy at fresh air, in this instance."

"How is it possible?" I took another step to the side, putting some more space between us. "Is that what you've been doing to me all this time here? That's why I'm here?"

The struggle to retain my sanity suddenly got harder. At the moment, I wasn't sure what was bigger in me—fear or utter disbelief.

"No need to be afraid, please." He extended his arm to me, but I recoiled from his reach. "I can only take your emotions once they've left your body. It's not harmful."

'They can do more harmful things . . .' Keller's words suddenly came to mind.

No matter what anyone said, the best thing was to stay cautious and guarded. The only one I could fully trust around here was myself.

"Let's just . . . walk." I gestured at the gravel path that led from the entrance door and seemed to circle the sprawling property.

Since I'd gained the chance to be outside, I figured I'd use this opportunity to scan the area for any escape route, in case either demons or the people who made deals with them backed off from their promises.

"What's your name?" I asked as we moved along the path, just to keep him talking while I took in every detail of the grey one-story building where I'd been held all this time. It didn't seem to be as large from the outside, but I suspected the place was probably a few times its supposed size due to the expansive basement. "You do have some kind of a name, don't you?"

In the receding light, I noted the tall concrete fence in the distance that enclosed the grounds and stretched in both directions as far as the eye could see.

"Yes. I do have a name," he replied finally. His answer was stilted, just like the speech of the guard at the entrance door. "It's Garrett. My human name is Garrett."

"Your *human* name?" My gaze returned to his mask. The building's outdoor lights flickered to life at that moment, instantly shrouding in darkness anything outside of their reach. Through the slits of his mask, I saw his dark-brown eyes squint from the sudden light. "Do you have *non-human* ones?"

"Except for Raim, the Grand Master, all of us have two names. I have a demon name, too. But it's not advisable to share it with humans, even though we're allowed to talk to you now."

"Why not?"

He cupped the back of his neck in a very human gesture of indecision.

"It gives you power over us, I believe. The power to summon us to do your bidding. I . . . I don't remember exactly how." He spread his arms to the side in display of frustration. "Even if I did, I'm not sure I could explain it eloquently enough. I'm too hungry for that."

"Hungry? Didn't you just eat my *joy of fresh air*?" I retorted, still unsure how to feel about his way of obtaining his *nourishment*, or if it was even true.

"I need much more than that to regain my full mental power. Taking your emotions simply allows me to stay awake and to function."

A sudden understanding brought me to a stop.

"Garrett. What was happening in the white room? The red lights in the eyes of the men in there? Were they also *feeding?*"

Wasn't that the exact word used by Keller to describe the proceedings?

"Yes," Garrett confirmed my suspicion.

"Why red lights, though?"

"The Council feeds on sexual energy, which reflects red in our eyes."

So, they weren't perverts watching after all—they were demons feeding.

The realization didn't change anything. All of it was still wrong—them feeding off me . . . and me enjoying it.

"Will I really be allowed to go home?"

He took his time to answer, but I didn't get the impression that the delay came from his hesitation to tell me the truth. Talking to Garrett generally proved rather painful. It felt like my words needed time to physically seep through his helmet before their meaning could be absorbed by his brain.

"To my knowledge," he started finally, "the decision between both Councils and The Priory has been made. All Sources are to be released from the base as soon as they are ready to return to their lives."

"Oh, I'm ready! I'm so freaking ready—"

"It's not up to me to release you, Kitty."

Was it a shade of regret I sensed in his voice muffled by the helmet? A hint of compassion?

"Garrett, can you produce your own emotions?"

"No." This time the answer came fairly quick. And definite.

So, whatever I thought I sensed in him, must have been simply my imagination, distorting the reality.

"I'd like to go back, Garrett."

He nodded and offered me his arm to lead me to the entrance. The walk and fresh air had made me lightheaded. After a moment of hesitation, I leaned on him for support.

Chapter 3

INSTEAD OF TAKING ME back to my cell, Garrett led me to a large bathroom I hadn't seen before. There was no sink or a toilet—just a white tub in the centre, filled to the brim with fragrant bubbles.

"You can take a bath before going to bed." He took my humongous jacket off for me. "I'll be back for you when you're done."

This was highly unusual, but Garrett exited before I had a chance to ask him any questions. I watched the windowless door slide close behind him, then turned back to the bathtub in the middle of the white tiled floor.

Fragrant steam rose from the snowy-white foam, beckoning me.

Maybe this was one of the signs that things had changed around here? Just as Keller said, I was a visitor here, not a prisoner anymore, and guests were allowed to take baths.

I kicked off my boots and padded around a small wooden table next to the tub. A folded towel and a basket of toiletries sat on top.

The water under the foam felt pleasantly hot when I dipped my hand in to test it, and I promptly got out of the grey pajamas and into the tub. A moan escaped me as I soaked in the fragrant warmth. I had forgotten how wonderful a hot bath felt.

With another happy moan, I slid all the way in, dipping my face and my head under the water too, then washed my hair thoroughly.

I stayed until the water in the tub started to cool and the skin on my fingertips pruned. Finally, with a lazy stretch, I got out of the tub reluctantly and unfolded the white, fluffy towel.

A faint blue flash to the side caught my eye, startling me. Quickly, I swept the room with my gaze, catching another flicker behind the ornate mesh covering the walls before all went dark again except for the dim yellowish glow from the sole light bulb in the ceiling.

My heart skipped, as a chill of suspicion prickled along my spine.

The blue light from behind the mesh appeared identical to the one flashing in the eyes of demons—I was being watched.

I had often been watched—openly while on the cross, through the bars of the door to my cell. Even during my walk outside, I had Garrett keeping an eye on me. This, however, felt like the biggest intrusion of my privacy. I hadn't been warned. In fact, I had every reason to believe I was alone.

Judging by the location of the white-blue flashes, there were more than one of them there. Two? Five? Thirteen?

Feeling suddenly exposed and vulnerable, I wrapped the towel tightly around me and clutched it to my chest.

The door to the bathroom opened that very moment, letting a uniformed guard in. I shrunk back to the tub, striving to stay in the middle of the room and away from him and the walls.

"It's me, Kitty," came the somber voice of Garrett from behind the mask. "I'll take you back to your cell if you're ready." He crouched to pick up my clothes and boots from the floor.

"There is . . . someone. Behind the walls? Isn't there?"

"They are hungry." Impassive like always, he stepped to the side, signaling for me to leave.

"So much for the promise of no more feedings, huh?" I hurried along the corridor next to him.

"It's different—"

"Hardly. I wasn't warned . . . or asked if I'd be okay with it."

"You weren't being harmed. Not even touched."

"It's still wrong, Garrett. Secretly watching me undress—" I shook my head in frustration. How was I to explain to this emotionless demon that this blatant violation of privacy went against all human ethics? What did he care, anyway?

"Would it be better if you knew about it beforehand, Kitty?" I could have sworn I caught a note of genuine interest in his previously monotone voice. "Would you have agreed to being watched then?"

He stopped, waiting for my answer.

"Honestly? No, I wouldn't. But I would've thought more of you if you gave me the choice and treated me with any kind of respect. One of the differences between a visitor and a captive is freedom of choice, Garrett." I couldn't believe I had to explain these basic things to someone who wasn't a child. I knew very little about these demons, but they seemed to know even less about humans.

"What would make you agree?" He inclined his head. "Anything?"

"Agree to being watched? Nothing. I like my privacy when I bathe. Like most people do, actually."

"What if you knew that the joy you felt at taking a bath would help several of us function through the excruciating pain ravaging our bodies every minute of every day?"

"Pain?" I tried to search for his eyes through the slits of his helmet, but the dim lighting in the corridor left them in the shadows. "Is that really what you experience?"

Gingerly, as if to avoid aggravating a physical injury, he rolled his shoulder and slowly stretched his neck.

"Yes."

I had no obligation to have any feelings of compassion for my captors and every reason to hate them. Garrett was one of them.

Still, I couldn't help but ask, "Does taking my emotions act like some sort of a painkiller for you?"

"It cools the flames of agony. Makes it easier to breathe, to think." The somber note in his quiet voice tugged at something inside me.

Immediately, a brief series of blue sparks illuminated the slits of his helmet.

"Your positive emotions bring relief and give us energy to go on." He drew in some air and rolled his shoulders back. "Even if temporarily. There is no other way for a demon to thrive but to feed off humans."

"What will happen to all of you now that we're being released?"

Worry and mistrust rose in me again. The way it had shaped out to be—the demons needed my emotions. Letting me go was against their best interests.

"I—I'm not on the Council, Kitty. My knowledge on their plans is limited. I trust there are some other arrangements being made to keep the army fed."

"An army of demons?"

"That's what we are. We are all soldiers under the orders of the Councils."

"Whom do you fight?"

"No one. Not anymore. We have been under the terms of a peace treaty with humans for . . . a while now."

I open my mouth for more questions. The more I learned, the more I needed to know, it seemed.

"Kitty," Garrett stopped me. "It's way past your usual bed time already. And I still need to feed you dinner."

"What?" I felt a smile tug at my lips at his words. "You sound like my nanny."

"I have been trained to take care of you. That's all I know how to do now."

Chapter 4

I LAY ON THE MATTRESS in my cell. The lights had been dimmed for the night, but I guessed they would be turned back on to daytime brightness soon enough—between the visit from Keller, the walk and the bath, my evening must have stretched out into the early morning.

Sleep evaded me, though. Recent events had been spinning through my head, as I was trying to make sense of everything I'd seen and heard.

Demons or humans. Councils or The Priory. Could I trust whatever promises came from either of them?

My conversation with Garrett had planted seeds of understanding and even something akin to compassion in me. It also showed that their way of thinking differed from ours.

I got up and moved my jacket and boots closer to the mattress, just in case.

In case of what?

No matter what they had told me about freedom, as long as I stayed here, I still remained in their absolute power. I had no control over anything here. The uncertainty fed my anxiety.

Giving up on sleep, I nervously paced around my cell then stopped in front of the door. When he left, I'd asked Garrett to leave it ajar. Otherwise what was the point in keeping it unlocked if I still couldn't open it?

Would they let me walk out of here, on my own?

Determined to test the promise of freedom, I threw the jacket on and slid my feet into the boots then shoved the heavy door open.

Once out of my cell, I headed into the direction of the stairs to the ground floor and then to the exit Garrett and I had used earlier.

The guard at the door blocked my way.

"I'm free now. I wish to take another walk." I lifted my chin up.

He stared at me for a moment. "It's not safe."

"I'll be fine. I'll make sure to stay within the fence," I repeated Garrett's words from the last time.

"It's too dark." The guard shook his head.

"I'll stay where it's lit."

"Too cold." He wouldn't give up.

"Really?" I replied, sarcastically, and pointed at my jacket. "I have warm clothes. If it gets too cold, I'll come back."

He seemed to ponder my words for a moment, staring at my jacket.

"Walking outside is not allowed at this hour."

"Who makes these rules?" I snapped. Frustration made it impossible to remain patient and calm.

"Raim."

Garrett had mentioned this name.

"The Grand Master?"

"Yes."

"Is it the one with the preference for white robes?"

"Grand Master wears the robe sometimes. Yes. However, I cannot speak to his preferences—"

"I don't care about that."

"But you said—"

"Never mind." I let out a sigh. The fight had fizzled out of me. I'd witnessed the absolute obedience of the guards to the demon in white and realized I had no chance of winning here.

"It's not safe for you to walk alone outside," the guard repeated mechanically, bringing the argument back where it started.

"Fine," I threw over my shoulder on my way to the stairs to the basement. "But I will come back tomorrow. When it's not *too dark* or *too cold*."

Instead of going back to my cell, though, I decided to explore the basement. I didn't think I'd be able to fall asleep tonight, anyway. And the knowledge of the layout might become useful if they ended up backing off on their promise to release me and I had to plan an escape after all.

The corridors seemed endless. The same grey concrete walls and bare light bulbs for what felt like hundreds and hundreds of yards, broken only by the occasional metal door with a barred window.

Cautiously, I peeked through each window, relieved and disappointed to see just empty mattresses inside. Relieved, because they didn't seem to be that many captives sharing my underground prison. Disappointed, because I could really use an honest talk with another human being right now.

After taking a few turns, I contemplated going back before I got lost in this concrete maze when another turn made me almost trip over a pair of long legs stretched across the floor. I leaped back in alarm, noticing the grey combat boots worn by the guards.

"Shh, Kitty. It's me." I recognized Garrett's gloomy cadence in the quiet whisper. "Don't be scared."

"What are you doing here?" Pressing both hands to my chest, I tried to calm down my racing heart.

"Waiting for the morning to come," he replied calmly.

"Here, on the floor?" I asked in a loud whisper. "Don't you have a bedroom? A bed?"

"I don't sleep." He shook his head. "But Simone needs it. And she doesn't fall asleep if I'm not here."

"Who is Simone?" My voice rose above a whisper, and he shushed me immediately by bringing his finger to the mesh part of the helmet over his mouth.

"She's just calmed down. Please, don't wake her up."

I nodded and crouched in front of him.

"Who is Simone, Garrett?" I repeated softly.

"She is my previous Source." He gestured over his shoulder, and I just noticed that he was sitting with his back against another metal door. "Raim only moved me to be your Handler this morning. Simone was my Source for months, but I only learned her name yesterday. *Simone*. I think it's the most beautiful name I've ever heard."

I rose to my feet to peek through the bars on the window. A small figure, with a dark mess of thin braids on her head, curled on the mattress with her back to the door. The row of metal buttons on her dress gleamed dimly in the semi-darkness of the cell.

"Does she know what you are?" I lowered myself to the floor next to Garrett. Somehow, the warmth in his voice when he talked about Simone put me more at ease in his company.

"I told her my name as soon as it was allowed, but since I've been moved, I can't see her through the day anymore."

"How long have you been her . . . um, *Handler*? That's what it's called?"

He nodded.

"Several months. Since an incident here at the base a few months ago, Grand Master has been changing Handlers and Sources often. You had four before me, I believe. But I managed to remain with Simone all this time. And now, she doesn't want to see me anymore." He shifted on the floor, bending one leg to place his forearm on his knee. "She requested a Janitor bring her meals." He sounded . . . crestfallen.

I couldn't help but ask, "You said you can't feel emotions?"

"We can't *create* them. Doesn't mean we can't recognize them or experience some of them."

He remained silent while I pondered his answer for a moment.

"So, if Simone doesn't want to see you, why are you here?"

"I respect her request and don't enter her cell. But I know that she is scared, lonely, and sad. She cries. A lot. She only seems to calm down when she knows I'm here. So, I come here. Every night."

"Why? Why do you care if she sleeps or not?"

"Because I want her to have balance inside, to be calm . . . happy?"

"To make more happy emotions for you to take?"

"*Skim* not *take,*" he corrected. Apparently, the terminology was important. "And no, I'm not allowed to feed on her emotions now that I'm no longer her Handler."

"Why is it important for you to keep Simone happy then?"

"Why?" He propped his forehead on his hand, seemingly genuinely puzzled by my question. "I—I don't know . . . There is often just muddy fog inside her, but a few weeks after she got here, she started recognizing me. I noticed that my presence brought her a hint of comfort. Once, I even saw her . . . smile."

The reverence in his voice made me wish I could see his face. Could this demon, who seemed barely a step up from a soulless robot, be capable of this depth of emotion?

"It was . . . magical, Kitty, when she smiled. Like watching sunrays flicker through the leaves deep in the forest. The tiny morsel of happiness I got to skim then was the most delicious thing I've ever tasted."

"But you wouldn't be allowed to taste it."

"I don't care. I just want to see it shine inside her . . . to light up her face again."

"Why doesn't she want to see you? Have you done something to her?"

"No . . . Um, yes. I have. Whatever was required from me to do as her Handler. I can see that she detests this place. I'm afraid she sees me as a part of it."

We sat in silence for a few moments. Starting to sweat under my jacket, I shifted to unzip it. My movement must have brought Garrett out of his thoughts.

"Do you think there is any hope at all that Simone would ever let me close again?" he asked me unexpectedly.

"Well, since we're supposedly all free now. Wouldn't she leave here soon?"

"No." He shook his head. "Not Simone. She can't leave. I won't let it happen." He leaped to his feet and faced the door then grabbed on to the bars in the window leaning his forehead against them. "I'll fight the Council . . . The Priory . . ."

"Garrett," I called softly, getting up from the floor too. "It's not up to any Councils or Priories here. If we're truly being released then it's only up to Simone herself whether or not she wants you anywhere near her. You can't *force* her to stay. If you try, you'll most certainly lose her for good. She needs to *want* to stay with you. That's how it works with humans."

"What can I do to make her want it? What would make you want to stay with someone like me?"

Everything inside me rebelled at once at the mere thought of staying in this place for any reason. However, I realized his interest lay with Simone's motivations, not mine, and made an effort to come up with an objective answer. "Well, I guess if I really cared about the man . . . the demon, I mean. Yes. I would need to care about him enough for the feeling to outweigh the animosity towards this place . . . and your kind."

"I have to make Simone care about me for her to stay with me?" The hope in his voice was almost palpable, leaving me no choice but to root for him.

"Really, Garrett, all you can do is show her that you're someone worth caring for. Treat her with respect. Give her a choice. And if she decides to leave, let her go. You can't force love, caring or affection. You can only invite them."

I wasn't sure if he heard me—his attention remained solely on Simone as he stared at her through the window.

Then I heard him whisper, "Do you think once she is free from here, she'll learn how to laugh again?"

Chapter 5

I SHOULD'VE ASKED GARRETT for a proper breakfast.

The thought of a coffee and a muffin made my mouth water as I entered my cell. I seriously considered turning around to give him my request, instead of having to face another day with a stomach full of green goo.

A dark figure rose from a crouch by my mattress. Dim light reflected off his uniform.

"Garrett?"

Had he taken some shortcut to get here before me?

"Shh." The demon brought a gloved finger to the mesh of his helmet.

A pair of arms suddenly circled me from behind. A hand covered my mouth to muffle the scream of panic ready to burst out of me.

Thrashing in the grip of whoever grabbed me from behind, I arched my back and kicked my feet violently. Twisting my body, I managed to knock one arm off me, almost getting away from him.

"The shot. Give her the shot," a hissing whisper reached me. The uniformed demon rushed to me, and the sting of a needle burned the side of my neck. The hand at my mouth pressed more firmly, silencing my scream of pain.

What's happening?

Why?

Terror exploded through my brain in bursts, each wave decreasing in its intensity, muffled by the numbing darkness descending over me.

Until all my senses shut down completely, plunging me into oblivion.

THROBBING PAIN POUNDED inside my head. The pressure threatened to explode into full-blown agony as awareness slowly trickled in.

I lay on my side, my arm numb and trapped under me. To free it, I had to turn over but couldn't. My muscles didn't cooperate when I tried. The effort only made my stomach churn. Then I heard muted noise.

Voices.

I heard them speak—two people—I believed, but I couldn't grasp the meaning of what was said. They must have spoken at a normal volume, but the fog in my head muffled them.

As the haze gradually dissipated and I was able to hear them clearly, I realized, I still couldn't understand them because they spoke some other language than English. German possibly, judging by the harsher sounds.

My fingers twitched. Could I move now? I shifted a little then stilled again, stifling the moan of pain in my throat. Instinctively, I remained quiet so as not to alert them that I was awake. Then I remembered what happened.

They took me. Again.

Something didn't make sense with my abduction this time, but I couldn't focus on it yet. Any effort to concentrate sent another burst of sharp pain through my head.

The voices got louder, it sounded like they were arguing.

Carefully, I half-opened one eye.

Still dressed in my jacket and boots over my grey pajamas, I lay in the back seat of a vehicle that wasn't moving. Save for the faint light from the car's console, it was dark. The two men talking were the driver and the front seat passenger. The driver opened the door, and I caught the glow of a cell phone screen as he stuck his hand outside.

Searching for reception?

In any case, judging by his frustrated groan when he pulled his hand back inside the car, he didn't find what he was looking for. The one in the passenger seat said something accusingly, and the driver snapped at him again.

It was pitch black outside. Was it still the same night?

The car moved again, and I was finally able to shift off my numb arm following the jerking momentum of the vehicle. Blood returned to my arm with a prickling ache, and I swallowed another moan, determined not to disclose my returned awareness to my abductors while I assessed the situation.

The car came to a stop, so suddenly, I nearly rolled off the seat to the floor. My head lolled with a sharp stab of headache, and I couldn't help a soft groan this time.

Thankfully, the men in the front were still arguing loudly. The passenger yelled agitatedly then got out, slamming the door behind him. The driver waited for a few moments then cursed under his breath and got out, too.

Left alone, I made an effort to lift my hand and gave a silent prayer when it obeyed. Then I tried to open the door next to my head.

Locked.

I didn't bother with the one at my feet. Instead, I heaved myself up over the centre console to peek through the windshield.

In the yellow beam of headlights, I saw the backs of the two men dressed in dark suits walking away from the vehicle. It appeared they moved to the crossroad sign at the intersection ahead.

Did my kidnappers get lost? The notion made me giggle uncontrollably even as my whole body tensed with nerves.

Must be the drugs wearing off.

As fast as I could muster with my limbs barely under my control, I crawled into the front passenger's seat. This door opened when I turned the handle as quietly as I could, and I slipped outside, crouching beside the car.

My attention fully on the two dark figures illuminated by the headlights, I closed the door carefully, afraid to breathe, and attempted to run in a crouch into the forest on the side of the road.

My legs gave under me, though, and I rolled off into the ditch, my body feeling like an uncoordinated sack of muscles and pain.

I needed to run or at least to crawl further into the forest somehow, but all I could do was just lie there, trying to calm my churning stomach, which was set on emptying itself any moment.

Throwing up would definitely make some noise, I feared. I flipped to my back and stared up into the dark sky, counting my breaths and desperately willing my insides to settle.

The arguing grew louder—they were coming back to the car. Soon they'd see I wasn't there. They'd search around and find me.

Everything inside me clenched with fear. Afraid to move towards the forest where I might make more noise in the underbrush, I rolled to my stomach and crawled along the ditch, away from the voices.

I stilled as soon as the voices paused, halting my breath while lying low in the dirt and dry grass. As if the whole world came to a stop, even my heartbeat seemed to pause the moment the car doors opened and closed.

The noise of the engine moved away. Only then I dared to release my breath. A painful knot twisted in my stomach, and I leaped to all fours just in time for my stomach to finally empty itself in the ditch. Again and again. Until the spasms came up in dry heaves, with nothing left in me.

My arms and legs shook. Feeling drained, I fought the urge to collapse back in the ditch next to my own vomit, pushing up to my feet instead, then staggered through the undergrowth into the forest.

Sooner or later the two in the car would notice I wasn't there anymore and come back to search for me. Determined to put as much distance between me and them as possible, I kept rushing though the dark woods as fast as my shaking legs would allow.

Chapter 6

I RAN AS LONG AS I could, in a general direction away from the road, without letting myself dwell on the odds of my surviving the wilderness of the Yukon—or wherever it was that they had managed to get me to—in my condition. I simply let panic and fear drive me as far away from my kidnappers as possible.

When I had no more energy to run, I walked, staggering through the forest, afraid to stop.

I had no idea how long I marched between the trees and through the underbrush, but the sky above me had turned lighter with the rising sun, and I noticed the trees around me had thinned, eventually being replaced by a valley.

Unnerved by being in the open, I scrambled to a copse of stunted trees in the distance and heard the sound of bubbling water when I reached it. A small creek wound its way between the trees and bushes, and I sank to my knees on its grassy bank.

I washed my hands and face in the chilly water and rinsed the filth from my mouth. Thirst forced me to drink it, too, outweighing the fear of any possible bacteria in the open stream.

Exhausted by trekking through the woods, I also felt ravenously hungry. My overall condition had improved, however. Whatever drugs my kidnappers had injected in me, must have worn off. Drinking the water had eased my headache.

I sat on the bank, resting my arms on my knees, and swept the area with my gaze as my surroundings emerged in the pale light of sunrise.

The valley that seemed to be an abandoned farm field ended in the distance with more woods visible on the horizon. Several forested patches were scattered throughout the open space. The unexpected sight of the hard line of a roof between the trees of one of them made me pause. My heart raced in my chest with hope filling it.

The adrenaline that fueled me during the escape had worn off. I was hungry and exhausted. A house meant people and civilization—and hopefully food, rest, and a phone to call the police for help.

I got up, every muscle in my body protesting with pain, and started towards the outline of the roof between the trees.

THE MOMENT I GOT A good look at the structure, it became clear no one had lived there for some time.

Disappointment shot through me—sharp and dark—as I stood in front of the house staring at the boarded windows. The gravel driveway was overgrown with tall grass, and white paint peeled off the garage doors and front porch.

The thought of more was daunting. Maybe, I could hide inside from the two men, who must be looking for me out there, and get some rest? Would the owners, wherever they were, forgive my trespassing considering my circumstances?

My stomach was so empty, it felt like it pressed flat against my spine. Maybe there was some food left in the house? Like a can of something. Anything.

I swayed on my feet with exhaustion. What choice did I have? Get inside or sit out here until my kidnappers found and drugged me again?

Decision made, I walked up the stairs of the front porch and tugged at the doorknob.

Locked.

I took a quick look around. The old porch was bare of furniture—no flowerpots, not even a doormat, under which the owner might have hidden the key. Wide pieces of plywood completely covered both windows on each side of the door. I hooked my fingers under the edge of one, trying to pry the corner off. It didn't budge. Whoever nailed it was very thorough in their job.

Walking around the house, I checked every window then the back door. Nothing.

Disheartened, I stopped in front of the garage, searching the ground for a stick or a big enough rock that would possibly break through the piece of thick plywood when my gaze fell on the handle at the bottom of the garage door. The house seemed old enough to have manually opening garage doors.

With renewed hope, I tugged at the handle with force. It gave in and moved up only to stop again almost immediately. I let go of the handle, leaving the door ajar, and crouched by the opening.

In the darkness of the garage, I could see the glimmer of the thick, rusty chain that held the door from inside. The chain was locked with a huge padlock that came in my view through the gap.

There was nothing big enough or strong enough around me to knock the lock off. The gap between the ground and the bottom edge of the garage door seemed too small to fit a person.

Too small for an average *person to fit through.*

Sitting on the ground, I unzipped my jacket and shrugged out of it then lay flat. First I wiggled my hips under, desperately hoping that whatever kept the door up would continue to hold, then squeezed the rest of me through. I had to turn my head to the side, glad the rest of me had shrunk with the weight I'd lost over the last few weeks.

Once inside, I pulled my jacket in, too, then wrenched the door, letting it drop back down to close the gap behind me.

Chapter 7

PALE MORNING SUN FILTERED through the thin gaps between the plywood on the windows as I made my way from the garage to the kitchen of the abandoned house. The air was stale and musty. The house felt unlived in inside as much as it appeared to be on the outside.

Flicking the light switch and turning on the taps, I determined that there was no running water or electricity. The fridge was empty and perfectly clean. I went through the kitchen cabinets methodically, searching for any scraps of food that might have been left behind and finding none.

Disheartened, I moved from the kitchen to the living room then down the hallway. Opening doors as I went, I still harboured the hope of finding a pantry stash with some canned food behind one of them.

A dark bedroom. A bathroom. A linen closet, with bedding and towels folded neatly inside. Most of the house was furnished—a dining set in the kitchen, a couch in the living room, beds in the bedrooms.

Was it too much to hope for a can of tuna lying around somewhere, too?

I pushed another door open and glimpsed a bed inside yet another dark bedroom then froze, shock nailing me to the spot.

Someone was in the bed.

The door slowly swung open all the way, and I jumped from its soft thud against the wall. The figure on the bed didn't stir.

Was the person asleep?

I ducked sideways to hide behind the wall in case they saw me. Now what? Get out of here before the owner caught me snooping around their house? Or wait until they woke up and ask for help?

Something was not right, though. The whole idea of someone sleeping in a house that seemed completely abandoned didn't make sense. The nagging feeling at the back of my mind formed into questions. Why was the house boarded, with no electricity, and not a crumb of food anywhere if someone actually lived here?

Lived?

An uneasy sensation churned in my empty stomach. Did the owner die, and I had just stumbled upon a dead body?

No longer afraid to wake anyone up, I stepped through the doorway, entering the room. The dead didn't scare me. Finding a corpse would be eerie and definitely unpleasant, but hardly dangerous.

Oddly enough, there was not a trace of the stench of a decomposing body in the air inside the bedroom. Instead, a faint tendril of pleasantly spicy scent reached me along with the dusty smell of an abandoned place.

As the rising sun filtered in through the boarded windows, it became apparent the person was a male. Dressed in a plain white t-shirt, he lay on his back with his arms stretched over the quilt that covered him up to his chest.

His enormous body appeared too large for the bed. Even at rest, his biceps stretched the short sleeves of his t-shirt to the limit and his shoulders spread wide.

The thick ropes of muscles in his forearms and the hard planes of his chest straining against the t-shirt spoke of vitality and strength. Yet the eerie feeling created by his utter stillness wouldn't leave me the more I stared at him.

There was something ethereal in the peaceful beauty of his face and in the pale glow of his long, golden hair fanning over the pillow.

The unearthly perfection of his features didn't seem to be touched by death, even as it hardly belonged to the world of the living, either.

The glowing beauty drew me in, making me forget any caution. I went and sat on the bed at his side.

From close up, I noticed the near translucency of his pale skin. The shadows around his eyes and in his sunken cheeks marred his perfect features, giving him an expression of eternal suffering. My heart ached with compassion for the complete stranger in front of me.

Only then I realized that his chest did not rise and fall.

He was a corpse, after all. Did he die recently?

Compelled by need to check for a pulse, I touched his neck.

His skin was cool but soft and pliable, far from the stiffness of dead flesh. I slid my thumb along his jawline, enthralled by the exquisite sensation of his skin under my touch.

A deep rumble rolled through the silence of the room.

With startling speed, his hand shot to mine, pressing it to his face with crushing force. His back arched, and snarling groan tore out of his chest.

An icy cold sensation seeped into my palm from his face then spread up my arm alarmingly fast.

Startled into shock initially, I finally jerked on my hand in a futile attempt to yank it free. It felt like my skin fused with his face, frozen solid, filling me with cold horror.

I jammed my knee into the mattress, leaning all the way back, away from him and off the bed.

For a brief moment, I believed my hand slid a little under his, giving me a tiny flicker of hope. Then I recognized the grey glove on his hand. I'd seen the same ones on every guard in my basement jail at the base.

My head swam, as my vision dimmed.

Thick veins bulged in his neck and across his face, turning it from beautiful to terrifying.

The last I saw before the darkness took me completely were his eyes opening wide with the white-blue light shining bright through them in the poorly lit bedroom.

He was one of them.

Chapter 8

Pain twisted his insides, cutting sharply through his whole body. Every muscle hurt. The agony spread everywhere—from his scalp to his fingernails. He could have sworn even his hair hurt.

A thin, delicate string of calm floated through the raging storm of pain, and he held on to the brief sense of relief it brought.

The sight of the white ceiling came into focus, making him aware he was in his bed in his bedroom. Awake.

Why?

He recognized the tendril of calmness as someone else's presence inside him. The life force of a human.

Some poor soul had woken him up. He closed his eyes with a groan, trying to re-claim awareness from the fog of oblivion.

Waking up brought nothing but trouble—a brief flash of relief from consuming a human life force then renewed suffering that came with falling back into Deep Sleep again.

He sucked in another gulp of air, putting his lungs back to work after who knew how many years of idleness.

How long had it been?

Did it really matter?

He dug through the few memories he could access, remembering what he had to do now. The list was short—get rid of the corpse and go back to sleep.

Slowly, he sat up, his gaze sweeping the bed for the body of the human who woke him up.

Nothing.

With a sigh, he threw the covers off and swung his legs to the side. His muscles listened well enough. It was just his mind that dragged way behind.

Getting out of bed, he almost stepped on the body but managed to halt his foot the very last moment.

Small and thin, a form was curled on the floor by the bed, drowned by a pair of loose flannel pajamas.

A child?

Regret twitched painfully somewhere in the area of his heart, adding to the agony wreaking havoc on the rest of his body.

All humans died sooner or later. However, draining children of their life before it had really begun didn't sit well with him. The fact that he had no choice and no control over what had happened didn't make him feel any better over this.

He kneeled by the body.

A female, judging by her delicate features.

Brushing the dun-brown hair from her face, he examined it. Small, slightly upturned nose with a dusting of freckles. Full, pink lips, still slightly parted after the release of her last breath. Fooled by her size, he was surprised to find fine lines and angles of maturity on her face.

Not a child, after all. A young woman.

Still the heavy feeling weighing on his heart didn't ease. Her death was useless. Completely unnecessary. And he knew humans well enough to believe that she would have preferred to live if given a choice.

Why did you come near me?

He sighed again. Curiosity afflicted humans of any age.

Carefully, he hooked his arms under her knees and shoulders and lifted her up, trying to think of the most suitable way to dispose of her body.

Her head rolled off his shoulder, and he felt a sudden, slight jerk through all of her.

She was still alive?

He stopped and scanned her carefully.

A tiny, faint spark of light glimmered inside her.

His breath hitched with shock. How was it even possible? He couldn't remember if any human ever survived waking a sleeping demon before. True, he only had a few memories at the moment, but the newness of the notion of one actually surviving it was rather clear.

Carefully, he lowered her on top of the covers then just stood there, staring.

Now what?

He had no list in his memory of what to do in this situation—a sure sign that this occurrence was irregular. How did she even manage to keep any life force to herself? He had been incapable of stopping before he took everything.

Her position on the floor when he found her indicated that she must have broken their connection just in time somehow by falling off the bed.

He shifted through his short stack of memories again. From what he remembered about humans, she would need sleep and food to regain her strength.

Something else nagged at the back of his mind, something about her that was not entirely right. The thought buzzed inside his head somewhere, unable to break through the fog, and he had no choice but to let it go for now.

Hunger hollowed him from the inside with more pain. He needed some food, too. What he took from her was not nearly enough to clear his head. And she had nothing else to give at the moment.

Well, it'll have to do.

He covered her with the quilt then got some money from one of the safe places inside the house and walked to the garage to fetch his car.

Chapter 9

THE HEADACHE HAD RETURNED with a vengeance. I rolled my head on the pillow and regretted it immediately, as the sharp pain shot in a series of arrows through my skull. I moaned then froze with fear, scared to make another sound.

Where was I this time?

My eyelids were impossibly heavy, but I pried my eyes open. There was almost complete darkness. However, I recognized the room by the smell of dust and stale air. I was still in the abandoned house, lying in bed—possibly the same bed where the beautiful corpse had lain.

The one that came to life.

The thought jolted me out of my hazy dizziness, and I sat up. A debilitating bolt of fire exploded through my brain, making me double in half as if from a physical blow.

"It will pass." A raspy, hollow voice sounded from somewhere in the corner. "Try to avoid sudden movements . . . for now." I heard a rustle of clothes, as though someone had gotten up.

Was it *him*?

"What do you want from me? Are you going to take me back?"

"Back where?" He sounded confused.

"To your base."

"Is that where you came from?" A slight note of interest filtered through his flat tone as he came close enough for me to see the pale outline of his tall figure in the darkness.

He wore a grey hooded sweatshirt over the white t-shirt, a pair of drawstring pants, and the leather gloves. My gaze slid down his thighs, and I recognized the material of his pants—the grey flannel that my own pajamas were made from.

Definitely a demon!

My worse suspicions confirmed, I bit my tongue, fearing I already told too much and afraid to say anything more.

"I'll get some light and food for you." He didn't insist on my reply to his question, I noted with relief. Then I heard the door open and close.

Not waiting for him to come back, I threw the covers off and leaped out of bed. My head swam with a severe bout of dizziness that threw me back. My ass bounced off the edge of the mattress, and I slid to the floor in a heap.

Dammit!

I couldn't even get up to all fours—my hands and knees shook so much, I collapsed face down as soon as I tried.

What did he do to me?

The door opened again.

"Why are you on the floor?" The genuine puzzlement in his voice would have been comical if I could laugh at the moment.

I turned towards the light from the candle in his hand.

"What did you do? I can't move."

He heaved a sigh.

"You need some rest . . . and some food to regain your strength." His voice impassive, his speech had the same halting pattern that reminded me of Garrett.

He placed a tray with the candle on the floor then reached for me.

"No! Don't touch me!" I shrunk away from him then muttered under my breath, "I'm so freaking sick and tired of your kind knocking me unconscious over and over again. You have no idea how an-noying it gets after a while."

Gripping the covers and using the bed frame to haul my non-co-operating body up, I attempted to climb back onto the bed again.

"I'm wearing gloves." He spread his fingers to demonstrate. "I can't take anything from you through them."

"Yeah, well, you already took. Didn't you?" I struggled to climb up.

"*You* touched *me*," he remarked calmly, taking away my argu-ment.

"Fine." I gave up, sliding back to the floor with a frustrated huff. "Could you help me, please?" I reasoned that if he wanted to harm me more, he would've done it by now—in my current position, I could offer zero resistance anyway.

Taking a step closer, he lifted me in his arms promptly and put me on the bed—all in one movement, as if I weighted nothing at all.

"Thanks." I crawled back under the quilt, panting from the ef-fort. "When am I going to be myself again?"

Will it ever be possible? To be myself in every way again?

He put the tray with the candle in my lap.

"Eat."

Only now I noticed a Styrofoam cup with soup next to a bottle of water on the tray, and my stomach clenched in hungry anticipa-tion.

"Oh, God. Thank you," I exhaled, quickly grabbing the plastic spoon from the tray and diving in the soup. It was lukewarm, with a faint synthetic aftertaste. Still, it felt wonderful, filling my empty bel-ly.

"Sorry, I'm not sure of its taste. I got it from the gas station in the nearest town, about a two-hour drive from here." He remained standing by the bed, watching me eat.

Normally, this attention would be rather unsettling, but right now I was focused on the food in front of me, too grateful to have something to eat.

"There is no power and no food in the house to cook," he observed evenly.

"You can cook?" I asked in surprise between the mouthfuls.

"Yes."

"What's your name?" I licked the spoon after finishing the last drop of soup and leaned back against the headboard. Having a full stomach seemed to have eased my headache but made me exceptionally sleepy.

"Ivarr." He took the bottle from the tray, opened it, and handed it to me.

The name had a Norwegian sound to it and combined with his appearance—large, muscular body and blond, wavy hair—brought Vikings to mind.

"You're a demon, too, aren't you?"

"Yes," he replied simply, taking the bottle from me. "Don't fight the sleep. You need to rest."

I gulped half of the water and now struggled to stay awake, despite the needles of apprehension inside me. Now more than ever I needed to be fully alert, yet it seemed to be taking most of my energy just to keep my eyes open.

"What will you be doing while I sleep?" I couldn't fight the fear and suspicion that made it into my voice.

"Me?" He rubbed his forehead, as if an answer to my question required some deep concentration from him. "I'll wait until you wake up strong enough to leave. Then I'll go back to sleep myself . . ."

"That's it? You'll let me go, just like that?"

"Yes."

"You won't take me to the base or call your demon buddies to fetch me?"

"No."

"Why should I trust you?"

"I don't know . . . Maybe because you don't have a choice?"

The demon was right. In my current position, I was as helpless as a fly. He didn't even need to lie. Had he announced that he was about to take me back where I came from, I wouldn't be able to do anything about it.

"I—I didn't mean to take your life force," he offered slowly, as if searching for every word. "I have no control over what happens when I'm in Deep Sleep . . . What I'm trying to say is that I am sorry for your condition and I feel responsible for your safety until you're better."

That came as a complete surprise, depriving me of the ability to respond for a moment. I had every reason to distrust a demon. Yet the sincerity in his tone reminded me of Garrett. Could demons be like people in that there were some of them capable of some decency, caring and responsibility?

With awareness gradually seeping out of me, I knew it'd be impossible for me to take care of myself any time soon. I could only hope that Ivarr was a demon of his word and I could count on him to keep me safe.

"Two of you," I hurried to warn him while I still could, "drugged me and kidnapped me from the base. They were transporting me in a car along the road not far from here. I managed to get away, but they will be looking for me." My heavy eyelids dropped, and there was no power in the world that would help me lift them again. "They may be here soon . . . Don't let them take me. And, please, don't take me back to the base," I mumbled, sagging to the side like a rag doll, all control over my body gone.

Demon or not, I was entirely at his mercy now.

"I'll keep you safe." Was the last I heard before exhaustion, heavy as death itself, pulled me into the darkness.

Chapter 10

He lifted a strand of brown hair that had fallen across her face the moment she'd sunk into the pillows. The silky lock, the same colour as the freckles on her skin, slid easily between his gloved fingers. He twisted the ends, admiring the copper highlights brought out by the lights of the candle on the tray.

I'll keep you safe, he'd promised. By whatever miracle, she'd survived waking him, and he felt the responsibility to nurse her back to health after she had the misfortune to touch him.

Now, he tried to focus all his mental power on how to accomplish it.

He saw her fear when she spoke of the Incubi Base. Personally, his own visits to that place were infrequent, as far as he could remember. They were short, too, lasting a few weeks each—the time between his arrest and sentencing.

Last time, the main condition of his being allowed to stay in this world and to avoid Inferno was that he remained in Deep Sleep. Being awake now violated this condition. If he went back to sleep as soon as possible, the Council would never need to know he'd woken up at all.

Except that the two Incubi—must be one of the Council's Source Retrieval Teams—were out there, searching for her.

In all the time of his existence that he could remember, he never heard of a Source running away from the Base. Something like admiration rose in his chest as he eyed the small figure curled under the quilt.

The petal of life inside her pulsated with growing force as she slowly regained her strength.

If they caught her, chances were she'd be dead within a year, all life in her extinguished.

He could possibly give her a chance. The strength of his body combined with the full mental power of her brain—together, they might be able to outrun the demons, get her somewhere safe.

Luckily, he was good at running. All he needed was some better nourishment, though, to remember exactly how to do it right.

The mental effort it cost him to build the simplest chain of logic felt exhausting. Unfortunately, she was filled to the brim with worry and fear—emotions more harmful than helpful to him. The power of her life force was wearing off quickly in him, and her enjoyment from the poor-quality meal he'd skimmed wouldn't last long, either.

With his car apparently gone, he'd have to take Sytrius's truck and drive south. South, because the Base was located north from here, and he needed to get away from the Base to keep her safe.

Safe.

He walked to the kitchen and took out a metal box he kept under the floorboards there. The box housed the paper currency of several countries and a few passports in different names but with the same photograph—his.

Money and documents. This was his standard get-away kit for when he was on the run from the Council, which was most of the time when he happened to be awake.

Not this time, though. Just the idea of running again filled him with exhaustion. No one waited for him out there. The distant sorrow of some long-forgotten loss echoed through his chest. A shadow of grief from his past threatened to break through the fog into his awareness, but the thought of the Source sleeping in his bed chased it away.

Run.

Before Raim's Soldiers made it here.

From the bottom of the metal box, he took out a heart-shaped pendant on a cord of red silk. Gold swirls of light came to life inside the pendant as soon as he lifted it up. A sudden image of its amber glow against the delicate skin of the Source, when she'd wear it, rose in his foggy mind.

In a few hours, she would wake up. Then she would either tell him what to do next or feed him, so he could figure it out for them.

And once she was safe, he would go back into Deep Sleep again, because for him there was no escaping the pain, and in Deep Sleep at least there was less awareness of it.

Chapter 11

THE HEADACHE WAS ALMOST gone. The pain in my neck woke me up this time. I realized it was because of the uncomfortable position I'd fallen asleep in.

Massaging the soreness out of my neck muscles, I groaned and stretched then surveyed my surroundings, blinking in the bright daylight.

I was inside a truck, parked on the side of an unpaved road with deep forest on both sides. Wrapped in a quilt, I had been strapped into the passenger seat by someone.

Ivarr reclined in the driver's seat. Eyes closed, he appeared to have dozed off. I moved my gaze away quickly, not giving myself a chance to admire his long eyelashes, his angelic hair, or the way his t-shirt stretched thin across his wide chest, lest I do something stupid like touch him again.

Should I wait until he woke up to demand answers, or run again? For all I knew we might be on our way back to the Base, despite his promise.

My attention was drawn to the water bottle in the cup holder in front of me, making me realize how incredibly thirsty I was. I grabbed the bottle and drank as much as I could in hungry gulps.

Next, of course, I needed to use the bathroom. Clicking the seat belt off, I slowly crawled from under the quilt and climbed out the passenger's door.

To my overwhelming relief, my legs held despite my head swimming with dizziness. One hand on the vehicle, I slowly walked to the back tire. Afraid I'd collapse to the ground the moment I let go of the truck, I quickly abandoned the idea of going to the bushes and did my business right there.

Both hands on the cool metal, I fought another bout of dizziness, wondering what to do next.

Obviously, I was still in no condition to run anywhere yet. I also had no idea how long I'd spent unconscious or where I had been transported.

Were we still in Yukon? British Columbia or Alberta? Or Canada at all? They had taken me across the border once before. It was entirely possible that Ivarr had driven me back into The States by now. The surrounding area, however, didn't seem to be much different than the woods near his house.

Well, at least I was still alive, awake, and feeling much better than the last time I woke up. More importantly, there didn't seem to be any other demons around here besides Ivarr.

I had to find out where he was taking me, though.

Keeping my hands on the truck, I slowly made my way back to the passenger's door then crawled into the seat.

Ivarr remained motionless, his head tilted to the side, and my gaze travelled to his face before I could stop it.

He had tied his hair back, but a golden strand fell across his forehead. I balled my hands into fists and sat on them to stop myself from reaching out to move it away for him.

No touching.

Besides, he might need a rest, too. I remembered Garrett mentioning that he didn't sleep. Ivarr obviously did. Maybe demons were more different than I thought?

Waiting for him to wake up, I let my gaze linger, studying his features. Straight nose. Strong jawline. Sensual mouth that just begged to be kissed . . .

What?

I blinked the sudden thought away, forcing myself to concentrate on other, more practical and less dangerous ideas.

Like where was the nearest police station?

A deep growl rumbled in Ivarr's chest suddenly, startling me. His peaceful expression crumbled, as his body tensed, back arching. Teeth bared, he groaned as if in pain.

"Ivarr?" I leaned towards him carefully.

He didn't seem to hear me. Hands squeezed into tight fists, he doubled over in his seat, and his forehead hit the steering wheel, the horn blowing.

"Oh, God. Ivarr!" I yelled over the deafening sound. "What's wrong?" Faced with his obvious agony, I forgot all about the potential danger of touching him and grabbed his shoulder. "Can I do something? Anything?"

Fear and worry for him filled me as I shook him gently, trying to get his attention.

Panting, he rolled his forehead on the steering wheel to face me. A series of blue-white lights flickered through his eyes as he stared at me, unblinking. Then his chest rose with a deep inhale and his breathing seemed to slow down.

"What's going on?" I asked, cupping his face to lift his head from the horn button and stop the blaring noise.

Concern won over fear inside me at the sight of his torture, and I didn't even pause to think about touching him this time.

I held his head in my hands, watching mesmerized as the dark clouds of pain cleared from the brilliant blue of his eyes. "Are you okay?" I whispered. Without the noise of the horn, the silence was deafening.

He closed his eyes and lifted his hand to mine, pressing it firmer to his face. The gesture was almost the same as the first time I touched him. Yet his hold was gentle this time, and there was no cooling sensation in my palm, just the feeling of his warm skin.

"Thank you," he whispered, and inhaled deeply again.

"What do you mean?" I brushed my thumb along his high cheekbone.

He unexpectedly brought my hand to his lips and kissed my palm. Startled, I didn't move away, and he trailed the kisses to the inside of my wrist. His caresses rippled through me in a light wave of pleasure.

"Ivarr?" I whispered a little breathy, leaning closer. "What are you doing?"

"I'm hungry," he murmured against the sensitive skin of my inner arm, sending a flock of warm tingles through my chest. "Will you feed me, sweetheart?"

"Feed you?"

A hair-thin thread of warning filtered in my brain through the syrupy warmth brought on by the touch of his lips.

"Mmhmm." His fingers circled my wrist, raising the inside of my elbow to his lips. "So . . . good."

The lights flashing through his hooded eyes had a pink hue now, reminding me of the crimson glow of the thirteen who had watched me on the cross in the white room.

"No." I shrunk back, and to my relief, he let go of my arm immediately, dropping his hands into his lap.

I shook my head, trying to clear the spell his kisses seemed to have put me under.

"What were you doing to me? You weren't just taking my emotions. Your eyes . . . the light wasn't blue this time." I'd never seen Garrett's eyes light red, only those of the members of The Council, while I was on the cross.

"You got aroused." He inclined his head. "The sexual energy reflects red in our eyes."

"No, I didn't!" I squirmed in my seat, mortified and angry at the same time—embarrassed over my reaction to him and mad at him for causing it.

"Yes, you did." His tone was certain. "A little."

He didn't seem to be mocking or teasing, just stating the truth.

"How do you know?"

"I saw it." He shrugged. "I see all emotions inside you, in light and colour. The pink blush—not unlike the one on your cheeks right now—is the shade of rising desire."

Renewed fear pushed aside my initial embarrassment.

"I've only seen red in the eyes of Council members, Ivarr." I moved as far away from him as the space in the truck would allow. "Are you with them?"

"I've never served on the Council or worked for them. In fact, I prefer to keep as much distance as possible between me and them."

"Sleeping in the same country as their base doesn't seem to be that far away," I pointed out.

"This wasn't me taking a nap. I was put in Deep Sleep as a punishment."

"For what?"

"For not following the rules of the Council."

"Why weren't you? Aren't all of you their *Soldiers*?"

"We are. Except that not all of us have enough self-control to stay away from humans and their emotions as the Council demands. At least, I don't."

"What do you mean?" *The rules* were outright criminal, as far as I knew. However, since I had some knowledge about how they were executed at the Base, I more or less understood what to expect. Here, one on one with a demon gone rogue—who knew what could happen.

He turned more my way, appearing eager to explain.

"Their feedings are forced." His voice filled with emotion, and his expressions became more animated. "The way it's done is . . . unnatural. It hurts both humans and us and solves nothing. I refused to go hungry as the treaty demands and instead fed *my* way—pleasurable for me and the woman whose emotions I shared, which was against the rules." He leaned back in his seat. "And that made me a deserter."

His brilliant blue eyes closed for a moment, as if he needed to focus on something inside him without any visual distractions.

"This here." He pressed his fist to his chest. "This calmness and peace . . . feels right. Sexual energy was meant to be our nourishment, but I don't agree with taking it by force. The only way they could stop me from running away and feeding on my own was to make me fall into Deep Sleep."

"How could they *force* you to sleep?"

"By starving me until all energy was gone."

"Sounds like death." A brutal one at that. The fact that any society, demon or not, would do that to their own kind was appalling. On the other hand, I knew far too well what entailed to keep one of them fed—the more demons there were awake, the more women there needed to be in the basement cells.

"Demons can't die. Deep Sleep is a state of immobility with no awareness but pain."

I remembered his tortured groans and the expression of pure agony on his face.

"How long were you supposed to *sleep* like that?"

"Until the Council decided to wake me up, which would most likely be never."

"So, they just left you there? Alone?"

"They may have sent someone to check on me here and there. However, their resources are rather limited to worry overmuch about me. They had reasons to believe I'd sleep or would go back to sleep if awoke by accident. So, I wouldn't be surprised if they've forgotten about me." He rubbed his forehead as if considering something. "Sytrius must have come by, though, took my car and left his truck behind."

"Who?"

"Sytrius. The Soldier who captured me and brought me to the Council for sentencing. In this very truck, by the way."

"Do you think he will be back, looking for it?"

"I really don't know. It puzzles me why he'd need my car in the first place."

"Is there GPS tracking on it?" Spurred by a shot of anxious worry, I frantically searched the front console for any devices. The truck seemed rather old to have one built in, not that I knew much about it.

"I don't think so. It is rather exhausting keeping up with modern human technology. Normally, it takes us a while to catch up."

I stopped searching, not because his words convinced me, but because I didn't find anything obvious and had no idea what else to look for.

"So. Where are we and where were you taking me?"

He briefly scanned the area outside the windows, an expression of deep concentration settling over his handsome face. "We need to come up with a plan. So far, I've been just driving south, away from the base."

"Has anyone followed us at any point?"

"Not that I've noticed."

"How far until the nearest police station?"

He remained silent for a few moments, his forehead creased in thought.

"The next town along the highway should have one—"

"Good."

"If you think the best plan is to go to the police, that is."

"Will you stop me?" I challenged.

"It's not about that. My brain is still rather foggy to do a full analysis of the situation, so if you're absolutely certain going to the police is the right thing to do, I'll take you there. However, women have been taken for as long as I can remember, and to my knowledge, human authorities have never come searching for them."

"Has anyone ever escaped before?"

He gave me a long, penetrating look, with a glint of interest and something like admiration in his eyes.

"Not that I remember."

"So, maybe this is my chance to alert the police and make the demons pay for all of this?"

Demons?

A sudden image of Keller came to my mind. He had seemed to be comfortable enough in a place full of demons. Moreover, they even appeared to take orders from him.

He also threatened *The Priory* would prevent anyone from obtaining a search warrant. His organization must have some power over the authorities then, not to mention their obvious desire to keep the existence of demons and whatever relationship they had with them in secret.

My determination wavered.

"Do you think the police are on their side, too?" I voiced my doubt.

"I—I don't know. But you do need to be careful."

"What do you know about The Priory?"

"The treaty signed between them and the two Councils outlines the rules that have been governing our existence in this world for, um, about six hundred years now, I believe." His voice sounded hesitant again, as if remembering the dates and facts still needed some effort on his part. "The agreement is about providing Councils with human sources for nourishment."

"The Priory allowed my abduction?"

"Right."

"Are you sure?"

Ivarr nodded.

My insides flipped with apprehension. Looked like I was right about trusting no one.

"What happened then that made them claim they'd release me?"

"Release you?" he asked with frown of surprise. "I thought you escaped."

"That's the thing that confuses me here. A man, claiming to be representing The Priory announced that I would be released within the matter of days. Apparently, that was in accordance with some new agreement. Then, that very night, demons abducted me from their base and were transporting me in a vehicle when I escaped. Why would they do that?"

"Because the Council didn't want to lose you as a source?" He suggested. "So they went against the agreement?"

"Would the Council do that?"

"I wouldn't put it past Raim. Being deceptive is not natural for us, but not impossible. It requires a lot of practice and some decent nourishment to invent a lie—both of which Raim has."

"But Keller, the man from The Priory, said that the idea of a new agreement came from the Council. Why would they demand any changes at all if they were happy with the way the things were?"

"I don't know anything about a new agreement."

"How long were you sleeping before I woke you up?"

Ivarr gazed at me with his baby-blues for a minute, and it cost me an effort not to get distracted. Having him this near in the confinement of the truck, made it somehow difficult to focus for me.

"What year is it?" he asked, bringing me back to our conversation.

I told him the year and added, "September, I was told."

"About two years then, since I fell into Deep Sleep. I'm sure there were no talks about any revisions to the treaty at that time. This must be very new."

We both went silent again.

According to Keller, The Priory was planning to provide me with a cover story and help me to get on with my life, keeping me safe from demons. I wished that was true, in which case the best option for me would be to find a way to contact The Priory. Going to the police, for example, might alert them.

However, the fact that they literally gave me to the demons in the first place made it impossible to trust them.

I shook my head, confused about the best course of action. Maybe, like Ivarr's, my mental abilities were still impaired, and I needed more time to fully recover.

"I think we should wait before going to the police for now, Ivarr. Let's see if we can find a place safe enough to rest and have some food first."

He nodded and turned the key in the ignition.

"Wait." Forgetting myself, I covered his hand with mine to stop him then jerked it away quickly. "Why are you helping me?"

"What?"

"You've violated your punishment. And now you're driving me away from the demons in charge. I don't think it'll improve your situation in any way."

"My situation could hardly get any worse." He gave me a faint smile. "I'm not too eager to return to Deep Sleep, and I'm good at running—I've evaded the Council for centuries at a time. I may as well help you get away from them now."

"What do you want from me in return?" I squinted at him, waiting for his answer.

"You'll need to help me form a plan."

"So, you won't expect me to be your *food source*?"

A wide, blindingly gorgeous smile broke out on his tired face, catching me completely unaware.

"Only if you offer."

"Not happening," I snapped quickly, afraid I might lose my resolve under the power of this grin.

"Then you will have to do all the thinking to come up with the plan. My ability at logic and analysis is impaired the hungrier I am. It would be too easy for me to make a mistake or oversee something essential."

"Okay." I considered this for a minute then continued, selecting my words carefully. "I don't want you to starve, I'm not your Council. Garrett, my Handler, said he fed off my positive emotions. You can do the same. I really don't mind you skimming anything that would help you stay awake and well."

By saying this, I realized I'd just willingly agreed to be his food source after all.

In a way that wouldn't harm me physically or emotionally.

Still, I specified, just to make sure.

"If you promise me that I can trust a demon, who has confessed to a lack of self-control."

His expression turned serious, any shadow of the smile completely gone. I realized, with surprise, that I immediately missed it.

"I may never be able to bring a woman to orgasm only to feed someone else—whatever sexual energy I make her create is always mine." The possessive firmness of his tone resonated through me. "But I lived among humans long enough to learn how to exercise restraint. I had plenty of practice to promise you with confidence—you don't have to be afraid of me."

The sincerity in his voice was comforting.

"Besides," he added with a glint in his eyes. "Nothing can compare with the taste of arousal from a willing woman."

His gaze lingered on my face—a little too long and a bit too intensely for my cheeks not to warm up again.

I shifted in my seat under his penetrating stare.

"Well. Um. *Willing* is the key here, isn't it?"

"Right."

"Good," I replied with an easy heart. Despite my resolve not to trust anyone, the honesty in his voice made me want to believe him. "So, when you say your abilities are impaired what exactly do you mean? I've noticed that your speech is more fluent now and, you know, overall you seem to be more . . . alive."

"The revitalizing power of human emotions." He lifted a teasing eyebrow at me. "That tiny taste of your desire was especially helpful. Thank you."

"Um. You're welcome?"

"That said, I still only remember as far as about six or eight centuries of my life. My physical abilities are renewed, but memories and the mental power to process information need much longer, with considerably better nourishment."

"So, my positive emotions alone wouldn't help much?"

"They'll sustain, but not improve. I'll try to get some sexual energy in the next town we come across. Meanwhile, you'll have to think and let me know if I miss anything."

For whatever twisted reason my insides dropped a little at his mention of getting sexual energy elsewhere, but I forced the sickening feeling aside.

"Where are we exactly?"

"In Alberta, Canada." He glanced outside again. "About twenty minutes away from the highway south. I got off when I started falling into Deep Sleep again—driving was no longer safe—" He stopped abruptly and shook his head. "I knew I was forgetting something. What's your name?"

"I'm Kitty."

"Kitty?"

"Well, my actual name is Katherine, but everyone calls me Kitty, so . . ."

He stared at me closely.

"Say your name again. Please."

"Kitty," I repeated, confused by his reaction. "Why?"

"No." He waved me off. "The other one."

"Katherine." I loved this name. To me, it sounded grand and regal, and truly beautiful. However, I didn't mind when everyone from my family to my co-workers and my now-ex-boyfriend called me Kitty. I agreed, visually, it suited me better. According to Derek, my ex, *Kitty* was 'short and cute' like me.

"Again."

"Katherine." I smiled awkwardly at his unexplained persistence. "You know. Like Catherine the Great, only with a *K*."

He nodded. "I'll call you Katherine then."

"Everyone calls me Kitty, Ivarr . . ."

"I'm not everyone," he reasoned. "Your name is Katherine. I can see how much you like it. Besides, it suits you very much."

"It does?"

"You've escaped from an army of demons, Queen Katherine. That must have taken some royal courage to get away."

"Well, I'm not done running yet," I reminded, feeling my face heat up from his compliment. Or was it from the way he said it? In that deep, low voice, quiet yet powerful? "Let's keep going, shall we? South, away from the base."

"Right." He turned the key in the ignition once again and brought the truck back in motion and on the road.

Chapter 12

DURING THE TIME IT took Ivarr to drive us back to the highway, I folded the quilt the best I could and put it in the back seat. There, I noted a camo backpack and my jacket from the Base. The grey material of the jacket was stained and torn in a few places, which must have been from my running through the woods.

I smoothed the fabric of my pajama pants over my knees—also ripped and dirty from crawling through the ditch. At least I'd been lucky enough to avoid getting any vomit on myself. Although, I still felt filthy and stinky.

I cast a furtive glance Ivarr's way. He had on a pair of jeans, a pure-white t-shirt, and a grey hoodie. Simple enough outfit, but he wore it impeccably well. Somehow things seemed to sit just the right way on him and hug all the right places.

I slid my gaze up along all those places of his. The thick thighs. A massive shoulder next to mine. Huge biceps, barely contained within the sleeves of the hoodie . . .

He caught me watching—a blue spark twinkled in his eye, and a smile of amusement touched his mouth.

Perfectly kissable lips . . .

What was going on with me?

"Are you . . . doing something to me?" I asked accusingly. There is no way I would normally admire a man I just met this hungrily. "Can demons manipulate people's emotions?"

"Only to some degree."

I knew it! It wasn't typical for me to react this way at a mere sight of a well-developed chest. I'd always prided myself on being practical and level-headed.

"How?"

"Like this." Ivarr tugged his sleeve up, exposing the thick, veiny ropes of his forearm muscles for my ogling pleasure.

"Oh, for crying out loud!" I huffed, turning away from him to stare out the window. The effort it cost me to focus on the forest outside instead of facing him again was almost painful.

Serves me right for waking up a demon. Should have kept my hands to myself.

"For whatever reason, most women seem to be attracted to this body type." His voice sounded contemplative, even detached, as if he were talking about someone else.

Until I met him, I didn't consider myself one of the *most women*. I never fell for athletic types.

My reaction to his physical appeal was unusual. However, as handsome as he might be, I was fairly confident that I would eventually get used to his looks, no matter how startling they might have seemed at the beginning.

It was the glimpses of his emerging personality—the glint in his eyes, the passion in his voice, combined with that smile of his—that I found truly intriguing. The more I saw of the person, the more I wanted to learn about him.

"Don't be mad, Katherine. My appearance is not my fault—all of us were created the way we are, to help us feed, I believe. But really, our looks are not much deeper than the clothes we wear. I spend no effort to have this body, and I don't pride myself for it." He inhaled deeply. "My mind is a different story."

"What do you mean?" I ventured a glimpse at him from the corner of my eye.

"My collection of memories. I've been generating them for centuries. They're the reflection of choices I've made. I've broken many rules—all of them, really—and I pay for it over and over again. But I have memories like no other demon in this world. Hunger often makes me forget many, but I treasure every one that I still have." He paused for a moment. "One of the reasons I feed is to remember."

"What kind of memories?" I asked quietly.

"Feelings, emotions, and experiences I had while living among humans."

"Tell me." I twisted in my seat to face him fully now. "Please."

"I still don't remember much from my early years on Earth—I'd need to feed well, for a prolonged period of time, for all memories to return. The earliest ones are not the best, to be honest. Hiding, fighting . . ."

"Fighting with whom?"

"Humans, mostly. As far as I can remember when people learned about us—they hunted us."

"Why?"

"The very nature of our nourishment is believed to be offensive and dangerous by some, even if the contact is fully consensual. With advancement of Christianity, the purpose of sex was narrowed to procreation only and was strictly limited to marriage. What we needed to survive could no longer be given freely. We had to steal whatever sexual energy we could find and fight for our very existence. If we failed, we fell into Deep Sleep."

"Doesn't sound like the type of memories one would treasure."

"Not all of that was bad. When awake, I lived on my own, skimming from people whenever I had a chance. I got to taste a huge range of their emotions, a rich kaleidoscope of feelings. Do you know that there are many flavours of sexual energy, too?"

"Are there? Did you . . . um. When you feed, do you have sex with women?"

"If they let me."

"Right." I exhaled a short laugh. "Like anyone would say *no* to you."

"Would you?" he replied quickly, glancing my way.

"Me? Oh, um . . ." Unable to meet his eyes, I stared at my hands clasped in my lap, while I collected my thoughts sent in disarray by his question. "I—I don't do casual sex, normally."

"Normally?" His tone was light, which eased my tension. "In the past few days at least, I believe, you've done many things you wouldn't do *normally*. Escaping a kidnapping. Waking up a demon."

"Yes, because I've been put in an unusual situation by a bunch of criminals," I bit out. "It absolutely doesn't mean that I should disregard all of my principles. I don't do one-night stands. Definitely not with demons who are merely interested in turning me on to feast on my arousal."

"There is more to it than that. With the right woman." His voice dipped dangerously low, its vibration making my skin tingle. "Any sexual energy is nourishing and revitalizing, but other emotions colouring it can make all the difference."

"What do you mean?"

"Anything a woman feels towards me, personally, makes her energy special."

He fell silent for a few moments, possibly lost in his thoughts or maybe letting me ponder his words.

"One of my most treasured memories is making love to a woman who cared about me," he said finally, his voice soft.

"Who was she?" I stared at his profile as he gazed straight at the road ahead.

"A widow. Her husband died at sea years before I met her. This was about two hundred years ago. She lived alone on a shore in Norway. We spent over six years together—the happiest years of my life."

"Did she love you?"

He said she cared about him, and for whatever inexplicable reason I needed to know how much.

"No." His reply felt bitter. "Her love remained with her husband to the end. But she found comfort in my touch, an escape from loneliness. Over time, she grew attached to me, which turned into an affection." He paused, his gaze on the road. It seemed like his mind had wondered back in time to that Norwegian shore and the woman he once knew. "But I always longed for more. Nothing she ever felt for me was as strong as the flame of love she carried inside for her husband. The most beautiful feeling I've ever seen. Endless and powerful. The more I took from it, the brighter it burnt."

"You fed on the woman's love for her dead husband?" I clarified, with a cringe inside.

"Yes." Unapologetic, he met my gaze with challenge. "I know exactly what undying love looks like and how it tastes. There is nothing in this world that could compare to that."

The conviction in his words subdued my judgment.

"What happened to her?"

Ivarr's chest rose with a deep inhale, and he released the air slowly.

"She died from an illness." His voice turned rough. "There was nothing I could do but hold her in my arms as her soul departed." His throat moved as he swallowed hard before adding softly, "Never before have I hated to be immortal as much as that day."

"Immortal," I whispered, trying to imagine what that would be like to carry memories and grief for an eternity.

A strong urge to comfort him rose inside me, if only I knew what to say or do to ease the pain of loss that lasted much longer than I'd been alive.

"I left Norway the very next day," he continued. "And let Sytrius catch me a few weeks later."

"You *let* him?"

"Well, usually, I make him work hard to try and catch me. When awake for a while, I am better fed than he is and therefore stronger and smarter, too. The Council's rations barely keep their Soldiers awake. But Sytrius has persistence and an indestructible sense of duty on his side, which makes him a worthy opponent." Respect and even something like admiration spread on his face. "Still, I had evaded him for centuries. With Margreta gone, everything, even freedom, lost its meaning."

Margreta. The name of the woman who managed to capture a demon's heart, without giving hers in return.

Suddenly, I wondered what it would be like to be made love to by him. Did he do everything with the same passion he spoke . . . and kissed? An achy feeling stirred in my chest, and I recognized it as envy—I was envious of a woman, who'd been dead for two centuries, of her getting to experience *him*.

Meanwhile, Ivarr continued, "Sytrius brought me to the Council, who sent me to Inferno for two hundred years for getting too close to a Source, without permission."

"What is *Inferno*?"

"A form of fiery jail for demons who break the rules of the treaty. Once I got out, I spent several years on the run, until Sytrius caught up with me again. This time, he somehow convinced the Council to let me fall in Deep Sleep instead of Inferno. Not much of a difference, but the lesser evil of the two. I'm not sure why exactly Raim agreed to it. But this time, I didn't live with a woman and didn't have much time to commit that many crimes against the Council, just feeding on my own."

"So, having sex with women in order to feed on their sexual energy is considered a lesser crime than living with one and having her care about you?"

The world of demons was still a dark place for me, and their extensive list of rules murky at best in its logic.

"It would seem that way, wouldn't it?" The now-familiar wrinkle of concentration appeared on his forehead. "I can't tell for sure, though. Every judgment is case-specific. And every decision is up to the Council."

"Not up to Raim?"

"Well, Raim basically *is* the Council. He's been Grand Master for centuries. Smart and ambitious, he seems to have the interest of our kind at heart. He's also the one with the most experience. I believe Raim is probably the only one of us who hasn't spent any time in Deep Sleep."

"Would he know that you're awake now? How long until they send Sytrius after you?"

"I'm not sure." Ivarr rubbed his chin. "For whatever reason, Sytrius stopped at my place to take my car. Maybe, I need to get hold of him."

I gasped. "Why would you even think about contacting someone who hauled you in front of the Council more than once? How can you trust him?"

"Why shouldn't I trust a demon who does his job well?" he replied calmly.

I shook my head.

Obviously, playing a cat-and-mouse game for several centuries must have established some kind of connection, even respect for Sytrius in Ivarr. Didn't necessarily mean that the feeling was mutual.

In any case, I felt some caution wouldn't hurt.

"Don't worry." Ivarr sent a quick look my way. "I won't call until I can analyze this idea and its consequences better than I am capable of doing right now."

"If you think he'd be a reliable source for information . . ." I rubbed my neck in thought. If there indeed was a safe way to connect with someone who could help us with answers, maybe I could ask a couple of questions on my own. With more information on The Priory, I could figure out whether or not it was safe for me to contact them and ask for help and protection, instead of continuing to run from both people and demons.

I felt a sore spot under my hand and turned the rearview mirror my way, to inspect the three little puncture wounds on my neck, each with a small circle of bruising around it. The coloring of the bruising in various shades of blue, yellow and purple suggested that the injections were done at different times, probably, to top me up as the drugs started wearing off. I wondered if my abductors missed a dose when they got lost, thus allowing me to wake up.

"Who did that to you?" Ivarr asked gravely.

"The guards. The ones from the base. When they kidnapped me."

"Are you sure they were the guards?"

"They wore those armour suits."

"Soldier uniforms?"

"If that's what they're called—"

"Hold on." He reached out and moved my head to the side slightly, giving the injection side on my neck a quick, penetrating stare. "These don't make sense. Why would they inject you?"

"To keep me quiet?"

"What difference would it have made if you screamed?"

Sad but true. I'd been loud enough at times at the Base, no one seemed to be bothered by my screams before.

"Maybe they didn't want The Priory rep to hear me this time? And to keep me from escaping, obviously, since I ran away the moment I woke up. Who are The Priory exactly? And how come they are the ones authorized to make any deals with demons?"

"The Priory has some religious roots, but I'm not sure if they adhere to any particular religion nowadays. At the time the treaty was signed, they had a vast influence on governments of many countries but were believed to be generally apolitical. New members are selected by existing members and remain with the organization for life.

That's all I know about them. The treaty allows the Council to obtain a certain number of Sources a year for feedings. That's how you would have been acquired in the first place."

I rubbed the sore spot on my neck, absentmindedly.

"Why would they take me from the base? And where would they transport me?"

Ivarr didn't reply right away. Eventually, the grim expression on his face changed to that of frustration.

"I don't know." He exhaled finally and shook his head, muttering under his breath, "I need to feed."

Chapter 13

MAKING SURE THAT NO one appeared to be following us, we agreed to stop at the next town for the night.

Ivarr drove the truck into the parking lot of the first motel we saw, just before nightfall.

"We both need some food," he stated, gesturing at the bar next to the motel. "And I'll get us some rooms so you can rest."

'Rooms' not *'a room'*, I noted. While I'd be resting in mine, I assumed, he'd be *feeding* in his.

"I'll have to leave, Katherine," he said after escorting me into my room on the second floor of the motel. "I'll bring you dinner. Don't open the door to anyone. And here, I was meaning to give you this, too."

He dipped his hand in a side pocket of the camo backpack he brought with him from the truck and took out a shiny piece of jewelry on a red, silk cord.

"What is this?" I inspected the heart-shaped pendant, realizing that it was not shining from the outside. Instead, the light was coming from within, twirling in the middle in continuous fluid streams. "This is so unusual."

"It's *soros* stone."

"Never heard of it." I turned the heart-shaped rock in my fingers, admiring the swirls of light within.

"*Of the demon world but carved by humans*," Ivarr replied quietly, as if quoting something he'd heard long ago. "Not sure yet how I got it, but I've had it ever since I can remember."

"Why are you giving it to me?"

"To protect you while I'm not here. If you wear it, it will prevent any demon from entering this room. It also glows only in the presence of one of us. When I leave, it should turn dull. If you see it glow, don't invite anyone in. Actually . . ." He rubbed his forehead. "Don't invite anyone in. Period."

"Not even you?"

"I'm already here. Even when I leave, I'll be able to enter freely."

IVARR BROUGHT ME A hearty steak sandwich from the bar for dinner. He also gave me one of his white t-shirts to sleep in and declared he'd find a store to get some more clothes for me tomorrow.

"Ivarr . . ." I stopped him when he had his hand on the door handle, ready to leave in search for his own *meal*. "How, exactly, do you feed? I mean, I don't need any details or anything, but how do you find your, um, energy source. Are there any specific criteria that you use to select her?"

"No, nothing like that." He took his hand off the handle.

"So, just any woman would do?"

Why on earth did I care? This looked too much as an attempt to stall him.

"For a quick feed? Any woman, willing to let me close, is suitable."

"So, you don't have any preference at all?"

"I didn't say that." He took a step in my direction. "Why are you asking, Katherine?"

Good question. Why did I ask? To make sure he wasn't out there, harming anyone? He had been rather adamant about a woman's consent. I might not have known him for long, but I believed that he wouldn't hurt a woman. Why did I need to know any more about the way he fed?

"Oh, just curious. I've only seen how it's done at the base," I rushed to explain, words tripping over each other on their way out. "And I know you don't agree with that, not that I agree either, of course . . ."

I should've just kept quiet.

"Anyway," I finished my blabbing. "I was just wondering how else it could be done."

"Would you like me to show you how I feed?" His voice dropped to the consistency of honey, and his gaze trapped me like a fly in a net.

"What?" I blinked, speechless, feeling my face heat up.

Did he just ask if I wanted him to feed off me? Or did he mean I'd watch him with another woman?

Not that it mattered either way—both were out of the question, of course.

"No. No, it's fine." Now, even my ears were burning hot. "Sorry, I asked. It's none of my business. As long as no one gets harmed . . ."

Because that was my true concern, the safety of everyone involved. Right?

"I told you, I don't force."

"And I believe you." I cleared my throat, trying to collect my bearings. "Well, you, um . . . have a good night, Ivarr. I'll see you later."

AFTER HE LEFT, I HAD a long shower and changed for the night. With probably close to a foot and a half of height difference between us, Ivarr's shirt reached to just above my knees.

Getting under the covers, I nuzzled my own shoulder—the faint smell of spice and male tickled my nostrils.

I forbade myself to speculate on what he might be doing at that very moment. However, the unbidden images still floated through my mind's eye. His big, strong arms propped on the sheets, holding his large frame over a woman spread under him. The muscles of his back rippling as his body undulated over her, his hips thrusting into her.

I turned in bed, tugging the covers over my head, as if that would help me shield my mind from the vivid pictures of Ivarr with the random woman.

It could have been me . . .

The thought shot through me like a hot rod, heat surging to my lower stomach before spreading through my whole body. My arms and legs felt weak at once.

No.

Having a one-night stand with a demon was not in my plan. There was no place for anything like that in the life I was trying to return to.

I survived the accident, which killed my parents. Raised by my mom's older sister, who had become another mother to me, I graduated with honours and worked as an Accountant in an excellent firm.

I believed I had a good head on my shoulders and a healthy set of morals. My ex-boyfriend was the first and only man I'd had sex with, and I found it satisfactory enough.

Ivarr might not have been the one who kidnapped me and held me in the basement, but he still belonged to the world I was trying to escape. A realm of the gloved hands of strangers touching me in the most intimate way.

It would be feeding time on the Base right about now.

I closed my eyes tight, struggling to keep those memories away, but it wasn't the nightmares that they brought. The heat between my legs turned into a pulsating ache as soon as I thought about the cross. I squirmed under the covers. This body reaction definitely couldn't be normal.

With a gasp, I sat up in bed.

One thing Keller was absolutely right about—I would need to seek counseling as soon as I got the chance.

At least the anxiety extinguished my arousal somewhat.

Despite it being night, the room wasn't really dark. The fluorescent light from the parking lot outside reached in through the thin curtains, tinting everything inside with a sickish grey. My gaze fell at the bottle of water left by Ivarr on the table for me. Suddenly thirsty, I tossed the covers aside, got out of bed, and padded to the table under the window.

I swept the mostly empty parking lot with my gaze as I drank. It stretched between the motel I was in and the bar where Ivarr bought my sandwich, and where I was fairly certain he went in search of his own dinner.

The unsettling feeling about him returned. Suddenly, I wanted him to be here, not necessarily in bed with me, but just here, in this room. I wished he wouldn't need to pleasure women to feed and could've just shared my sandwich with me, instead. Then he would've told me more about what he'd done and seen during his incredibly long time on Earth.

The image of his eyes, full of sorrow, when he talked about the one woman he cared about and his longing for more came to mind. I believed I'd glimpsed into his soul then, and I wished to see more.

What made him feel so strongly about a woman whose heart could never be his? And why did I feel a sting of sadness, knowing that I might never find out?

Envy, or maybe even jealousy, raised its obnoxious head inside me. And I wasn't even sure which one of the women I was more envious of—the one who had his heart long ago, or the one who was probably having his body right now.

The doors of the bar across the street opened at that moment, letting a couple out. I recognized the man and almost choked on my water.

Ivarr.

A tall, willowy blonde was glued to his side, her arm around him, her other hand splayed on his chest under the open zipper of his hoodie. The low neckline of her tank top under her fitted leather jacket and the platinum-blonde pixy cut emphasized her long neck, which bent gracefully as she inclined her head his way.

The faceless, random woman from the images in my mind was now here, in flesh and body . . . a rather gorgeous body, I had to admit.

I swallowed hard and put the near empty water bottle back on the table.

Ivarr's arm was around the woman's waist, the thumb of his other hand hooked in the pocket of his jeans as he casually led his companion across the parking lot to the motel—to his room. To be devoured by him for dinner . . .

Why shouldn't it be me?

The thought exploded in my head again, blinding as lightning, incinerating whatever logically constructed objections I had.

As they crossed a poorly lit part of the parking lot, a flicker of orange-pink flashed across Ivarr's face—the demon was feeding.

And there was nothing I could do about this.

He might look like a man, but he was something else entirely, someone who had to have sex for nourishment. That was what he'd done for centuries and that would be how he would continue long after I went back to my life as Kitty Jones, the accountant.

Our paths had crossed but for a very short time here and now. Sooner or later, they would part again. He'd be a demon on the run, and I'd find my way back to Seattle and to the life I used to have.

A few days from now, everything would be different. We could be miles apart by then and any gorgeous blonde could have him.

But not tonight.

The idea came so suddenly, it made my head spin. I swayed on my feet and braced myself with my hands on the table.

Tonight he could be mine.

There was no one to judge and no one to stop me . . .

Suddenly, nothing else mattered. Common sense must have deserted me completely. I rushed to the door, shoving my bare feet into the snow boots on the way then sprinted down the stairs outside.

Tonight, he was mine.

"Ivarr." I stopped in front of them the moment they'd reached the door of a room on the first floor.

I panted from running. My hands started to shake from nerves. I didn't give myself a moment to contemplate how ridiculous I must have looked, wearing nothing but an oversized t-shirt and a pair of winter boots. "I've decided."

"On what?" He lifted an eyebrow in question.

"Your dinner," I blurted out. "You can have it . . . with me. If you want."

"Who is this?" The blonde's hand patted his chest under the hoodie. He didn't seem to notice that, staring at me intently.

I straightened my shoulders under his gaze. If he was watching my emotions, I really hoped he could make some sense of what he saw. Because the way I felt, there must have been just a lot of jumbled, muddy chaos inside me. I wasn't even sure if there still was any hint of the desire that had been simmering just under my skin since the moment I met him. Right now, I felt like one ball of tight nerves.

And anger, I realized with surprise.

Irritation buzzed inside me as I watched the woman's hand slide down his stomach until her fingers dipped under his belt.

"Is this your little sister or something?" she cooed then tossed my way, "We already had dinner, sweetie."

Ivarr's arm dropped away from the blonde's waist, and I was finally able to exhale the air that had sat tight in my lungs.

"Hey, you, asshole!" came loud and sharp from the parking lot. "Get your hands off my girl!"

A group of leather-clad men came running to the motel from the bar. The short, wiry one in the front spat on the pavement on his way to Ivarr.

"You're not fucking this moron, Jessa!" he yelled again. "I swear to God, I'll fucking break your legs if you do!"

Sizing up the approaching men, Ivarr quickly stepped in front of the seemingly unconcerned Jessa, shielding her and me from the approaching crowd.

"Get in the truck, Katherine." He tossed me the keys, tipping his chin at our truck parked about thirty feet from where we stood. "Lock the doors."

His face remained calm, his voice even. But I noticed more men rushing through the doors of the bar into the parking lot. Whether they simply hurried to watch the short guy fight or intended to join him remained to be seen. However, the odds were potentially turning against Ivarr.

"We should go." I made a tentative step towards the truck, reluctant to leave him to face the horde alone. Even with all his strength, he couldn't possibly fight a whole gang of them. Could he? Not that I would be much help here, but I simply couldn't run, leaving him behind.

"Go. I'll catch up." Ivarr nodded reassuringly then addressed the short guy, his voice friendly enough. "Sorry, man. She was alone."

"Fuck you!" Jessa's admirer stopped just a few feet away from Ivarr. He appeared pumped up and itching for a fight, making up in enthusiasm what he was lacking in size. "She's with me!"

Rolling her eyes, Jessa attempted to walk around the short guy, a bored expression on her face.

"Where are you going, you slut?" he shrieked, shoving at her shoulders with both hands. She staggered back, balancing on her mile-high heels.

"Hey!" Ivarr stepped between the two. "No need to be an asshole. We were leaving anyway." He sharply gestured towards the truck to me, urging me to get going.

I nodded, taking another step back ready to run for it.

"We?" The short guy's gaze flickered my way. "Who is this thing?"

Thing? Really?

"Is she with you?"

A shudder ran through me. I did not like the glimmer in his eyes when he ogled me. The t-shirt wasn't keeping me warm in the chilly autumn night. I resisted following his leering stare at my chest, knowing very well that my nipples must be poking against the thin material in the cold.

"See how you like *this*, big guy," the wiry man gritted through his teeth, menace thick in his voice.

I didn't wait to see what *this* was and whipped around to sprint to the truck the moment he lunged for me.

"Katherine!" Ivarr's voice cut through the night, low and dangerous, when the man caught up with me and grabbed me around my middle, swinging me back to face the fight scene in front of the motel.

The others from the bar had pounced on Ivarr. His fists turned to a blur as he swung them left and right, knocking his attackers to the ground, even as more kept coming.

Struggling against the arms that held me tight, I slammed my heel into the man's foot. Now I wished I wore something like Jessa's stilettos—the flat sole of my winter boot didn't do much damage. Still the guy hissed at my ear, jerking his foot away.

"Hold still, you little bitch! Or I'll fucking cut you."

I heard a click of a spring being released—a blade flashed, reflecting the streetlights, as my attacker slashed the knife through the air around me.

Panic shot cold through me. Using the strength of adrenaline coursing through my veins, I twisted in the arms restraining me.

"Let her go," Ivarr gritted out, from somewhere behind my shoulder, and the loud sound of his fist connecting with the skull of the man holding me drowned the noise of the hoarse breathing at my ear.

The man jerked. His arms dropped from me. Without so much as a glance around, I bolted for the truck hitting the 'unlock' button on the way.

Chapter 14

PANTING, I JUMPED INTO the passenger's seat then peered out the window at the demon fighting men.

It looked more like a slaughter to be honest. With incredible speed and unstoppable power, Ivarr threw punches in every direction, piling up bodies all around him.

A few more men ran out of the bar. I noted some of them dash to the row of parked bikes to grab some tools they obviously intended to use on Ivarr.

A tattooed guy in a leather vest yanked a thick chain from a compartment on one of the bikes and was now rushing Ivarr, swinging the chain over his head.

Another one produced something that blinked with a flash of reflected light, and I tensed in fear. A gun?

Ivarr was holding his own against them all, but I was sure someone from the motel or the bar must have called the police already. With armed bikers ganging up on him, like a pack of hyenas on a lion, Ivarr's situation seemed to become more dangerous by the second.

Unfortunately, the horde swarming Ivarr prevented him from getting to the truck, cutting off his retreat.

I had to do something.

Cursing under by breath, I crawled over the centre console into the driver's seat then slid all the way down to reach the pedals and started the engine before moving the seat closer.

Plowing through the fight to reach Ivarr, I pressed hard on the horn as the only warning, letting the guys decide for themselves whether they wanted to get out of my way or be mowed over.

"Ivarr!" I shouted through the rolled down window.

He glanced up, a flash of amusement lighting up his expression of surprise. Not a hint of fear or even concern for himself.

"Come on!" I yelled, not amused at all. "Get in."

Clutching the wheel, I couldn't reach across the wide cab of the truck to push the passenger's door open for him. He punched a couple of guys out of his way then jumped into the seat.

Without opening the door.

Mechanically, I pressed the gas pedal all the way into the floor, revving the engine to send the truck flying through the parking lot and onto the street.

What was that? How on earth did he get in?

"They're after us." Ivarr's calm statement yanked me out of my bewilderment.

In the rearview mirror, I caught the sight of a few shapes on bikes and wrenched the steering wheel to the right, taking a side road into the fields instead of going back to the highway.

"What are you doing?" There was more curiosity in his voice than alarm.

"The bikes are faster than this truck," I gritted through my clenched teeth, focusing on the dirt road lit by the headlights. "They'll catch up with us either way." I threw a quick glance his way. "Out here—there're less witnesses."

I trusted his ability to deal with our pursuers, their chains and guns notwithstanding. Whereas attracting attention on the highway could be dangerous for both of us, especially if demons were out there, looking for us.

From the corner of my eye, I noted one bike getting awfully close to the back of the truck.

"Buckle up," I warned Ivarr, quickly throwing a seatbelt across my chest, too, and clicking it in. Then I slammed on the breaks, the seatbelt digging painfully into my shoulder.

The bike behind us rammed into the tailgate, spinning on its side and off the road.

I shoved my foot against the gas pedal again, and the truck lurched ahead.

Another bike pulled to the side of the truck, and I twisted the steering wheel sharply to the left, sending him off into a ditch.

Taking my eyes off the road ahead for a moment, I scanned the rearview and the side mirrors, watching for more bikes gaining on us. But the headlights of our pursuers seemed to come to a stop at the spot where the last bike had crashed.

Obviously bored out of their skulls to attack Ivarr with so much fervor in the first place, the bikers, I hoped, had finally come to their senses and would leave us alone.

"Are there any more?" I asked Ivarr.

"No. They stopped," he replied with certainty.

Only then I ventured a shaky exhale.

"Did I kill anyone?"

"Well, none of them wore a helmet." He shrugged staring back over his shoulder. "If you did, it would be on them, not you."

"Huh!" I huffed sharply. "Why doesn't that make me feel any better?"

This was by far the craziest thing I'd ever done. Until now, my behaviour had been perfectly law-abiding. I'd never even got so much as a speeding ticket.

The shock of it all threatened to suffocate me.

"Well." Ivarr turned in his seat to face forward again, apparently satisfied that there was no further pursuit. "The last guy has just crawled out of the ditch, on his own. So, he is alive," he added brightly.

"Did *you* kill anyone?" was my next question.

"I don't think so. Not this time." He rubbed the back of his neck. "There were definitely quite a few broken bones, though."

I nodded and kept driving along the road, without having any clear sense of where we were after a while.

"How are you?"

"Don't worry about *me*, Katherine." His voice was full of unidentifiable emotion.

Adrenaline wearing off, my fingers began to tremble on the steering wheel.

"Are we okay?" I asked, needing to make sure there was no longer any immediate danger, in case I broke down. "Are they gone?"

"Yes."

I stopped the truck right in the middle of the dirt road between two empty fields.

"Fuck," I exhaled.

I hardly ever swore, but the situation warranted it.

Slowly, I uncurled my fingers and peeled my sweaty hands from the steering wheel, dropping my head to my chest.

"Just . . . give me a moment," I whispered to Ivarr, waiting for my pulse to stop pounding in my ears.

"Katherine."

He covered my hand with his, and I stared at it for a moment, trying to figure out what struck me as unusual about it.

His hand was bare, I realized. He had taken his ever-present glove off and was touching me skin to skin.

I tensed and fought the impulse to jerk my hand away from him.

"Shh," he whispered soothingly. "I just want to help you calm down."

The slight cooling sensation enveloped my hand, and I looked up in alarm. "What are you doing?" But the heavy anxiety seemed to be lightening inside me with every passing moment.

"Don't be scared," he stroked the side of my hand with his thumb in a comforting gesture. "I've learned to control this."

"Control what?"

"How much I take. When I'm awake, I can stop."

"Take?"

His words should still alarm me. Only, I was not worried. On the contrary, with every breath I took, I felt calmer.

He watched me with the same intensity I had noted in his gaze before, although, no lights were flashing through his eyes this time. Instead, I gasped at the black swirls taking over the brilliant blue of his irises, like ink dissolving in water.

"Ivarr?" There was no fear, no worry inside me, just an easy emptiness. I drew in a cleansing breath, and it came out as a sigh of content. "Your eyes. Are you okay?"

The cooling sensation stopped, and I took his hand in both of mine.

With a soft groan, he leaned back in his seat but didn't take his hand away from me.

"No," he panted heavily. "I'm not okay, but I will be."

"What's wrong?" Concern for him spiked inside me, only to disappear the very next moment with another gentle sweep of cooling sensation between our clasped hands.

He rolled his head on the headrest to face me and opened his eyes. The black swirls in them receded to the very edge, dissolving completely as he spoke.

"Thank you, Queen Katherine. Much better now."

"What was that?"

"Negative emotions are harmful." He lifted my hand to his lips—my pleasure from his soft caress against my skin immediately reflected as a bright blue spark inside his eyes. "But any positive ones have the power to heal the negative effects." He gave me a strikingly bright smile that made my breath catch for a moment.

More blue sparks came.

I was beginning to like seeing them. Not only were they pretty to look at, but their presence meant that Ivarr was well. When he fed, he grew stronger. Strong enough, apparently, to take on a whole biker gang.

The tender expression on his face hardened, deepening the wrinkle between his eyebrows.

"What is it?" I smiled in confusion at his obvious concern.

"I'm so sorry, sweetheart, but I'll have to release the pain now. I can't take it all. It's ongoing."

"What do you mean?" The smile disappeared from my face, as I slowly became aware of the dull pain in my arm. "What is this?" I reached to touch it, but Ivarr caught my hand in the air.

"Don't. You'll make it worse."

My gaze fell on a spreading bloodstain that soaked the right sleeve of my t-shirt.

"I can't believe it. I didn't even notice it!" Until now, the adrenaline must have numbed the pain before Ivarr took it away. I nudged my hand from his to lift the sleeve up and faced the long wound on my upper arm. "The bastard cut me after all." Swearing again. Twice in one day. But I really didn't have a better name for the short guy with a knife right now.

"You'll need stitches," Ivarr stated grimly.

He tore off a wide strip from the bottom of his t-shirt and deftly bandaged the wound. The whole arm throbbed now, but the trickle of thick, dark blood from the cut had almost stopped.

I noticed a few red drops on his chest.

"You're hurt, too!" I pointed at the small cut above his ear.

He brushed his hand over it then glanced at the smear of blood on his palm.

"Just a scratch," he dismissed.

"Let me see." I cupped his face and turned his head to the side. A cut was about an inch long. "It's deeper than a scratch, Ivarr. You may need some stitches, too."

"It'll heal on its own," he insisted. "But yours will definitely need medical attention."

I dropped my hands, and he rummaged through the glove compartment, taking out a folded road map.

""Since we don't have cellphones, we'll need to find a hospital the old-fashioned way." He waved the map. "I'll drive." Without waiting for my reply, he lifted me out of the driver's seat and placed me in his lap. I assumed his intention was to slide from under me and into the driver's seat next, but he paused with his hands on my waist.

"You smell . . . nice," he said softly, and touched his nose to my shoulder.

"Thank you," was the only thing I could think of in reply, incredibly grateful for the motel shower.

A strand of his hair brushed against my cheek. In the dark, the gold shine in it made it appear luminous. I leaned my face closer, enjoying the soft caress of silky tresses against my skin.

"You smell very nice, too," I whispered, filling my lungs with his spicy masculine scent. Splaying my hand on his hard chest, I traced the outline of his pectorals under his t-shirt, firm and solid, like the rest of him. He made the night feel safe, even as both of us were on the run.

Here in the dark, surrounded by his scent, the moment was filled only with the sensation of his hands on my waist, his warmth soaking into my skin through the thin material of the t-shirt.

"The soft glow inside you," he murmured just above my ear and slid his hands up to my shoulders, bringing us closer, "is irresistible."

I raised my hands to dip my fingers into the golden silk of his hair, my whole body singing with awareness, tempting me to simply enjoy the sensation. My movement pulled on my wound, however, making me flinch.

Ivarr stilled.

"We'll need to get you to the hospital," he said with resolve, but did not release me from his arms.

Instead, he leaned in and gently pressed his lips to my forehead. His kiss left a dusting of frosty sensation on my skin, and the budding desire in me dissipated instantly.

I shifted in his lap uncomfortably, promptly removing my hands from him. With the warmth of arousal gone, the awkward feeling of unease quickly filled the void left behind.

Sliding to the side, I let him move into the driver's seat.

"Hospital it is."

Chapter 15

WE DIDN'T LEAVE MUCH in the motel. Ivarr took his backpack to the truck before going to the bar, and the only things left behind were my filthy clothes—nothing I wanted back, anyway.

He used the first aid kit in the truck to clean the blood off my arm and to cover the cut by his ear with a Band-Aid. Then in the yellow light of the cab, I figured out the map, and Ivarr drove us to the next town south along the highway.

Before going to the hospital, though, he pulled into the parking lot of a shopping plaza.

"A women's clothing store and a lingerie boutique right next to it," he announced with satisfaction in his voice, and placed his hand on the door handle, ready to exit.

"They'll be closed at this hour." I stopped him. "Are you planning to break in? Or are you going to seep through the wall the way you did to get in the truck at the motel?"

He squinted my way.

"You noticed?"

"Of course I did. What was that?"

He frowned. "There was no time to open the door."

"All of you can do it? The other demons, too? Walk through doors like that?"

"Yes. Any door, wall or fence."

Another new thing I learned about them. "Why have I never seen the others do it?"

"They're not allowed to walk through walls in front of humans at the base. That's a rule."

The list of rules proved even longer than I thought.

"Is that how you're planning to get in the store now?"

"Do you see any other way?"

I glanced at the storefront, a neon 'closed' sign glaring bright on the door.

"No. I guess not."

"I'll go in, take some clothes for you and leave the money by the cash register along with the price tags." He took a wallet out of the back pocket of his jeans. "What's your size, by the way?"

"You've done this before, haven't you?"

He just gave me a non-committal shrug in reply.

I'd just have to add this to the long list of unusual things that I got to witness lately.

"What about the cameras? Motion sensors?"

"Unless things have changed drastically during the past two years I spent in Deep Sleep, Katherine, many cameras have blind spots. Small mom-and-dad stores like these aren't likely to have many motion sensors, either, if any. Here." Ivarr inserted the key back in the ignition, obviously humouring me. "Be ready to start the truck and get out of here if you hear any alarms blaring. Now, what are your sizes?"

"THESE ARE RATHER DRESSY." I lifted a pair of black slacks from the pile of clothes Ivarr had shoved in my lap, admiring the faint shimmer of the material in the dim light entering the truck.

We made it to the parking lot of the hospital, and I was about to get changed, with him turned to the side window to give me privacy.

He zipped up his hoodie to hide the blood stains and the torn-off hem of his t-shirt he used to bandage my arm. Astonishingly, this was all he had to do to appear impeccably dressed despite his casual clothing.

"Those were the simplest things I could find," he grumped in reply. "Lots of evening gowns and stuff."

"Oh, I don't mind. They are beautiful. Thank you." I fingered the red lace of the bra and panty set next. "It's just if you want our story to the hospital to be that I cut my arm by fixing some farm machinery, these clothes may raise some questions."

That was how Ivarr suggested to explain my wound to the hospital staff, since I was positive that telling the truth would send the police—and possibly demons—our way.

"I'll deal with the hospital staff." He shrugged my concerns off.

I sneaked a glance his way to make sure his back was still to me, before slipping the t-shirt off over my head, then quickly put the underwear and the pants on.

Carefully, so as not to aggravate my injury, I slid the straps of the bra over my arms.

"I'll . . . um, I'll need your help," I realized that I wouldn't be able to close the hooks of the bra with only one arm fully functioning.

With my back turned to him, I felt the light touch of his fingers as he deftly closed the little hooks for me.

"Red suits you." He traced the satin strap with one finger after he was done.

"I—I don't believe I own anything in red."

I wore a lot of grey. Black shoes. White blouses. Sensible clothes. Derek, my ex-boyfriend, used to appreciate my choices. He was planning to run for public office one day and used to say that I had the perfect style for the wife of a future politician.

"Well, now you do." Sliding up along the bra strap, Ivarr's finger reached my shoulder.

"I'll give you the money for it. When I get back home," I whispered. My throat went suddenly dry, as sweet little tingles prickled my skin under the strap he touched.

"It's a gift." His lips unexpectedly brushed against my shoulder blade.

My cheeks burning hot, I halted my breath, but he just gave me a small squeeze on the forearm.

"Get dressed, I'll take you in."

Chapter 16

"KATHERINE IS MY COUSIN from The States. I live on a farm just north of here," Ivarr explained to the triage nurse at the hospital. "She insisted on helping me to sharpen the lawn mower blades." He shook his head dramatically and added, following the nurse's gaze that flickered to my red silk top with gorgeous beading on the shoulders. "She wouldn't leave the house without changing out of her work clothes first." He let out an exasperated sigh.

The nurse's smile shone with warm sympathy as she talked to him over my head, "Does she have travel insurance?"

I shook my head in response to her question, but I didn't think she noticed it. All her attention was directed at Ivarr standing next to me. She had to crane her neck to maintain eye contact with him, but she didn't seem to mind the inconvenience.

"I'll pay." He reached for his wallet in the back pocket. "It's my farm, I'm responsible."

"It's so very nice of you," the nurse cooed, taking the cash from him to process the payment.

"YOU DID PRETTY GOOD out there," I said as we sat in the examination room, waiting for the doctor. "For someone who finds lying unnatural, you sounded very believable."

"Lying costs a lot of energy."

"So I've heard."

Ivarr shifted in the green pleather chair next to my cot. The chair groaned under the weight of his massive body.

"I've had practice—lying is unavoidable when living among humans. Even though I tried to keep away from people, I still had to lie, pretending to be one of them, whenever I came close to feed. I've had enough experience over time."

"You said you're about eight hundred years old?"

"At least. That's how far my memories reach right now. Most likely, I'm considerably older."

"How much of this time did you spend asleep?"

"I missed most of it. Between Deep Sleep and Inferno, probably about five-six hundred years."

"Centuries of pain," I whispered. "Why? What is the purpose of your being here?"

I shouldn't be asking him questions. Being ready to jump in bed with him for the thrill of physical pleasure I believed he could deliver was one thing. Getting to know him on a personal level was entirely different and, I sensed, more dangerous for me, because the more I learned about him the more things I found in him to admire.

Learning about his past helped me understand him as a person. By now, I no longer viewed him as a demon, a creature vastly different from me. When I looked at Ivarr, I saw a man, capable of feeling pain of loss, pride for his life choices, and concern for people like me. A man with solid principles and quiet dignity.

"No one knows why we're here, Katherine." A gloomy cloud shadowed his features, making his face appear truly world-weary for a moment. "The most common belief is that we came to this world as a punishment. But no one remembers exactly what the crime was or what to do now to be forgiven for it."

"Would you ever remember? How long do you need to have sex with women for all of your memories to come back?"

I asked this without judgment. Now that I understood his world a little better, I couldn't hold the way he had to obtain his nourishment against him. At least Ivarr, as opposed to the rest of them, had found a way to feed without harming anyone.

Some unpleasant note must have still slipped in my voice, because his frown deepened.

"It depends. What exactly do you mean by *sex*?"

"Well . . ." I sensed an unbidden flush of warmth spread up my face. "Whatever it is you do to get yourself fed."

He nodded slowly, his eyes on me. Unable to hold his gaze, I dropped mine. He sat with his elbows on his knees, hands clasped together. And I focused my attention on his large hands that I knew could equally deliver a bone-crushing blow and a gentlest of caresses.

"I don't *fuck* random women, Katherine." His gruff voice reached me, and I flinched. This was the first time I heard Ivarr curse.

"What do you do?" I asked quietly, knowing it would be best not to go there but unable to stop.

"Whatever gives pleasure to the woman I'm with."

"Without the actual intercourse?" I ventured a glance at his face.

He nodded, his mouth pressed into a firm line.

"I don't take my clothes off when I feed, Katherine, not even the gloves. I give the women pleasure and take their sexual energy. There is no other exchange that takes place."

"How about your own pleasure?"

"Mine?" He lifted an eyebrow, as if I'd asked something unreasonable and out of place. "That's not what feeding is about for me."

"So, it's really just about nourishment, then?"

"For the past two hundred years, yes."

Two hundred years? Since Margreta then.

"You haven't . . ."

"I haven't been inside a woman for over two centuries, Katherine. If that is what you're trying to ask."

His directedness, the way he opened up to me, laying his life bare for me to examine and judge made me want to do anything but that.

Another glimpse in his soul, dark and turbulent as it might be, revealed to me a man, who remained loyal at heart to the woman he cared about, even as his very nature left him no way to stay physically faithful to her.

"Hunger is the most prevailing urge." Ivarr spoke while I remained silent. "It overpowers everything, even arousal in the likes of me. It takes someone very special to make a demon lust after them in *every* way."

His words tugged at my heart with a new jolt of ache.

"Was Margreta that special woman for you?"

"Yes."

"Did you remember everything when you were with her? Were you no longer hungry then?"

"I'm sure I must've had more memories than I do now. The hunger was definitely more bearable during the six years I spent with her, but it was still there. It's inescapable. They say it only stops with forgiveness."

Six years were not enough? Demons were truly insatiable.

"Miss Jones?" The doctor walked in, holding a clipboard in his hand and interrupting our conversation.

It was a man, I noted distractedly, hoping he would be able to pay more attention to my stitches than to Ivarr's handsome face.

IT WAS STILL EARLY morning when we left the hospital. The sky had just begun to change to a lighter grey on the horizon.

My wound neatly stitched, my arm freshly bandaged, I clung to Ivarr's forearm, almost running at his side, trying to keep up in the gold-lace Mary Jane shoes he had gotten for me.

Less than ten feet from the truck, I tripped, and Ivarr lifted me in his arms, without skipping a step.

"You need some sleep, sweetheart," he said with a concerned frown. "There should be a coffee shop somewhere around here. They generally open early. I'll get you breakfast. You can sleep in the truck while I drive."

Curled against his chest, I felt I could just sleep like this right now—no breakfast necessary.

Reaching the truck, Ivarr shifted me in his arms to open the passenger's door, then placed me gently into the reclined seat.

"What should I get you for breakfast? Herbal tea or milk? No coffee. Coffee will keep you awake."

"Tea, please." I figured I'd fall asleep before he found a coffee shop anyway. It would be an iced tea by the time I woke up.

"Are you wearing your amulet?"

I nodded, lifting my hand to the silk cord around my neck, just to make sure.

"I'll lock you in the truck afterwards, Katherine, and find a phone to call Sytrius."

"Oh, can you ask him about The Priory?" I perked up. "What's their part in the new agreement? I need to figure out how much I can trust them."

We'd been driving south, towards the border and my home. I had to know if it was safe for me to return to my life back in Seattle. On one hand, I could definitely use The Priory's protection from demons. On the other, I was uncertain whether I could wholly trust the organization that made deals with them in the first place.

I hoped whatever news Sytrius might share would help me make a better-informed decision on what to do next. Ivarr seemed to believe we could rely on Sytrius for an accurate update, and at the moment, I had no other way to get the information I needed.

I fought to keep my eyes open. "I want to know what Sytrius tells you."

"Sure." He undid my shoes and slid them off then rubbed my feet gently.

"Those shoes are so beautiful," I mumbled sleepily as he took off my black coat and tossed it into the back seat, then buckled me in. "I feel like Cinderella wearing them." He grabbed the quilt from the back and tucked it neatly around me. "Thank you," I whispered, my heart warming with gratitude. "Thank you for looking after me."

"You're welcome," he said quietly, smoothing my hair out of my face. "I have no idea why I am in this world, Katherine. But this . . ." He tugged the quilt up to my chin. "This right here gives me a true sense of purpose."

Chapter 17

IT FELT AS IF I'D ONLY managed to doze off for a moment when my throbbing arm woke me up.

"Ivarr?" I called, blinking in the bright sunlight flooding the cab of the truck. "What time is it?"

"Almost two in the afternoon." The answer came from the driver's side.

"Did you talk to Sytrius?" I rubbed my eyes, straightening in my seat.

"No. The phone number I had for him has been disconnected." He flexed his jaw, his mouth forming a hard line. "I got a cell phone while you slept, but I don't trust anyone else at the base enough to call them."

So much for getting more information. Disappointment spread through me, raising more concerns.

"Do you think he's been sent after you again?"

"There is no way to tell for sure."

My anxiety accelerated. In addition to demons who might be searching for me, we could also have Sytrius on our heels.

"Don't." He glanced my way. "Please don't worry yet. Sytrius is not that quick. The way the Council feeds him, it'd take him a while to catch up with me."

He took his hand off the steering wheel and squeezed mine reassuringly.

"I just wish I knew what's going on . . ." I exhaled, stroking my thumb along the side of his glove.

"We'll figure it out," he promised reassuringly. "I got you a sandwich and fruit salad for lunch." He gestured to the paper bag on the front console. We'll be in Calgary in a few hours. There, we'll stop for dinner and a better rest for you."

I was more than willing to forgo all comfort for the sake of getting home faster and opened my mouth to protest.

"In a real bed." He cut me off before I had a chance to say anything.

'Real bed' sounded amazing after being curled up in the seat of the truck for hours. Still, I worried about the delay from stopping.

"Are you sure it'll be safe? Shouldn't we just keep going?"

"First, we really need to figure out exactly where we're going. Otherwise, I'm afraid we run the risk of making a mistake."

With everything that happened last night, I remembered, Ivarr never got fed and still couldn't properly analyze our situation. The lack of information didn't allow me to make a confident decision, either.

"I wonder if I should get hold of anyone at the base after all." Ivarr sounded as if he were thinking out loud. "Someone from the Eastern Council may be safer."

"Right. There is more than one Council." I recalled him speaking of them in plural before. "How many?"

"Two. One in each hemisphere."

Twice as many demons.

"Fortunately for us, neither of them are fast to act. From what I know about life at the base, it's slow like molasses. It takes a while for the Council to reach a decision and even longer to act on it."

"Why?" My monotonous days at the Base and the fittingly slow manner of Garrett's speech rose in my memory.

"There is no concern about running out of time. Ever. All things get done, eventually. Sooner or later, they will catch me again, but it may not even happen in this decade. Meanwhile we'll have lots of time to figure everything out for you."

"Okay. Good to know." I relaxed a little. *'Next decade'* sounded comforting.

"WE'LL STOP HERE." IVARR pulled into the underground parking lot of a hotel in Calgary a few hours later. "You'll have a decent rest and some food. We can leave sometime after midnight to reach the border before the morning. I'll have to make the decision of whom at the Eastern Council to call by then."

"I don't have an ID to cross the border," I reminded. For all I knew, my passport could be still in the desk in my apartment where I left it last.

"That is not a problem. I'll take you through a passage in the mountains I use when I don't want to bring anyone's attention to me. Unless things have changed drastically between Canada and The United States in the past couple of years, I'm fairly certain we'll cross without trouble."

It sounded so easy coming from him, but then again, Ivarr had been traveling the world for centuries, crossing borders, oceans, and continents many times.

"I'll get you a room and bring you dinner." He parked the truck, walked around the front, and opened the door for me. "Then I'll have to feed, too."

Feed?

My stomach flipped at hearing this word.

He must have noticed my reaction—his voice softened.

"I have to clear the fog in my head, Katherine. It's too easy for me to make mistakes in my current state. This . . ." He tipped his chin at my bandaged arm. "Cannot happen again. It was my responsibility to keep you safe, and I failed."

"It wasn't your fault." I argued, my voice small. "I shouldn't have . . ."

Shouldn't have done what? Run to him? Stopped him from taking Jessa to his room by offering myself in her place?

He said nothing more, but I sensed the unspoken question in his silence. Less than twenty-four hours ago, I literally propositioned him. Now, he was giving me the chance to confirm the offer, giving me a choice once again.

Everything felt different, however. Within the past hours, Ivarr had become much more to me than simply an impossibly attractive demon. He could no longer be just a hot man for one night, someone I could easily forget afterwards.

The night spent with him was sure to leave memories and regrets. And now I knew, the regrets would be not of what I'd *have* with him, but of what I'd *lose* once he inevitably left me.

Everything inside me already felt hollow at the thought of having to part with him, possibly within days. Any kind of intimacy added between us, I sensed, would only make the loss greater.

"Come, Queen Katherine." Ivarr finally broke the silence, taking my hand in his and heading to the exit.

He didn't need to voice it. I understood from his tone that he was not going to hold me to my impulsive promise.

A heavy weight settled over my chest nevertheless.

IVARR SENT ME TO THE hotel store to buy some painkillers for my arm, while he checked into a room. Then he snuck me upstairs.

"Would you like to have a nap now? There is still time before dinner. Or are you hungry already?"

Hungry.

Even the word itself sounded wrong to my ear somehow.

"No." I shook my head. "I'll just have a quick shower and go to bed if you don't mind. Feel free to lock the door when you leave." I gestured at the heart pendant around my neck. "Either way, I'll be fine."

The only sleep I managed to get last night were the few hours in the truck. This would be the first time I'd get to sleep in a proper bed for over a month.

Feeling truly exhausted, I desperately hoped to pass out the minute he left the room. Then when I woke up, his *feeding* would be over, and I could try to ignore the fact it had ever happened.

IT WASN'T THE BEST sleep I ever had, but it turned out to be re-vitalizing. I woke up, feeling physically completely myself. The fog in my head had fully cleared. My energy returned. And the pain in my arm had numbed, possibly mostly due to the painkillers, still it was a relief.

"Good evening, Sleeping Beauty." Ivarr sat in the armchair by the window, facing me.

"Have you been here all this time?" I sat up in bed, with a thud of selfish hope in my chest.

"No, I went out for a little while."

"Feeding?" I blurted out before I could stop myself as my heart skipped with a jolt.

"No." He got up and grabbed a white box from the nightstand. "Not feeding. Shopping."

I slowly released a breath, reminding myself that any relief his words brought to me was only temporary. If he hadn't fed yet, he'd have to go soon.

He'd changed while I slept. A pair of charcoal pants and a black button-down shirt replaced his jeans and ripped t-shirt. His thick, golden hair had been tamed and tied back.

He sat down on the bed next to me. A whiff of expensive cologne mixed with the warmth of his scent reached my nostrils.

I held my breath, willing to stop my pulse from racing.

"Let me see your arm." He opened the box filled with medical supplies and reached for me, his long fingers almost touched, circling my puny bicep.

Carefully, he removed the bandage covering my injury and inspected the stitches.

"Looks good."

I thought about the long centuries of his life.

"You must have seen a lot of wounds," I said, partially to distract myself from the overwhelming mix of feelings brought on by his proximity.

"Cut, stab, burn." He nodded, cleaning the skin around the stitches before applying some gel and a fresh bandage. "All kinds of them. My own wounds heal, regardless whether I treat them or not. The ones on humans have always been much more difficult to deal with. Especially, before antibiotics were invented."

He nimbly bandaged my arm while he spoke, his head leaning over just an inch or two away from my face. I braced myself against the inexplicable urge to bury my nose in his hair.

"Why didn't you feed?" My voice came out soft, barely more than a whisper.

Would it be better if he had fed already and it was all over by now?

"I got distracted."

His hand slipped into mine.

"By what?"

"This." With a gentle squeeze, he let go off my hand and rose to his feet to place an elegant paper bag from the table by the window into my lap. "I saw this and wanted to see it on you."

I peeked under the gold and silver striped tissue paper inside the bag.

"Red?" I gasped at the glimpse of crimson silk.

"Your colour." He nodded, watching me pull the dress out.

I got off the bed, holding the ankle-length gown up. "This is gorgeous, Ivarr. So beautiful." I pressed it to my chest and kicked my foot out, sending the flared skirt to flutter around my legs in scarlet waves of shimmering silk.

"The exact colour of my favourite emotion in you."

I glanced up to catch him staring at me.

"It's too much."

"It's a gift," he dismissed.

"Another gift? It's too much, Ivarr," I insisted. The dress was impeccably tailored and must have been expensive. The fabric felt rich and luxurious in my arms. "It's unnecessary."

He came closer, his chest brushed against my forearms clutching the dress in front of me.

"You like it," he stated confidently.

"Oh, I do," I exhaled. "I love it—"

"Then wear it. I want to take you to the restaurant downstairs for dinner."

"But . . ."

Surely, I could wear the clothes I already had. They were dressy enough for any restaurant.

"You'll enjoy wearing it, Katherine. And it would please me to see you in it. Who else do you have to worry about?"

Who else?

"Just you and me?" I craned my neck to see his face high above me, calming warmth melting in the vivid blue of his eyes.

"No one else matters tonight," he replied, his lips curving into the wide smile I liked so much already.

Any resistance had evaporated in me under the effects of his grin combined with the growing desire to wear the spectacular creation I clutched to my chest.

"No one else," I whispered, smiling back at him, then dashed to the bathroom to get ready.

Chapter 18

I WAS ON MY SECOND flute of champagne. The effervescence bubbled inside me, heating my cheeks. However, I had a strong feeling that the warm pleasure spreading through me had as much to do with my surroundings as it did with the wine.

The soft music, muted voices, and the glow of the subdued lighting in the restaurant created the atmosphere of intimate comfort. The sight of Ivarr's smiling face across the table completed the picture, filling me with excitement head to toe.

"Tell me what you see," I asked for the third time since we got here.

He tilted his head, squinting.

"Right now, you are a kaleidoscope of happy colours, Katherine. A sunny yellow, warm caramel, and bright orange. All swirl with bursts of every tint of pink from magenta to blush."

"It sounds so beautiful." I sighed. "The way you describe it."

"It's gorgeous," he agreed, his eyes flashing bright blue below his hooded eyelids. Since he sat with his back to the rest of the room, this was my own private lightshow.

"I wish I could see what you see."

"You *feel* it. That's what matters."

He lifted a glass with whiskey on the rocks, and I watched his lips touch the glass when he took a drink from it. Ivarr had explained that demons couldn't get drunk from alcohol, but he enjoyed the scorching sensation of a good whiskey in his mouth. The burn made him feel alive, he claimed.

"Thank you," I said softly. "Thank you for everything, Ivarr. For this evening. This dress. For taking care of me all this time. Without you, being on the run would've been so much more dangerous and definitely much less, um, enjoyable." I smiled, taking another sip of my champagne. "I really don't remember the last time I enjoyed myself this much."

Derek and I used to go out regularly. Most of our dates involved some important political or social functions. But even when we were alone, I always had the persistent feeling of being watched and judged.

It occurred to me now that it wasn't other people who made me feel that way, but Derek himself, with his constant obsession about how he was perceived by everyone around him.

I blinked, chasing the memories of my ex away, refusing to let anything mar this moment, but it seemed Ivarr had picked up on the dip in my mood already.

"Who is waiting for you at home, Katherine?"

Slowly, I put my glass flute back on the table, stalling my answer. "No one."

"Where are your family?" He took another drink of whiskey. A plate with a steak dinner sat in front of him, too. He'd picked at it a little to keep me company, but hardly ate much. Almost all of the food was still there.

"I don't have a family. My parents passed away a while back."

"When?"

I glanced up at him, unused to those types of questions. Normally, people avoided going into the details, choosing the tried and true *'sorry for your loss'* at this point.

"A long time ago. I was seven." I swallowed, reaching for the glass of water at my side and bypassing the champagne for now. "A car accident."

That was all anyone needed to know.

Only a few people knew that I was there with them, the day when the load of steel rods slid from the flatbed of the truck in front of our family car and hurtled through the windshield.

The rods speared my parents in the front. One went through my father and through the driver's seat, piercing my stomach, as I sat in the back seat right behind him.

They said I got lucky. The blow to my middle made me fold in two. Otherwise, my head and chest would have been stabbed by more rods that pierced our vehicle like a pincushion.

Most of this I learned from others when I got older, because I didn't remember much myself. Whenever I thought back to that day, I could only recall a complete vacuum of horror—void of colour or sound—hollowed in time and space, and the feeling of terror that still came back in nightmares sometimes.

My stare glued to the plate in front of me, I felt Ivarr's hand covering mine and squeezed his fingers in return before continuing, "I was raised by my aunt, my mother's older sister. She passed away four years ago. Auntie Sue."

She was the one who stayed in the hospital with me, day and night, while they were stitching my internal organs back together. Years later, she was also the one who told me the devastating news that I would never be a mother—the rod went through my uterus, and it had to be removed.

Derek never wanted children. He actually seemed to be glad when I told him I couldn't have any. Something that I had considered a horrible defect about myself for years, he treated as an advantage. His acceptance was probably one of the main reasons I fell in love with him then.

"What happened to your man?" Ivarr asked unexpectedly.

I stared at him in surprise.

"Why do you think there was a man?"

"Wasn't there?"

Awkwardly, I tugged at my hand in his, but he just shifted closer, not letting me break the hold.

"I—I had a boyfriend, but we broke up a couple of months ago." This was the first time I spoke about Derek with someone who didn't know him personally. Except for giving short answers to the questions of my friends, I didn't discuss our breakup with anyone.

"Why?"

Nosy demon.

"Does it matter why?" I replied, marveling at his insistence, which bordered on being intrusive.

"I want to know. What didn't work for you?"

"For me? Actually, I thought everything was perfect. We were together for over two years and talked about getting married. At only thirty-two, Derek has done very well for himself as a motivational speaker. He is the author of several bestselling self-help books and has very good prospects in politics." I recited all the facts that used to fill me with pride every time I talked about Derek. Now, all I felt was sadness.

"What happened then?"

"Nothing."

That was the part that hurt the most. Nothing happened. There was no fight, no disagreement between us. At the time when Derek told me he didn't think that things would work out between us, I still honestly believed they had already worked out very well.

I'd tried hard to be everything I thought he needed in the woman at his side, content to live in the shadow of his greatness. It thrilled me to be the woman behind the successful man, his support in public, the source of his strength behind the scenes.

"One day he came over and said we needed to talk." I crumpled the white napkin in my free hand. "Always scrupulously correct in everything he did, Derek broke up with me in a very proper manner, too. At my apartment, not at a restaurant or some other public place.

In person, not over the phone or anything. He said he needed to focus on his future and could no longer give me the attention I deserved. Honestly, I'm not sure what he meant." The old hurt made me frown. "We used to go out once or twice a week, mostly to events which would benefit his career—fundraisers, public rallies, galas . . ."

I trailed off, still confused about his reasons. After Derek left, I spent weeks wondering what I had done wrong for him to end it. Had I asked for too much extra attention? Had I called him or texted him too often? He hadn't complained about anything before.

Everything seemed to be fine, until the day he left me alone in my apartment. I held it in as long as I could, waiting until the door closed behind him and the elevator dinged in the hallway. Only then I slid to the floor in a crying heap—the man I'd thought I'd grow old with gone, leaving me with nothing but a void in place of our carefully constructed future.

Ivarr squeezed my hand gently, bringing me back to the moment. I'd tried so hard not to spoil this evening. Though, even with my bubbly mood subdued, I didn't regret his asking. It felt liberating, in a way, to be able to talk about everything freely.

"Why do you blame yourself for this?"

"I do?"

He nodded firmly.

"No. It's not that," I protested. "It's not about a blame, really. It's just . . . It's a two-way street, right? Any relationship requires effort from both partners. So if it falls apart, it's a failure of both people. I've just been trying to find my part in it, to see what I did wrong."

"Why? To what purpose?"

I shook my head, letting my shoulders drop.

"I don't know. To avoid making the same mistake in the future?"

"Are you planning to get back together with Derek? In the future?"

"No. Why?"

"Well, unless you're trying to figure out your mistakes—and by *your*, I mean both of your mistakes, his and yours—to make sure you'll avoid them in a future relationship between the two of you, it makes very little sense to dig through the past. With another person, there will be other mistakes, right? And just because it didn't work out with this man, doesn't mean it won't work with the next."

Staring at him, I considered his words for a moment. What he was saying was simple but made a lot of sense. Obsessing about what it was that I did wrong in this relationship wouldn't help to put the breakup behind me and move on. Neither, learning what the mistake was would ensure a happy relationship with someone else.

"It is rather sad, though, if you really think about it, because it means that there is no way to prevent what happened. No matter how hard I'd work on it next time—"

"Does it have to be a hard work to be with someone?"

"Well, doesn't it?" For me it was. Back then, I even prided myself on how much effort I'd put into being with Derek, giving it my all to be the perfect girlfriend I thought he needed.

"Okay, I'm not claiming to be an expert here. I mean my one and only relationship with a human happened two hundred years ago. But for me, being together with someone I cared about was not *work*. In fact, it would have been infinitely harder to stay apart."

My chest tightened from the simple truth in his words, and I inhaled deeply before breathing out the acknowledgement, "Derek was the wrong man for me?"

Ivarr just shrugged his shoulder.

"Like I said, I'm not an expert, but it might be time for you to let go of your guilt and get over that man."

"Who told you I'm not over him?"

"I don't need to be told. I see it, remember?" he replied, matter-of-fact.

"Just because you can see emotions doesn't mean you can read thoughts."

"Thoughts are connected to emotions. It takes some practice—every person is different—but sometimes I can figure out what you may be thinking while you're feeling a certain way."

"So, since I have some lingering guilt about my breakup, it means I'm not over my ex? Is that what you mean?"

"Something like that. Emotions are often attached to people in your life. Let go of one, get over the other."

"Really?" I narrowed my eyes at him but was unable to stop the corner of my mouth from curling up in a smile. Despite the topic of our conversation, I didn't seem to be able to stay sad for long tonight. "Sounds so simple."

"I may be wrong. What do I know, I'm just a demon." A teasing glint in his eyes betrayed his good humour. "But human life is so heartbreakingly short, and your youth is evanescent. It seems a shame to waste them both, obsessing over things you can't change and a man you don't need."

"Well, if you put it that way . . ." With a smile on my face and the glass of champagne in my hand, I considered his words for a minute, swaying a little to the restaurant music.

"Dance with me?" Ivarr asked, completely out of the blue.

"What?" A blues melody played softly in the background, luring me into its rhythm. "Ivarr, this is not for dancing. There isn't even enough space here—"

"We'll find space." He tossed his napkin on the table, getting up. "Come." He tugged at my hand still held in his.

"I—" I glanced around the restaurant nervously. It wasn't busy this late at night, but a few tables were occupied, people already giving us curious stares.

"It's just you and me tonight, Queen Katherine," Ivarr reminded, his expectant gaze on me. "No one else."

No one else.

My stomach fluttered with excited anticipation.

Wine might have played a big part in it, but for once, I didn't want to be the quiet, sensible Kitty. Suddenly, I was Katherine—the daring, fearless queen in a blazing red dress and golden shoes.

Quickly, I grabbed his glass from the table and took a swig. Whiskey burned my throat like molten lava.

"Fine." I got up resolutely. "Let's go."

"You're not charging into a battle, my queen." Ivarr chuckled, taking my hand. "It's just a dance," he murmured, tugging me forward.

My skin tingled from being this close to him, as though a wave of champagne bubbles rushed through it.

Hand on the small of my back, Ivarr maneuvered me between the tables towards the open space in front of the bar. Mindful of my injured arm, he lifted my hand in his and stepped even closer, almost flush with me.

The first few steps were unhurried, following only every other beat of the music, as Ivarr led me in a slow dance. The confidence of his movements betrayed his skill. As soon as he sensed that I was able to keep up, he increased the tempo and took a few more complicated steps.

"You're a great dancer, Katherine." His voice held an approval that warmed me from the inside. He extended his arm to the side, prompting me to twirl.

The silk of my skirt swirled around my legs, hugging my hips in a twist before cascading down in soft folds again when he caught me back in his arms.

"Thank you, but I wouldn't say *great*." I laughed. "Just whatever the few years of dance lessons through middle school taught me. Besides . . ." I admired the blue of his eyes above me. "Everything is easier with a good partner."

Following his confident lead, I allowed myself to get completely lost in the melody. The whole world seemed to fall away, leaving me with him—the only place I wanted to be at this moment.

The soothing flow of music.

The feeling of being safe in his strong arms.

An effervescent swirl of happiness curled through me like luxurious gossamer silk.

I was in a fairy tale, completely detached from reality, above any worry or fear. Right now, I truly felt like a queen.

Ivarr's queen.

As if in a dream, I felt him release my hand. He wrapped both arms around me, pulling me into him. I rested my head on his chest, enjoying the feel of the hard muscle concealed under the crisp material of his shirt against my cheek.

He slid his hands higher up my back, and I felt the warmth of them against my shoulder blades. His thumbs skimmed the edge of my neckline on the back, teasing my skin, as he led me in a slow dance.

I turned my face to burrow my nose in his chest, breathing him in. Wrapped in his scent and body, I suddenly understood acutely the meaning of his words *'life is so heartbreakingly short.'*

People had hardly any time to do what they wanted, and I'd wasted so much of it doing what I believed others expected me to do.

Right now, I knew with absolute certainty what I wanted. Or rather *whom.*

"I want you, Ivarr," I whispered into his shirt. He was so much taller than me, I would never reach to his ear, and I didn't expect him to hear me. But I felt his body tense and his arms flex around me as soon as my words left my mouth.

Tilting my head back, I met his gaze. His eyes darkened to the colour of the ocean before the storm. The hungry heat in them sent my heart flutter, fanning sparks down through my belly.

Sudden applause brought me back into the restaurant, making me aware that we'd stopped dancing. I swept the room with my gaze. The few people present clapped their hands smiling at us.

"A bow, my queen?" Ivarr said, his voice low and raspy, then extended his arm to lead me to his side.

My cheeks flushed hot from the acute awareness of the silk of my skirt swishing against the heated skin of my thighs when I dipped in *grande révérence* to our small audience.

"Let's get out of here?" Ivarr tossed a few large bills on the bar counter.

"Let's," I agreed, breathless.

Chapter 19

WE ONLY MADE IT OUT the door and into the short wide hallway that led to the lobby, when Ivarr swung me to the side, pressing my back against the wall.

"Don't go out tonight," I exhaled quickly, searching his eyes, as my pulse thundered in my ears. "Stay with me."

I lifted my hands to his shoulders, as his large body covered mine, and dug my fingers in his hard muscle, bringing him to me.

"Tonight, feed off me." My voice was firm, carrying my determination. There was no way I could let him go out right now in search of someone else. No way at all.

"I couldn't feed off another," he rasped, leaning with his arms on the wall above my head. "While you slept, I went to the bar and . . . I couldn't even talk to anyone there. I knew I had to, but the taste of your emotions in me—I couldn't bring myself to soil it with anything else."

He slid his hands along the wall, to cage me in, and buried his face in my hair. "What are you doing to me, my queen?"

"Me?"

"I've been watching your feelings for me change and grow into a delicious mix. There are so many emotions in it now. Just for me. Too powerful to resist . . ."

"Don't resist." I linked my fingers behind his neck and lifted my face to his. Champagne might have given me the courage to voice it now, but I knew I'd felt it all along. "I want this."

"There's always doubt in you." He groaned low, and I felt his arms tremble with restrain.

"Oh God, Ivarr, of course there is! Doubt, anxiety, fear . . . But there is this overwhelming need for you, too. I know you can see it. I want this to happen. Even if only once."

This entire night might feel like a dream. But if all I was left with at the end was just a memory of the dream, I had to have it. "I want to know what it's like to be with you." I rose to my tiptoes to bring our lips closer. "I want to *feed* you."

Without saying another word, he lowered his mouth to mine, swallowing my gasp in a scorching kiss. His teeth grazed against my lower lip as he parted my lips with his tongue, demanding access with the desperate hunger of a starving demon.

Swept into his kiss, I ran my hands up his hard chest, the fine fabric of his shirt smooth under my palms. Arousal heated my inside, licking up my inner thighs and swelling in my breasts. A moan escaped from my throat into Ivarr's kiss.

"*My* dinner," he rasped against my mouth, his expression wild. "Now."

I hugged his neck as he swept me off my feet and carried me to the elevators.

As if through a haze, I caught a curious glance cast our way by the night receptionist at the desk of the otherwise deserted lobby and hid my face in Ivarr's shoulder.

"You're a true Viking with caveman tendencies." I giggled softly.

He shifted me in his arms to press the elevator call button.

"A true Viking would've tossed you over his shoulder and run, which would have been much faster, too," he groaned. "I have to hold back and act civil to avoid questions that would slow us down."

He carried me into the elevator and kissed me again before the doors even closed.

"There must be cameras in here," I panted between his kisses, cupping the side of his face.

He leaned away a little, and my breath caught at the sight of him. The passion of his eyes on me, the pools of blue rimmed with bright crimson. It didn't scare me in the slightest to see the red glow this time.

"Your eyes," I whispered, gliding my hand up his smooth cheekbone. "They are so beautiful." I smiled. "You're too handsome to be a Viking. You need some ruggedness to go with your muscles. A couple of scars? A beard, maybe?"

"Scars don't stay on my kind. Everything heals eventually." He kissed my hand at his face. "But I can grow a beard for you." He chuckled. "Just say the word, my queen."

I wrapped my arms round him, bringing us closer as he kissed my neck—hot and urgent. My eyelids drooped, and I melted into him, cascading waves of warmth spreading through me with his every kiss. Breathless, I couldn't get enough of his mouth on me.

I was only half-aware of him unlocking the door of our room then kicking it shut behind us.

Lowering me gently onto the bed, he trailed kisses down my collarbone while blindly searching through my expansive skirt with his hands.

I felt his hot mouth close over my nipple through the fabric of the dress the same moment his large hands landed on my naked thighs. A sharp charge of desire shot through my lower stomach and pulsed between my legs.

The need for him flooded my veins with liquid heat.

"Ivarr," I pleaded, curling my fingers in his hair as he rolled my nipple between his teeth.

He flashed me a crimson glance and tugged on my underwear as I lifted my hips to help him slide it down my legs.

Rising to his knees on the bed next to me, he clicked his belt buckle open.

"This course will be fast," he warned, pulling his zipper down. "Control is hard around you." He grabbed my hips and yanked me to him along the bed then covered my body with his. "I'm starving," he murmured against the side of my neck as his hand moved down between us. "And everything about you is so delicious."

I gasped when I felt his fingers parting my folds. His touch ignited a new fiery rush of arousal, and I eagerly ground my core against his hand.

Dipping his finger inside me, he pumped it in and out, slowly at first, circling my most sensitive spot at the end of each thrust, until my legs trembled, and my inner muscles clenched with need to come.

"Soon, sweetheart," he soothed in response to my whimpers. His fingers left me, then I felt the heat of the thick crown of his shaft press against my entrance.

With a guttural groan, I arched into him, prompting him to close the distance between us.

Slowly, he eased in, stretching me and filling me completely.

"Ivarr . . ." I breathed out, savoring the taste of his name on my lips along with the exquisite sensation of having him fully inside me.

He paused for a moment, and a small shudder rippled through his powerful body.

"What is it?" I slid my hands up and down the tight, corded muscles in his neck and shoulders, hard like rock under his shirt. "Ivarr?"

"It's just . . . been a while," he whispered through his clenched teeth and pressed the side of his face to my temple. "And you . . . This is more than I could've imagined."

Gently, I caressed his back, chasing the tension out of his body. Slowly, he began to pump his hips.

Long and sensual at first, his thrusts increased in speed and intensity.

I yanked the leather cord out of his hair, setting it free, and fisted my hands in the golden mass. Burying my nose in his shoulder, I breathed him in, eager to absorb all of him as he took me higher with every thrust.

"Now, my sweetness," he whispered, and I felt his hand dip between us. One slide, one swirl of his dexterous fingers set the orgasm shuddering through me in powerful spasms, the rhythmic pressure of his thrusts extending it and making my climax feel like it would last forever.

With a loud growl, he pumped his own release inside me, matching my rhythm.

His arms tightly around me, he rolled us in bed, placing me on top, then let his arms drop wide to the sides. "You are incredible," he panted.

"Me?" I nuzzled his chest, the frantic excitement slowly giving way to the cozy afterglow inside me. "I didn't do much."

"You did everything. You *are* everything." Gently, he caressed my arm from wrist to the shoulder. "You make me feel—"

"Fed?" I giggled.

"No, not just fed, darling. You make me feel special somehow. Important. And your energy is . . . There is this flavour to it that I can't seem to get enough of."

"How does it look?" I rose from his chest to see his face.

"Mesmerizing." His warm smile softened the receding scarlet in his eyes. "Like the tiny tendrils of a rainbow pulsing hot through every emotion you have. And it tastes—" He paused, as if in search for a perfect word. "Incredibly addictive."

The light caress of his fingers up and down my arm stopped at my shoulder where he hooked his thumb under the thin strap of the dress and slid it down, setting my breast free. The edge of the neckline tugged at my nipple on its way down. My breast immediately felt heavier as the tip pebbled.

My breath hitched in the back of my throat, and my skin tingled with a renewed wave of anticipation. I shifted my hips a little, in an attempt to alleviate the achy need building up between my thighs again.

His eyes immediately flashed bright red.

"I want more," he gritted through his teeth.

"More?" I sat up. The skirt of my dress draped over our hips in scarlet waves of silk.

"That was just the first course, sweetheart." With a teasing smile, he lifted my skirt and slid the dress over my head then sent it flying across the room.

"How many courses are there?"

"Well, it's a classy establishment." He eased hairpins out of what was left of my up-do, tossing them to the floor one by one. "Seven? Eight?"

"Eight!" I gasped. "That would never happen for me. Not even close." Reaching two orgasms in one night was already a huge stretch in my case.

He cupped my breast and brushed my nipple with his thumb. I arched my back, pressing into his touch.

"Make it nine," he rasped before leaning in and sucking my other nipple between his lips. "Dining at its finest," I heard him murmur between the nibbles and licks that quickly made heat spread in waves through me all over again.

Chapter 20

SOMETIME LATER THAT night, I'd lost count of Ivarr's *'courses.'* With relentless hunger and infinite passion, he reaped a never-ending cascade of orgasms out of me, rendering the world around us non-existent.

For a few blissful hours, it was just he and I, lost in each other.

Ivarr's lovemaking was all-consuming. I never had anyone enjoy me so thoroughly inside and out, obviously savoring every touch, every taste, and every sensation. His relishing my body this reverently did extraordinary things to me. I felt appreciated, cherished, worshiped.

Losing all inhibitions, I delighted in giving this joy to him, wanting to give more every time he took.

"Full?" I asked softly, threading my fingers though the silk of his hair when he collapsed at my side, his face pressed to my shoulder.

"Never," he groaned against my skin, visibly struggling to catch his breath. "I don't think I could ever have enough of you." He lifted his head, his eyes blazing red with the passion of every orgasm he'd given me. "But you need a break." He smoothed the tangled hair out of my face.

I stretched head to toe at his side, the delicious ache of thorough satisfaction rolling through me.

"Mmmm. Feeding a demon is exhausting." My eyelids half-closed, I snuggled into the warmth of his body.

"I'll have to ask you some questions, sweetheart," he said softly, an apologetic note ringing in his voice. "You'll need to stay awake for a few more minutes."

Turning on his back, he curled his arm around my shoulders, and I settled my head on his chest.

"Fire away," I mumbled, marveling at his high level of alertness when I myself felt as if I slowly descended into a warm pool of melted chocolate—soft, sweet, and thoroughly delicious.

"Tell me more about the ones who took you from the base."

I frowned, remembering that night.

"I didn't get a chance to take a good look at them. The one I saw wore the uniform like the rest of them at the base, so I didn't get to see his face." Thinking back to my second abduction somewhat cleared the sleepy fog of afterglow from my brain. "There was at least one other there. He caught me from behind. I heard someone give orders to the first, but I didn't get to see him at all."

"Did you get a chance to see them better in the car. Were they the same two who were in the cell?"

"No. I still didn't see their faces, but the two in the car wore suits, not uniforms. They argued and seemed to be lost, but I can't say for sure because I didn't understand what they were talking about. They spoke German, I think, definitely not English."

"German?" The incredulity in his voice prompted me to rise on my elbow to see his face.

Ivarr starred at the ceiling in visible concentration. The sharp focus of his features no longer held the confusion that I had often spotted on his face before tonight.

"Do you have your own demon language that you would speak to each other when you're alone?" I asked.

"No. We don't have one of our own. Normally, we would speak whatever language is spoken in the country where we are. So, I'd expect them to use English in this part of Canada. The only reason they would speak German would be if they had a German-speaking human with them."

"Do you think one of them was a human?"

Turning to the side, he rose on his elbow, too.

"I'm pretty sure both of them were, Katherine. A retrieval team would not be wearing suits. They'd either have their uniforms, or if they planned to sneak unnoticed, grey hooded jackets to keep their faces out of sight as much as possible. You said they used drugs to make you unconscious."

"Yes." That was one major difference between my two kidnappings. "There was the sting of a needle in my neck before I passed out."

"Can I see the marks again, please?"

I sat up, and Ivarr flicked on the lamp on his night table.

"There are several." I tilted my head to the side, to expose the injection area to him.

Ivarr gently skimmed his fingertips over my neck.

"You were right, these were made at different times."

"To keep me under during the car ride."

"Demons wouldn't do that, Katherine." His fingers wrapped around the back of my neck, he slid his thumb gently up and down my throat. "There is just no need for drugs. Taking a part of your life force would be enough and much more efficient. It would give them some additional nourishment, too."

"So, not demons?"

"I'm positive. Besides, most of the Council's Soldiers are half-starved drones under Raim's control. None of them would have enough creative energy to come up with a detailed kidnapping plan on their own."

I recalled their hold on me and how it gave under my struggle. The unnatural strength of the demon guards would've never allowed me to move an inch in their grip.

"But why? People have no use for my sexual energy. Frankly, I have nothing that humans would find of much value at all." It wasn't like they could even demand a ransom from anyone for my release. "Besides, it was a human who told me that the rules have changed, and I was going to be set free soon."

"I don't know, sweetheart." He kissed the corner of my mouth, his hand gently stroking my arm. "But I will figure it out. As soon as we cross the border, I'll try to get hold of Andras. He was the other half of Sytrius's team during the wars. I don't know him well and have no reason to trust him, but in this situation, the risk is worth the chance to gain any knowledge we can. I want us to be on the other side of the border first, though. Just in case Andras lets others know about my call." He stopped himself, as if another thought entered his mind. "If it's humans who are after you, I never should have left you here alone. The amulet would not stop them."

In one swift movement he got out of bed.

"Ivarr?" I called, unnerved by the grim focus of his expression.

Standing by the bed, he turned to face me abruptly, and my heart all but stopped at the sight of his strong, completely nude body. Unable to resist, I slid my gaze down his massive frame, taking in every hard ridge of muscle under the golden tan of his skin.

At this point, it wasn't even about my sexual desire for him. After the multi-course *dinner* we just had, I felt completely satisfied without any lingering lust burning through me. My admiration right now was mostly of aesthetic nature. It was impossible not to admire the classic beauty of his tall, strong body.

My gaze stopped on his thick erection nested in the mass of curls the colour of old gold. It twitched under my shameless, appreciative stare, and I blinked, forcing myself to stop ogling him.

"Sorry, you were saying . . ." I mumbled, organizing my thoughts.

Resting his eyes on me for a moment, he shook his head, a flash of regret crossing his face, then reached for his boxers. "Even if they'd made it to my house, humans wouldn't know what vehicle we're driving. But we did leave a trail—your pajamas in the motel, the hospital visit. In any case, they would figure out you'd be most likely going south."

Quickly, he threw on his jeans and a new white t-shirt then picked up my pants and top from the chair and laid them on the bed next to me. Propping his fists into the mattress, he brought his face close to mine, trapping me with his vivid blue gaze.

"We should get out of here, Katherine." He brushed a soft kiss on my parted lips. "One of the advantages I have over humans—I don't need rest. Sorry, but you'll have to sleep in the truck again." He shoved himself off the bed, and I began to throw my clothes on, too.

"So, are you sure that demons are not hunting me?"

"They might be." He grabbed his backpack and collected his things around the room. "The Council could very well have sent someone after you, too, once they realized that you were gone. Catching a human may give them a sense of urgency, as opposed to hunting me. I'm still not sure what to do with them claiming you were free in the first place. That's what I need to find out next."

"Could those two be from The Priory?" I did up my shoes and found my coat in the closet.

"Well, Priory members are the only humans permitted to enter the base. Beside the Sources, of course."

"I was hoping The Priory would protect me from the demons. Now, I really don't know whom I need to be running from."

"All of them. We'll stay away from both the Council and The Priory until we know more."

"Humans are much weaker than you, physically," I pointed out. "Why would The Priory have any power over your Council at all?"

"The Priory has a reach that is far greater than the power of an individual human, but I could never figure out what gives them their strength." He took my hand in his and took a hold of the doorknob, ready to leave. "For centuries they had been instrumental in shaping the rules governing all of us. Until now, though, they exercised their power exclusively through the treaty. I've never heard of them meddling in the affairs at the base or abducting Sources." He shook his head and added, "I need to find out what's happening here."

Chapter 21

Eyes fixed ahead, he drove along the narrow road that skirted the side of the mountain. They had been heading south then west into the mountains where he had crossed into The States many times before.

Katherine dozed off for a short while, but fear had been building up inside her with every minute they spent on the deserted road, keeping her from getting a decent rest.

He hated to see her natural, sunny happiness marred by the muddy cloud of fear. He longed to make her feel safe to have that bubbly ray of light reign over her again, but he couldn't figure out how to do it. Without having enough information, he didn't know how to ensure her safety.

So, he did what he'd always done. Ran.

Over the centuries, he had become good at running. Except that this time, he had so much more at stake than his own freedom. He had Katherine's life and happiness to guard.

He decided to cross the border, reasoning that the farther from the Incubi Base they got, the hungrier and weaker the demons chasing them should be. The easier it would be for Ivarr to deal with them if it came down to a fight.

Back in Seattle, Katherine had an established life to return to, and he hoped to be able to give it back to her soon. Although, he couldn't bring himself to think about having to part from her then.

In the brief time they had spent together, her vibrant emotions had become addictive. The distinct taste of her attraction to him was too alluring to let it go easily. In her, he had glimpsed a trace of the same warm feeling he'd seen in Margreta.

Except that in Katherine it was for him and only him. Unlike Margreta's, her heart was unoccupied, with plenty of room for the feeling to grow and thrive.

Her dimwit of an ex never claimed her heart, it seemed. And Ivarr longed to take it for himself. Grab it, conquer it fully, and keep it for him alone.

He could take her budding affection for him and grow it. Make her his, and keep her for as long as she should live.

Would it be fair to her, though? To take her on the run, something that would most likely last all her life. What could he, an age-long criminal offer a sweet, innocent person like Katherine? He couldn't even guarantee her freedom. What would happen to her once he inevitably got captured again?

The possible answers to these questions made his heart ache in a way, more torturous than the pain of Inferno.

In any case, the main priority right now remained her safety. First, he needed to figure out exactly who was after her and why. Then he had to get her away from them for good. After that, he'd work on finding the strength to part with her.

"Ivarr," her soft voice came from the passenger's seat.

"Yes, my queen." He made an effort to keep his voice neutral, but the warmth he felt in his heart for her found its way into his words.

"What will happen after you smuggle me across the border?"

"Technically, it wouldn't be smuggling." He couldn't resist a smile. "You are a US citizen, aren't you? You have the right to enter the country. You just don't have the documentation to prove it."

Her concern seemed to lie elsewhere, though. She shifted in her seat, uneasily.

"Then what? After we cross?"

"I'll make sure you're safe to go back to your old life."

"Will I ever get to see you again?"

He glanced her way, before returning his attention to the twisting road ahead. He couldn't decipher her emotions in that one glance. They seemed to be tangled into a knot that required longer examination.

"Would you *want* to see me again?" Her answer shouldn't matter—he knew what he had to do. Yet her reply was the most important thing to him in the world right now.

Watching the continuous turns of the road winding along the site of the mountain, he tuned all his other senses on her, halting his breath in anticipation.

"I—I don't know . . ." Her voice trailed off. Then, she added with much more confidence. "One thing I am certain about, though—I do *not* want to live the rest of my life, knowing I'd never see you again."

His chest deflated—all air left it at once, even as his wayward heart sang with hope.

"Katherine . . ." He wished to give her the world. He longed to promise her everything her heart desired, to clear every dark trace of fear and worry inside her.

Following the tight curve of the road close to the mountain, he was momentarily blinded by the headlights of a vehicle parked in his lane ahead.

He slammed on the brakes.

Jerked forward in her seat, Katherine cried out and braced herself with her hands on the front console. He spotted the second vehicle, parked across the road behind the first, and threw the truck into reverse.

The blinding light of the approaching car behind them blurred his vision through the rearview mirror for a moment, forcing him to hit the brakes again.

"Oh God, what's happening?" Katherine breathed out, barely audible.

Nothing good, my sweet darling queen.

"They caught up with us," he announced grimly, quickly scanning all three vehicles to get a grip on the situation.

"Who?"

Good question.

He clicked his seat belt off.

"I'll find out."

"Wait!" She leaned to him. "Ivarr, please. They can hurt you . . ."

"They can't kill me." He shrugged, but the usual fatalistic indifference to his own wellbeing was greatly overshadowed by the need to stay fit in order to be able to defend her.

The sound of car doors opening forced his attention to the windshield. In the headlights, he caught the blinding white of Raim's flowing robe.

Incubi.

It seemed he'd get some answers after all, even if not from Sytrius.

He grabbed his handgun from the backpack.

"Get in my seat," he said quickly. "If they get me down, back up through there." He tipped his chin at the section of the road still open between the car behind them and the sharp drop-off of the mountain.

"Let's do it now, let's back up now . . ." she begged in a frantic whisper. "You and I, together."

But he shook his head.

"I'll have to stop them from following you."

"Can't you just . . . shoot them?" Her gaze flickered to the gun in his hand.

"A bullet wouldn't do much against them. This is for the tires. The most effective way to incapacitate a demon is to break his bones, so he can't move. I can do it more efficiently with my bare hands. If I get Raim out, the rest of them wouldn't be able to organize a chase."

He put the gun on his thigh and took hold of her slender shoulders, staring into the bright hazel of her eyes which were shimmering with tears.

"Whatever happens, stay in the truck." He traced the red cord around her neck down to the amulet nestled between her breasts. "Don't let them in."

He hit the door lock button for a good measure, useless as it may be.

"If things go . . . bad, then drive like you did when you got us away from the bikes. My fearless queen."

Her chin quivered, and his chest tightened painfully with worry and an overwhelming tenderness.

He trusted she would get out of here. She had more strength inside her than she realized. But he had to keep Raim away from her.

"No matter what, I will find you. Wherever you are," he promised with absolute certainty in his heart, vowing to make it happen.

With one quick kiss on her soft lips, he whispered, breaking the only Incubi rule he'd never broke before. "My demon name is Eligor. Repeat."

"Eligor?" Fear overshadowed her misery. The fear was for him.

"Remember it. Dream about me."

Without opening the door, he slipped out into the night to face the demons.

Chapter 22

HIS KISS STILL LINGERED on my lips as Ivarr appeared outside the truck window backlit by the headlights of the car in front of us.

Squinting in the bright lights cutting the darkness, I watched Raim's robe whip in the mountain breeze.

Demons, not people, had caught up with us.

Quickly, Ivarr fired a shot at the tire of the car behind our truck then swung his arm, shooting at the two vehicles in the front.

Two uniformed guards jumped out of the large, black car and ran towards Ivarr, not bothering to duck away from his shots. A bullet meant for the car hit one in the chest, without so much as slowing him down.

Tossing the gun aside, Ivarr swiftly walked to Raim, who stood in the middle of the road. I had no chance to hear their exchange. A few moments later, with a brief glance my way, Ivarr leaned back and landed a blow on the side of Raim's face that made the Grand Master stagger.

I remembered Ivarr's instructions and scrambled into the driver's seat with full intentions to follow them, when the two guards rushed him at the same time as two more jumped out of the car.

Panic rising to my throat, making it hard to breathe, I watched in horror as they swarmed Ivarr.

Quick on his feet, he deflected most of their blows, moving with fluid grace and shelling out powerful punches left and right.

Raim stepped aside, observing the scene coolly, his arms folded across his chest, as two more guards emerged from the parked cars and joined the others in their attack on Ivarr.

For whatever reasons, Raim didn't seem to be paying any attention to me or the truck. His focus, as well as that of his Soldiers, appeared to be entirely on Ivarr.

I should have used the demons' lack of interest in me and try to get away, but I frantically searched for a way to get to Ivarr first. With the demon vehicles disabled by his bullets, maybe we could have a chance to get out of here together?

A fourth vehicle pulled in behind me, completely blocking the road and cutting off my escape route. With a mountainside to my right and the sharp drop to the left, we were essentially boxed in on this section of the deserted highway.

My heart thundering in my chest, I turned my attention back to Ivarr.

He continued to fight his attackers with steady efficiency, despite their greater number. One of them dipped in a crouch and kicked his leg out, planting the heel of his armoured boot into Ivarr's shin.

The way Ivarr staggered and crashed to the side sent my heart plunging into an icy abyss.

"Ivarr!" A choked cry ripped from my throat as I clenched my fists so hard my fingernails dug painfully into the skin on my palms.

Lying on his side, Ivarr grabbed the ankle of the guard closest to him and yanked him to the ground. Then he managed to rise to one knee and continued to defend himself from the blows until another guard kicked at his other shin, knocking it from under him. The angle of his leg when Ivarr fell again indicated it was broken.

My stomach churned, seeing him on the ground, swarmed by the guards.

"Oh, God. No!" I flipped the lock open and shoved at the door with both hands.

The sight of the guards still attacking Ivarr with both his legs broken turned me into a ball of fury, stripping my mind of any fear or self-preservation or even commonsense.

Aware that I had no way to defeat the demons attacking Ivarr, I jumped out of the truck and went straight for Raim.

"Make them stop!" I screamed, running at the figure draped in white.

Raim moved his gaze from the fight to meet mine. It felt like an avalanche of pure ice rolled over me, suffocating me with its crushing cold.

"Kitty." He tilted his head to the side.

I had no idea he knew my name, but right now it didn't really matter.

"Call back your drones!" I demanded, struggling to keep eye contact with his freezing glare.

"Miss Jones!" A feminine voice called suddenly from somewhere behind me. "Step away from him."

"I no longer have use for you," Raim stated calmly, paying no attention to whomever was approaching us. "Leave."

"I'm not going anywhere," I said firmly, also ignoring the clicking sound of high heels at my back.

"Stop this." I pumped my fist through the air in the direction of the demons beating up Ivarr.

"Miss Jones." A hand landed firmly on my shoulder, and I finally shot a glance at the tall, dark-haired woman in a sharp pantsuit at my side. "Kitty, we need to go. I'll take you home."

"Who the hell are you?" I shrugged her hand off me. "And I'm not leaving until he calls them off." Not even then. Ivarr was injured, he needed help . . .

Raim's gaze slowly glided over to the woman at my side, and the indifference slid off his face for the first time ever. His eyes narrowed, his features sharpened with concentration. His arms dropped to his sides as he stared at her face then down at her chest.

I followed his gaze to the tear-shaped pendant that appeared to be made of the same stone as the amulet I was wearing around my neck. Both of them glowed fiercely in the darkness of the night.

"Hmmm." The woman briefly touched her pendant. "I've never seen it do this," she muttered softly.

"Who are you?" Raim gritted through his teeth.

"Doctor Delilah Neri." She looked up, meeting his gaze, then blinked as if in a momentary stupor and even went to offer him a hand in greeting but stopped herself halfway, obviously thinking better of it. "I'm here to take Miss Jones home. I was told you'd been notified. Well, I'm not sure if it was *you* specifically, but someone in your *lair* was given the information." Her tone held authority, but it was the undeniable resentment in her voice that immediately bred a sense of camaraderie in me. Her tone softened when she addressed me. "We need to leave, Kitty—"

"No." I glanced at the demons crowding Ivarr and made a move to dash past Raim to him. Raim's sudden firm grip on my left arm stopped me in my tracks.

"Call off your thugs!" I yelled in his face, struggling against his hold. Fear for Ivarr was quickly turning to panic. Tears streaming down my cheeks now, I slammed my fist in the arm holding me. "Get them off him!"

His grip on my arm was like a steel vise. My blows didn't even make him flinch.

"Leave, and I'll stop them," he retorted, his voice as cold as his stare, the black wing of his hair whipping in the wind behind him.

"Let go of her." Doctor Neri's voice came in low and threatening.

Incredibly, Raim immediately released me at her command. Even more unbelievably, he took a step back and raised his arm.

The guards halted their assault in an instant, as if he'd pushed some invisible button, cutting off their power supply.

Several uniformed bodies lay on the ground next to Ivarr, incapacitated. Two others stood over him. He rose on one elbow, the other arm hanging motionless from his shoulder, his head bent down, the golden hair matted with blood.

"Ivarr!" Tears blurred my vision. I went to run to him, but a pair of arms around my middle stopped me.

"We need to leave, Miss Jones." Doctor Neri held me in place, with strength that rivaled that of the demons.

"Go." Raim held up his arm with a threat. "Or I'll set them off again."

"Please, don't hurt him," I begged, swiping at my wet cheeks.

Obviously unmoved, he held my gaze in silent command.

"Come, Kitty." Doctor Neri literally dragged me away, my heels tripping over the pavement. "It'll be better for everyone if we leave," she said in my ear soothingly, hauling me past the truck to the vehicle that arrived last at the scene.

"They've hurt him," I sobbed, only half-aware of her opening the door and shoving me into the seat.

"He is a demon. Just like them." She blew a long strand of black hair out of her face and buckled me in then ran around the front of the car to the driver's side.

"What are they going to do to him now?" I groaned, leaning forward. With a soft snap, the seatbelt held me in place.

"It's not our concern, Kitty." She started the engine, reversing the car to drive away.

Through the blur of my tears, I watched the headlights of the disabled vehicles disappear behind the first curve of the road.

"They have their own laws," she continued. "Your presence there wouldn't help him. For us it's best to stay away, as long as they keep their distance, too."

I glanced her way, rising suspicion prompting questions.

"Where are you taking me, Doctor Neri? Who exactly are you? And how do you know about them?" I placed my hand on the door handle. Although, I realized that the dark abyss of the mountain drop on my side of the road left no hope of jumping out of the moving vehicle.

"You can call me Delilah."

"Fine." I sniffled and wiped my cheeks dry. "Where are we going, Delilah?"

"I'm taking you home, to Seattle."

"Really?" I asked skeptically.

"Since you took off without discussing your release plan, The Priory sent me to get you, soon after the Council notified us about your escape. I'll help you get your life back on track and take you to your first counseling session on Monday."

"What do you mean by *escape*? And, wait a minute, do you work for The Priory?"

My mistrust grew stronger. A chill ran up my arms, and I realized that I'd left my coat in the truck along with everything else.

"No. Not officially. My father did, and I have strong ties with the organization because of him."

"So, are you aware then that I didn't simply *take off*? I was drugged and abducted from the base."

"By whom?" She shot me a glance, her eyebrows knitted in a frown.

"You tell me. Whom did The Priory send to take me?"

"I really have no knowledge of what you're talking about, Kitty." Delilah shook her head.

"Funny they didn't share that important detail with you," I scoffed.

"Because it can't be true, Kitty. Someone from The Priory called me yesterday, asking to pick you up. They said you ran away from the Incubi Base, but the Council had located you. The organization didn't have any members nearby to get you, and they couldn't get anyone fast enough to make it here in time. So, they asked me. I live in Seattle, and I drove here—"

"Well, I certainly didn't knock myself unconscious with drugs then drove my motionless body from one province to another." I yanked down the neckline of my top, displaying the bruised injection site to her.

Delilah's gaze flickered to my neck for a moment before returning back to the road ahead.

"It makes no sense for The Priory to do that to you, Kitty. You were about to be released. There is just no point for The Priory to stage another abduction right now."

"Who did it, then? In your opinion."

"Demons. Who else?"

"There is even less sense for demons to take me from their own base."

"On the contrary." Delilah's frown deepened. "They knew they were about to lose you. I wonder if they decided to move you to another location, to possibly hide from The Priory."

"Why would they dress in uniforms?"

"Most of them wear uniforms, don't they?"

"Sure, but they used drugs. Why would they use drugs?"

She shrugged a shoulder.

"To make you believe they're humans?"

"Oh God, really?" I groaned, my head pounding with confusion. "Demons dressed up as demons and used drugs to pretend they were humans? It's too stupid, even for their hungry brains. Makes no sense."

"Why did they lie about you running away, then?"

"Maybe they didn't know themselves what happened?" I hated to defend the demons but blaming them lacked any logic. Although,

I could see Delilah's point on how useless my abduction would be for The Priory, too. "Besides, most demons can't lie very well."

"That's what I've heard." She nodded. "But doesn't their ability to lie depend on how well they've been fed?"

"Yes."

"I also heard that Raim has been feeding long enough to invent any lie," she retorted grimly and added, "It was Raim, wasn't it? The one in white?"

"Yes."

"I've never come this close to him—to any of them—before. Those eyes . . ." she whispered, a shudder rippling through her body, "Beautiful and deadly. Dangerous combination." She went silent for a moment. "Did one of them help you escape?"

"Again, I did not escape. I was abducted by someone dressed in demon uniforms then transported in a car by two men in suits. They spoke German and apparently sucked at reading road maps."

"This is bizarre." The puzzlement in her voice sounded genuine.

"No kidding."

"I'll forward this info to my contacts in The Priory. They need to know this."

"Please do, by all means, if you think it would accomplish anything. Somehow, I still doubt I'll be safe, even if you're telling the truth and will deliver me home in one piece."

"You're under the protection of The Priory now, Kitty."

"It doesn't make me feel any safer to know this," I bit out.

"It's a very powerful organization, with a wide reach and influence."

"Apparently, that means nothing. They don't even have the resources to come 'rescue' me."

"The membership is very exclusive. It's for life and limited to men only, but they have people all over the world helping them. The Priory has been maintaining the fragile peace with Incubi for centuries, keeping it in a complete secret, so the rest of the world can go on undisturbed."

"With whom?"

"Incubi."

"Is that what you call the demons?"

"That *is* what they're called."

"So, one of them would be—"

"An Incubus. A sex demon, Kitty."

I should have known, my constant, irresistible pull to him from the very moment I lay my eyes on him sleeping in the abandoned house couldn't have been natural. The attraction that came fast and fierce, quickly followed by inescapable affection—both very unusual for me at this pace.

And maybe—just maybe—Ivarr, the sex demon that he was, ended up manipulating my emotions after all. Despite his insisting on the contrary, how much of my feelings for him were natural. Could any of it have been genuine?

Still, the longing that squeezed my heart at the memory of him—and the ache it brought—felt very real now.

"They feed on human sexual energy." Delilah's voice reached me.

"I know. I've been their food source. Remember? And, apparently, my kidnapping was legal, according to that treaty your organization signed with my captors."

"When the peace treaty was signed, its terms were deemed appropriate for the times."

"Appropriate?" I scoffed with sarcasm.

"Listen," Delilah's voice rang with the passion of conviction. "There was an unstoppable force of thousands of vicious, starving demons to contain—deadly in their insatiable hunger and their complete disregard to human life. You can argue about the means that were chosen to achieve the peace at the time, but the treaty served its purpose."

I drew in a lungful of air.

"I would agree with this, Delilah, except that I ended up on the other side. The world was saved at the expense of *my* freedom and the lives of many other innocent women."

"That's why The Priory is working with the demons to revise the system now. There is a strong push from the Incubi side to allow them to feed freely again, but the concern is that relaxing the rules would potentially expose more of human population to danger."

I thought about Ivarr's relationship with Margreta. The most "offensive" thing he, the breaker of all rules, did while free was to feed off one woman for six years straight, giving her the comfort she needed in return.

"Has anyone ever tried to give them a chance, instead of beating them into submission with rules?" I asked.

Something in my voice must have made Delilah pause.

"Who was the demon with you?"

"Ivarr," I exhaled. At the sound of his name, a painful lump formed in my throat.

"How did you meet him? Why was he with you?"

"I—I just happened to run into him, shortly after my escape from the car transporting me."

"I'll need details to report to The Priory. Was he involved in your escape in any way?"

"Only that he looked after me and protected me afterwards."

"Do you think you love him?" she asked completely unexpectedly.

"What?" I blinked in confusion. "No. Of cause not. I've only just met him . . ."

"Good." She nodded. "Don't trust Incubi, Kitty. The purpose of their appearance is to lure innocent victims. It's enthralling and hard to resist. But they're not like us. They have no feelings, no emotions of their own except whatever they have absorbed from humans over their endless lives. Their sole purpose is to feed."

'Taking care of you is giving me purpose', Ivarr's words rang through my mind.

"How well do you know them, Delilah?"

"Well, like I said, this is the first time I've seen one of them close up. But this encounter only strengthened my beliefs. I've read transcripts of the accounts of the women held in their captivity." She shuddered. "I am a psychologist specializing in relationship counseling, which is not the right area for me to be on the team to help counsel the released women. But I want this to stop, to end all kidnappings and release everyone. I volunteered to help integrate women back into their lives."

"Would you be able to find out what will happen to Ivarr?" I asked, unable to mask the desperate hope in my voice.

"I wouldn't spend too much time worrying about him, Kitty. As a couples' therapist, and a happily married woman myself, I would strongly advise you to search for happiness among your own kind."

She raised a hand to her chest, touching the tear-shaped pendant in a distracted movement. The diamond of her wedding ring glistened in the faint light from the dashboard. Both, her pendant and mine, were just two dull pieces of dark quartz or amber. All spectacular fire inside them completely gone.

"I hate to say it," she said. "But I'm fairly certain the Incubus wouldn't remember you for long. You see, one of them deserted from the base recently, taking one of the kidnapped women with him. Somehow, he managed to get her pregnant, which shouldn't be possible between a demon and a human. This made the demon mortal, which is apparently their ultimate goal on Earth. You see what it means, Kitty? Now they view human women as their ticket to earn their right to die."

"By getting a woman pregnant, they earn their forgiveness?" I whispered.

"It appears so." She nodded. "They get to be forgiven, earning the right to die and ascend to heaven . . . or something along those lines. Getting a woman pregnant grants them forgiveness from the Divine. It has something to do with their being here in the first place. The Priory is looking into this. If all demons became mortal, it would eventually help clear this world of them. However, the cost of this is concerning, as each of them would have to gain unlimited access to a woman. Also, the nature of the offspring of such a union is still unclear . . ."

I tuned out Delilah's speculations about the potential dangers of demon-human relationships.

The lump in my throat grew, threatening to suffocate me. I might be able to feed an Incubus. But if getting a woman pregnant earned him the coveted forgiveness, he would never get it with me.

Chapter 23

WE CROSSED THE BORDER a little while later. Delilah had my passport along with hers in her purse, claiming it was couriered to her at the time of the phone call from The Priory.

As soon as we entered Seattle's city limit, she took me to the nearest hospital.

"We need to make sure there is no physical damage as a result of your time at the base and your escape. And that . . ." She gestured at the bandage on my arm. "What is that?"

"Um. It was an accident."

"There might be a risk of infection."

"No, I'm fine. I got proper medical treatment for this." I fingered the bandage lightly, remembering Ivarr's large hands applying it with so much care just a few hours earlier.

"It wouldn't hurt for a professional to look at it again," she insisted undeterred. "Let me do all the talking here for now," she warned, pulling into the hospital's parking lot. "Later, I'll have several cover stories for you to choose from to help you get on with your life with as little disruption as possible."

"Why would I want to cover up The Priory's shady dealings with the demons," I snapped.

"Kitty, they are trying to help—"

"Their help wouldn't be necessary had they let me be in the first place, instead of having Incubi kidnap me. So, stop painting them as my saviors."

I closed my eyes and leaned back in the seat, not loving my irritation with Delilah or my tone of voice with her at the moment. These temper flare-ups were not typical for me. I was tired, definitely sleep-deprived, and on edge.

She heaved an exasperated sigh.

"I don't want to start an argument—"

"Of course not. What's the point? All your hate is directed against the beings you never took your time to understand. You never even met them until today. But you're talking about The Priory—the other side responsible for all this mess—as if they're the holy saviors of us all. What good did this organization do, beside hiding behind the backs of kidnapped women for centuries?"

"These are not some poor misunderstood creatures, Kitty." Delilah leaned towards me, her dark-blue eyes gleaming with conviction. "Their supernatural allure might have altered your perception, after your spending time with one of them. But believe me, I'm not indifferent to the plight of the women. I do have strong reasons to mistrust Incubi." She swept back the few loose strands of her dark hair that had made their way out of her neat bun. "My family suffered directly at their hands. My brother was kidnapped by them as small child. It broke my mother's heart, killing her within a year of his abduction. My father never was the same again. He dedicated his entire life to manage the relationships with Incubi. He worked hard to make sure there were no leniencies for them to ever take more than what was given."

She leaned back and shook her head before continuing.

"No one liked those arrangements. No one was happy about giving our women to them every year. But you can't kill the demons. There is no way to get rid of them. The only way to keep them in check is to regulate their hunger."

"Why would Incubi take a little boy?" I blinked, reeling from her revelations. "Your brother?"

"Because they are creatures incapable of love, Kitty. They're void of compassion and are beyond all human morals." Her voice rose. "They can't comprehend right and wrong. All they know is hunger. It hollows them with pain and they'd do anything to feed. Obviously, they needed leverage, knowing of my father's position within The Priory, and wanted to weaken him. But they've failed—his hatred for them grew and only made him stronger in his fight against them."

Her face flushed with the passion she'd put in her words. Navy blue eyes glistened, reflecting the unwavering strength of her beliefs.

"What happened to your brother? Do you know?"

"No. I'm still searching." She exhaled heavily. "The demons deny knowing anything about him. But I swore on the memory of him that sooner or later I would find what happened to him. And I'll make those responsible pay."

Chapter 24

I SAT ON THE EXAMINATION table, wearing a hospital gown, my clothes folded neatly on a chair nearby, the golden shoes tucked under it. Straining my hearing, I tried to listen to the muted voices of Delilah talking to the doctor on the other side of the curtain.

"The doctor has cleared you to go," she announced, shoving the curtain aside. "I'll drive you home." She tossed my clothes to me and folded her arms across her chest, waiting for me to change.

Turning my back to her, I started getting dressed.

"Where did you get that necklace?" Delilah asked unexpectedly as I struggled with the hooks of my bra. "I saw it glow last night, just like mine." She stepped closer, and I felt her fingers on my back, as she quickly closed my bra for me.

"Where did you get yours?" I asked her instead of giving an answer.

"Family heirloom. This one was my mother's. My father had one too, shaped like a claw. He gave it to my brother." She paused. Over my shoulder, I saw her twirling the pendant between her fingers. "But I've never seen either of them light up before."

"Ivarr gave me mine." Fully dressed now, I shoved my feet in my shoes. "To protect me from the Council. It glows when demons are near and prevents them from entering the room you're in."

"I never knew." She stroked her pendant, her brow furrowed in thought. "I don't think my parents knew, either, otherwise they would've told me."

"Miss Jones?" A nurse poked her head behind the curtain. "There is someone to see you. Mister Stratton."

"Derek?" I exhaled in shock.

"How did anyone know she was here?" Delilah moved on the nurse menacingly.

"Mister Stratton asked to be notified as next of kin if Miss Jones ever came in . . ." The nurse retreated, shielding herself with the curtain.

"I don't have a next of kin."

"In the absence of a close family," the nurse explained carefully, "as your fiancée—"

"Derek is not my fiancé. We're not engaged."

"This can't be standard practice, surely?" Delilah narrowed her eyes at the nurse, who almost completely hid behind the curtain from her by now.

"It doesn't need to be," I muttered.

Derek's local celebrity status, along with his all-American boy-next-door charm, compelled many into bending rules for him.

"Kitty!" He burst through the curtains, instantly filling the small enclosure with his cologne and his presence.

Ignoring everything around us, he rushed to me and enclosed me in one of his energetic hugs.

"They told me you were dead, but I just couldn't accept it. Not even when they said they'd found a body."

"A body?" Over Derek's shoulder, I glanced at Delilah in question. She waved me off, mouthing '*Later.*'

"Obviously, a mistake," continued Derek. "Good thing I never stopped searching."

Still, he appeared visibly shaken by my sudden resurrection. The familiarity of his arms around me relaxed me somewhat, and his distress triggered my compassion.

"I'm so sorry," I said softly.

"Where have you been?" He moved back to see my face and grabbed my arms.

I winced at the pressure of his hand on my bandage.

"Are you okay?" He jerked his hand away and stared at my arm. "What happened?"

"It was an accident," I replied, fully aware that his question applied to my disappearance as much as to the cut on my arm.

"Miss Jones is not at liberty to divulge the details of recent events at this point." Delilah stepped in, clearing her throat. "An investigation is still ongoing."

"And you are?" Derek straightened out, letting go of me.

"Doctor Delilah Neri." She offered him her hand, and he shook it coolly.

"Doctor? You're not the police?"

"No. I'm a psychologist. I'm here to ensure Miss Jones is delivered home safely."

"*I* will be in charge of Kitty's safety now," he declared with authority and turned to me. "Have you been cleared by the doctors to go home yet?"

"Derek." I shook my head, staring at him in confusion. "Why are you here?"

"Because who else *is there*, Kitty?" He wrapped his arm around my shoulders. "You have no one else to take care of you."

"We broke up," I reminded him.

"And I've been kicking myself over it since you've been gone. I should've never left you. None of this would've happened if I'd stayed."

"You don't know that. Besides, I'm not your responsibility."

"Yes, you are." He nodded with conviction and turned to face Delilah again. "I'm going to take her home if we're done here."

"Kitty?" Delilah turned to me. "Do you trust this man?"

"I do," I said without reservation. I would never trust Derek with my heart again, but I trusted him with my life. At least as far as all the known dangers in the world went.

Everything that had to do with demons and secret Priories, on the other hand . . . "Delilah, can you promise me with absolute certainty that it's safe for me to go home."

"Yes," she said firmly.

"Okay."

Despite us disagreeing on pretty much everything so far, I sensed a certain level of integrity in this woman that compelled me to trust her word.

Derek obviously didn't share this trust.

"I'll contact the police for any updates on the investigation," he declared, leading me to the exit, his hand on the small of my back.

Delilah gave him a glare, taking a wider stance.

"I don't think the police would share any information—"

"They will," he cut her off. "I have contacts there, too."

She tilted her head, her mouth pressed into a thin line.

"Here is my phone number, just in case you don't get any answers." She offered him a business card. Without giving it a glance, Derek shoved it in the breast pocket of his crisp, blue shirt.

"Can I have one, too, please?" I asked, taking a step her way.

At that moment, Delilah seemed to be my only connection to everything that happened, the only link to Ivarr, too. I couldn't leave here without having a way to contact her.

"Sure." She gave me her card then closed the distance between us and unexpectedly gave me a firm hug. "I'll take you to therapy on Monday. We'll talk more." She then whispered so soft, only I could here. "Until then, Kitty, please keep quiet."

Chapter 25

RIDING IN A CAB WITH Derek by my side felt surreal. It was as if I had spent time in an alternate reality.

Now, here I was, driving through the streets of Seattle, sitting next to my perfect boyfriend again as if the past few weeks never happened.

He took my hand in his, and I let him, my head reeling from the struggle to readjust to my old surroundings.

"I paid this month's rent for you," Derek said, unlocking the door to my apartment.

"Thank you." I walked in, surprised he still kept my key. "I'll transfer the money to you as soon as I get my bearings."

"Don't, Kitty. You know it's not about the money. No matter what they said, I wanted you to come back. And you needed to have a place to return to."

"Thank you," I replied mechanically, took a few steps across my tiny living room, and plopped on the couch. Dropping my head down, I blankly stared at my shoes.

"Those are pretty." Derek must have followed my gaze. "Completely not your style, though. Where have you been, Kitty? What have you been doing all this time?" He crouched in front of me. "Tell me what happened."

For a moment, I regretted not going through the available cover-up scenarios with Delilah after all and not choosing one to have prepared answers for him. Then I realized that I was in no condition to discuss any of it, fake or real.

Exhaustion weighed heavily on me, dragging me under.

"I'm so tired, Derek." It was early afternoon, but all I got for sleep last night were a couple of interrupted hours in a moving vehicle—first in the truck, then in Delilah's SUV. In addition to the physical exhaustion, I felt emotionally drained, too. "I'll need to take a quick shower before I crash here. Thank you for everything." With a huge effort I rose from the couch and went to the bathroom.

"Do you need my help in there?" His concerned voice was void of any innuendo.

"No. Thank you, I'll manage. I'll call you tomorrow?"

"I'm not leaving." The hard note in his tone made me pause. "I cleared my schedule for this week as soon as I got the call from the hospital. I'm staying here tonight."

"Why?" I braced myself on the doorframe to the bathroom.

"I don't want to leave you alone again."

"You can't babysit me day and night, Derek."

"Apparently, I have to," he bit out, making me flinch at the accusation in his tone.

"I'll be fine," I assured him solemnly.

"Kitty . . ." He came closer and put his hands on my shoulders. "Listen, I can see you're tired." His tone softened a little as the light green of his eyes warmed somewhat too. "We can have this conversation after your nap. But I'm staying here while you sleep."

"Fine. You can stay," I conceded, too tired to fight and disarmed by genuine emotions in his expression. "As a friend. If you want."

LYING IN BED, WITH the door closed and Derek guarding me in the living room, I stared at my closet. The dark curtains on my bedroom window let a few slivers of the afternoon sun through. The faint light glimmered off the gold of my shoes on the closet shelf. That and the bright crimson of my silk top on the hanger were the only splashes of colour among the usual monochrome palette of my wardrobe.

My chest tight, I struggled to breathe around the lump lodged in my throat. Where was he now? How was he doing? Broken, in pain, detained . . .

Incubus.

A sex demon, who in the short time that we spent together managed to crawl deep into my heart.

'He is a demon, like them.'

'We have no place in their world.'

Maybe. But now that he had made his way into my world, what was I supposed to do to get him out of my thoughts?

Chapter 26

IT WAS COMPLETELY DARK when I woke up. Physically, I felt rested. Mentally, I was disoriented. Waking up in my own bed after so many weeks, I felt uncertain how to go on. Getting back to my old life didn't seem as easy as slipping on an old pair of shoes.

Unsure of what time of the day it was, I only knew that I didn't feel like sleeping anymore. Instead, I threw a bathrobe on and shuffled to the kitchen to make some coffee.

"Good morning." Derek sat at the kitchen counter, his laptop open in front of him. "Did you sleep well?"

"Yes. Thank you. What time is it?"

"Quarter after five. You slept over fifteen hours." Derek'd always been an early riser. He appeared freshly showered and was fully dressed in his usual outfit—a crisp blue button-down and a pair of khaki pants, his reddish-blond hair carefully tousled, the top button of his shirt intentionally left open. Derek put a lot of effort into his casually effortless look. "I had Jake get some groceries last night. Milk for your coffee is in the fridge."

Jake was Derek's personal assistant, extremely helpful and super-efficient.

"Thank you," I said again, starting the coffeemaker, then sat on the barstool next to him. "Sorry," I rubbed my face, feeling awkwardly out of place with my sloppy appearance next to his impeccable self. "I'm . . . um, somewhat out of it, right now."

"It's understandable," Derek said in his best coaching tone, and took my hand in his. "I called several therapists yesterday and set up appointments for them to see you. I figure you can do an initial consultation with all of them then choose which one turns out to be the best match."

"But I already have someone. Delilah, I mean Doctor Neri, is taking me to see them on Monday . . ."

"Do you trust this Doctor Neri to act in your best interests, Kitty? Why?"

I didn't have one specific reason to trust Delilah, except that she had delivered on everything she'd promised so far. She got me home, safely.

Besides, she was in on the whole truth about Incubi, as would be the therapist she'd take me to see, I assumed. It seemed useless to talk to any professional if I had to lie about what happened to me in the first place.

"No more and no less than I'd trust any therapist right now. I could at least start with that one and search for someone else if it doesn't work out."

"I called some of my contacts in the police last night," Derek changed the subject, obviously avoiding an argument. "None of them are aware of any investigation in regard to your case. Apparently, you're still confirmed dead. But now that you're here, the police want to question you. I was able to postpone that, to let you rest, but someone will be here later this morning."

"I have nothing to tell them." I wrapped my arms around my shoulders, shifting on the stool.

"Will you tell *me*?" The expression on his face was that of a parent questioning their child—kind and insistent. "About where you've been?

"Not right now, no. Sorry, I just need some time . . ."

It wasn't even about the Incubi or the Priory or their centuries-old secrets. I simply had no idea how I could talk about any of this either to Derek or to the police, without making myself seem completely insane.

"Maybe . . . after I speak with a therapist," I added in a pacifying tone, very aware that nothing I could say to him at the moment would satisfy his inquisitive nature.

The coffeemaker beeped, and I got up to get a cup from the cabinet.

"But I'm here. Alive." I gave him a weak smile. "That should count for something, right?"

"Kitty." He shook his head. "You have no idea how terrible I felt learning about your disappearance. Then when they told me they found your body . . ." His voice broke off, and he shook his head again.

"I'm sorry." I left the mug on the counter and walked around to enclose his tall, lean figure in a hug. "I'm sorry you took it so hard."

"I care about you, Kitty. Even when I left, I never stopped."

"You didn't call me once after our breakup." I released him from my arms and sat on the barstool again. There was no accusation in my tone, I simply stated the fact.

"I didn't," he agreed. "But I knew you were okay. Until the night you disappeared."

"Did you spy on me?"

"I kept an eye on you. Kitty, you have no one else. And I should have never left you."

"Why?"

"All the time you were gone, I regretted leaving you all alone. You shouldn't live on your own." He closed the laptop, shoving it aside, and turned in his seat to face me. "Kitty, I want you to move in with me."

"What?" I didn't trust my brain without the coffee and was afraid I heard him wrong.

"I have this week off. We can move you within the next couple of days. It's not like you have that much to pack." He swept the room with a quick glance.

"What are you talking about? Why would I move in with you all of a sudden?" Maybe, it was he who needed some strong coffee?

"Kitty, don't you see? We are perfect together. You are the best partner and companion I could ever have. I was an idiot not to appreciate it enough before, but I swear I'll never take you for granted again."

"Oh my God . . ." I ran my fingers through my tangled hair, willing my thoughts into focus. "You want to get back together again?"

"I want us to get married." He produced a small leather box from his pants pocket. "I want you to be my wife, Kitty." He placed the opened box in front of me on the counter.

"What?" I repeated stupidly and stared at the diamond ring. The thought crossed my mind that even a month ago the sight of the ring would have filled me with delight. Now, confusion was the biggest emotion inside me. "Derek, why on earth would you want to marry me? You broke up with me for a reason . . ."

Even if the reason was never clear to me, it was obviously important enough to him to part from me.

"It was a mistake. And I'm so sorry that it happened. We can have a beautiful life together, Kitty. You've always believed in my work. And I may not have shown it as often as I should have, but I treasure your unwavering support."

Somehow it sounded more like a campaign speech than a marriage proposal at this point.

"Being good work partners is not nearly enough for a successful marriage." I combed my fingers through the mess of my hair again. "You shouldn't feel responsible for anything that happened to me. You're a good man, Derek, but I don't think getting married out of some sense of responsibility or misplaced guilt would solve whatever problems you thought we had to break up with me in the first place."

"We can work out any problems, Kitty," he insisted. "There are some excellent couples counseling programs we can do—"

"We're not even married, and we already should go to counseling?"

"If that's what it takes, I'm willing to work for it—"

"Being together shouldn't be hard work," I said. Someone else's words echoed in my mind, bringing the intimate conversation in the restaurant back to mind. "When you're with the right person, it is harder to stay away from them than to be together."

The full meaning of this resonated through my heart, and I felt exactly what Ivarr meant when he said this.

Derek didn't seem to get it, though, or at least he didn't accept it. Leaning in, he took my hand in his.

"Don't you see what really is important here, Kitty?" His voice rang with conviction. His clear green eyes implored me to understand. "We are a perfect fit. I'm so lucky to have found you. You are the best wife a man like me could ever have. I need a life partner who understands me and my work as well as you do. That's what marriage is all about. Not having someone you feel like ripping her clothes off and ravaging her against the wall or something. The mutual trust and respect—"

"Is that what it was?" I whispered, as understanding exploded in my chest with painful clarity. "Was that why you broke up with me?"

"What do you mean?" He leaned back, his eyes shifted from mine.

"You don't find me attractive enough?" I withdrew my hand from his and fought the urge to smooth my hair once again, hating the insecurity that washed over me.

'It's not what you look like, it's what you do,' my aunt used to say. And I grew up perfectly comfortable with my appearance. I wasn't a beauty queen, but I wasn't a hideous monster, either—I was *me*.

The fact that Derek made me feel this self-conscious was irritating and sad.

"You didn't think I was sexy enough to be your girlfriend. Now, you think you can *work it out* and make me your wife?"

Come to think of it, our sex life was rather lukewarm and monotonous for a young couple supposedly in love. I had too little experience to compare it with anything and didn't see a problem before.

Now that I knew exactly what it was like to be with someone who completely and utterly enjoyed every inch of me, I realized how little physical attraction Derek and I had really shared.

"It would never work." I shook my head, sliding the box with the ring his way.

"Kitty." He sighed, looking deflated. "I can change. I want to make you happy. We could have a good life together, a solid future."

"You really can't promise me that, can you? You left me once—you could very well leave me again. Guilt is not a solid foundation for marriage, Derek. And deep inside I'm sure you know it, too."

His shoulders hunched, he dropped his head.

"I've never felt more of a failure than I do right now," he muttered.

His crestfallen expression triggered the unreasonable urge to comfort him in me, and I didn't fight it. Leaning in, I gave him a quick, friendly hug.

"It's not your failure, Derek. You can't force yourself to feel a certain way, even if it seems like the right thing to do. The most you can do is to be honest with me and with yourself. I'm sure the perfect woman is out there for you. Also, just to be clear." I smiled. "If I ever do get married, I fully expect my husband to rip my clothes off and ravage me against the wall. And other surfaces."

He stared at me, eyes wide as I finally went to get my coffee.

Chapter 27

NO ONE CAME TO QUESTION me later in the morning. Derek got a call from the police about them re-opening my case only to promptly close it again as solved. They assured him that I was in no danger. An official statement had also been released, confirming the mistake in DNA analysis that resulted in the false positive identification in my "dead body" weeks ago.

Hearing this information from Derek only confirmed Delilah's claim of The Priory's far reach. Not only were they able to make me disappear from the face of the Earth, they literally "resurrected" me within hours, too.

I spent the rest of the day—and a large chunk of the following one—filing paperwork to get my life back.

Derek still insisted on sleeping on the couch in my apartment every night, refusing to leave me on my own at least until he was fully convinced in my safety. I agreed to him staying with me, vowing to choose a more or less viable cover-up story with Delilah on Monday, to be able to give some answers to him to put his mind at ease.

Going to bed on Sunday night, I paused in front of the mirror over the dresser in my bedroom.

A familiar face stared back at me. Pale skin. Eyes of non-identifiable color—blue, grey, and green mixed together without any dramatic effect. Brown hair, the shade more ash than auburn. Freckles.

Definitely not a beauty queen.

I slid my hands down the sides of a body that lacked any luscious curves.

Obviously, Derek didn't find this appealing.

I blinked, tearing my gaze away from my reflection. I hated that his opinion—or rather his lack of attraction to me—had this effect on my perception of myself, however fleeting.

'Looks are not much deeper than the clothes we wear.'

Ivarr's words rose to the surface of my mind. He saw much deeper, didn't he? Ivarr could see every single emotion inside me plainly, in light and colour, and he seemed to like what he saw.

I sat on the bed. The faint glint of gold from behind the half-open door of the closet caught my eye.

Ultimately, it was not about what either one of them, Derek or Ivarr, thought about me.

It mattered how I felt about myself.

And that night, dancing in my golden shoes, I felt beautiful, strong, and confident. For one night, I became the whole focus of a man's undivided attention. I might not have been able to see the colourful palette of my emotions the way Ivarr did, but that night I experienced a full range of them.

I felt alive.

And I enjoyed it all.

From the moment of my return home, the weeks of my abduction had moved into the distance in my mind, becoming a blur, sitting there, waiting to be brought into the light during the upcoming therapy sessions. Some of it the muddy cloud of a nightmare, some, like Ivarr, the light of a warm dream.

That was what the night with him was supposed to be, wasn't it? A beautiful dream, the memory of which warmed my heart with tenderness and a little sadness.

The intense longing I felt at the memory of his arms around me would ease with time. It had to. Nothing more could ever be between us. I knew it, even when I offered to feed him.

Now, I had to focus on moving on and learning how to live a normal life once again.

Chapter 28

"HOW IS IT? BEING BACK?" Delilah asked me after her greeting, as I climbed into the back of the limo and sat next to her.

"Fine. Thank you." I smoothed the skirt over my knees and sat my purse down then glanced around. "A limo?"

"Well, we need to talk. In private." She gestured at the partition dividing us from the driver then gave me a penetrating stare. "It's been only a few days, but you seem to be doing remarkably well."

Stable. Keller's assessment came to mind.

"I deal well with stress." I shrugged.

"Or hide it well." Delilah narrowed her eyes at me, and I could no longer hold her stare. "Just a note of warning, Kitty." Her voice softened. "The more you hold it in, the more it hurts once it finds its way out. I hope Doctor Yung turns out to be a good fit for you, but if not, please, let me know right away. We'll get you someone else. You need to be able to trust them enough to open up." She leaned in to cover my hand with hers.

"Thank you." I swallowed the faint tickle at the back of my throat. The genuine concern in her words touched me.

She nodded and took out a thick folder from the briefcase at her feet.

I caught the glimpse of her teardrop pendant in the opening of her blouse. That she would've possibly developed a habit of wearing it all the time, maybe out of some sentimental value it held to her as the family heirloom, did not surprise me.

Why I myself still wore the heart-shaped amulet, though, I couldn't really explain.

Could it be out of the lingering fear of demons snatching me in the middle of the night, despite all the assurances that I was safe? Or was it out of desire to hold on to the memories of that night, because the slight weight of the amulet around my neck and the sensation of its smooth warmth between my breasts reminded me of the one who gave it to me?

"So." Delilah cleared her throat and opened the file folder. "We have a cult here."

"What?" I blinked, needing a second to catch up.

"A semi-religious cult whose members kidnap or lure young women to use as wives or servants. Whatever you prefer."

"Okay." I realized she was going through the scenarios of the cover-up stories with me.

"The cult has now been discovered—its leaders arrested, and all women returned back to their homes. This one is good because we can use the same story for several women at once. You won't be the only one. But there may be some publicity involved."

"Publicity?"

"Possibly some news coverage and maybe a talk show interview? You can decline them all. The case will still gain some publicity, which may send reporters and cameras your way."

"No." I shook my head.

I could accept a small white lie to calm my friends and co-workers for the sake of their peace. This, however, sounded like it might require some more elaborate lies, with a number of details.

"I'm not a very good liar. Besides, it wouldn't be easy to convince my friends that I could be that easily brainwashed into anything."

"An abusive relationship?" Delilah offered the next scenario. "You met someone, went on a date with him, and ended up abducted. The amount of publicity can be greatly reduced if we imply you left voluntarily. Generally, adult women running away attract far less public attention than kidnappings."

"It'd be way too out of my character for anyone to believe." I was known as a practical, sensible person. Expecting people to believe I would fall head over heels for someone and run away without telling a soul would only be asking for more questions.

"Hmmm." Delilah leafed through the papers in her folder, muttering under her breath as she turned each page. "Medical emergency? Amnesia? Or lost in the woods? Would it be too late to convince everyone you spent the time lost in the wilderness in northern Canada?"

"God, Delilah." I sighed. "All of these read like a plot for a soap opera."

"Don't forget." She pinned me with her stern gaze. "What we're trying to keep a secret is much more incredible than any of these. I'm just trying to make the transition smooth for you, so you won't have to deal with questions you can't answer without risking to be put in an institution."

"Fine." I rubbed my forehead. "How about amnesia, then?"

This sounded less complicated than the rest. If I didn't remember anything, there was less risk of getting caught in my own lie, wasn't there?

"This has the potential of fewer questions," Delilah confirmed my unspoken assumption. "We can get medical reports to establish the head trauma that caused it, as well as to assure your full mental competency to return to work. How nosy are your co-workers?"

"They'll give me side glances for a while, but it should be fine eventually."

"Friends?"

Pat and Coco, my two closest girlfriends, didn't even know about my return yet. After being unable to answer Derek's questions, I decided to postpone calling them until this afternoon, after my meeting with Delilah. There was not a chance that Derek would have told them either. Since our breakup both Pat and Coco completely refused to talk to him.

"My friends will have questions, for sure. I'll need to be able to give them some solid answers."

"How about your boyfriend?"

"Ex," I corrected automatically. "Ex-boyfriend. We're just friends now. Derek will be the hardest to satisfy. He can be relentless in his search for truth, especially, if there is something as silly as an amnesia story involved."

"Amnesia may be rare, but it is real, Kitty. Every case of it is unique, and many could be considered bizarre."

"Okay, but I don't think this would be enough to convince Derek. Besides, he has a number of reliable sources throughout the city to verify any story you throw at him."

"You could tell him to mind his own business." Delilah's mouth pressed into a firm line.

"I could," I agreed. "But he simply won't stop digging if something doesn't sit well with him."

"Fine." Delilah took a pen out and started taking notes on the paper in her folder. "We'll make sure to feed the information to his sources, then. Anyone else?" She lifted her gaze at me.

"Nope." I bit my lip. "I've no one else."

She shuffled through her papers for a few moments, putting everything away, as I watched the streets of Seattle pass by through the tinted windows of the limo.

We stopped in front of a midsize building with a wrought-iron railing around the entrance stairs.

"Here we are, Kitty," Delilah said softly. "Do you want me to come in with you?"

"No." It was bad enough that Derek hovered over me day and night. I didn't need Delilah to lead me to the therapist by my hand. "Thank you. I'll be fine."

"You can be completely honest with Doctor Yung, Kitty. She's been recruited by The Priory and is fully aware of the situation. You won't be her only patient from the Incubi Base. I'm picking up two more women at the border next week. They went through the initial counseling in Canada but will be completing the program here with her."

"Okay." I put a hand on the door handle.

"I'll call you right after you're done here, to see how it went and to give you the details of your amnesia story."

"Okay," I repeated, squeezing the handle tighter but not opening the door. "Delilah." I couldn't meet her inquiring gaze, but I had to know. "Are you able to have any contact with the base at all? Through The Priory, I mean?"

"Oh, Kitty." She leaned against the back of the seat. "Don't do this to yourself. Let it go."

"I wish I could," I exhaled. "I mean I will. I absolutely will. But I need to know how *he* is."

She looked away, folding her arms across her chest, unyielding.

"Please. Remember how I left him? Lying in the middle of the road like that? With possibly every bone in his body broken . . ." I felt my chin tremble and stopped before my voice broke.

"Incubi heal perfectly fine, without any medical intervention."

"But they feel pain, just like we do, don't they? Please, I just need to know what's going to happen to him. He broke their laws. Will he be punished?"

"Most likely." She pursed her lips. "Kitty, for demons there are no happy endings. In fact, for them, there *are* no endings. Period. They just go through life, feeding and following the rules. Or not following, and then they get banished. Once they serve their time, they get out and start the cycle all over again. There is no end."

"There could be," I argued. "Didn't you say one of them found his forgiveness with a woman?"

"Do you want to be that woman for Ivarr?"

"No. I couldn't. But I do wish him well. Please," I repeated stubbornly. "I just need to know what happened to him, to be able to let go."

I held my breath, watching the severe expression on her face finally ease somewhat.

"Fine." She drummed her fingers on her arm. "I'll see what I can do."

"Thank you." I was able to release the air pressing inside my chest.

Chapter 29

THE NEXT WEEK, I RETURNED to work. They would've let me stay home longer, but I insisted on coming back. I needed the familiar routine of the office to help me get back on track as soon as possible.

As I'd hoped, blaming my absence on amnesia helped me avoid pretty much any personal questions. Whenever asked, I simply repeated the official statement released by the police.

I went to Canada for the weekend and was hit by a car while hiking outside of Vancouver. The elderly couple in the car took me home instead of the hospital for several reasons. First, besides a brief blackout and apparent memory loss, I didn't seem to show any signs of physical injury. Second, I had no identification papers on me for them to figure out who I was when I couldn't tell them that. And finally, they were initially worried about the consequences, feeling responsible for causing the accident.

After living in their house for several weeks, I finally started remembering enough to confirm my identity for them to send me home.

The story did cause some skeptics to raise their eyebrows. However, even Derek had to back off with his suspicions, faced with solidly documented proof of every point of the story.

There were records of my buying an airplane ticket and boarding the flight to Vancouver that Friday night. Full testimony from the Canadian couple, who hit me and then housed me in their home for weeks, was also provided by the Vancouver police. I wasn't sure if the testimony was a pure falsification like the rest or if or if there indeed were a couple who worked for The Priory and agreed to lie to the police on my behalf.

One of the hard parts turned out to be convincing everyone that I would just spontaneously travel to another country on my own. But since any memory of everything that happened after I came home from work on that Friday was supposedly gone, I didn't need to explain any of it.

With both of my closest friends being out of town that weekend and with Derek out of the picture by then, it was reasonable to assume I felt no need to notify anyone of my plans of a change of scenery, shortly after a breakup with my boyfriend of two years. Someone at the office even recalled a conversation we had a year ago when I apparently expressed the desire to see Vancouver one day.

In any case, cleared by medical professionals to return to work, I was free to get on with my life.

Everything seemed to be back to normal—waking up to the alarm in the morning, making it to the office on time, having lunch with colleagues, going for drinks after work or reading and watching TV at home.

Through the day, I managed just fine. At night was when I struggled.

With the expert help of Doctor Yung, I had been successfully dealing with the effects of being held in captivity. However, no matter how much she'd made me feel at ease talking about my sessions on the cross, I still couldn't bring myself to tell her everything about Ivarr.

The memories of my time in the cell were not the ones that haunted me most when alone in bed at night.

Regardless if my eyes were closed or open, staring into the darkness of my bedroom, I still saw his face framed by the golden halo of his hair as he moved over me, his expression that of passionate hunger and reverence.

The sensation of his skin against mine, his hands on me, his lips caressing every inch of my body—those were the memories I knew I had to let go, yet dreaded forgetting.

To leave behind the night I spent with a sex demon turned out to be not that simple. What was worse, the experience proved to be highly addictive—I wanted more.

More of him. More of the way he made me feel.

Lying alone in my bed at night, I went through every single detail of our time together, torturing myself with the memory of the vivid blue of his irises circled with bright red passion directed at me.

What worried me the most, though, was that it wasn't just the sex with Ivarr that I missed.

I wanted to dance with him again, feel the safety of his arms around me, just the two of us swept away with the music.

I longed to hear his voice, strong and powerful, even as a whisper.

In a very short time, he managed to learn enough about me to get me open up to him. In one conversation, I ended up telling him more about me than I'd ever did to anyone after months or even years of knowing them.

When I talked to him, he really listened, with all his senses focused on me, and I felt no fear of judgment or rebuttal from him. I missed that, too.

In my mind, I understood the sensible thing to do was to let him go, all of him, but I couldn't find a way to get him out of my heart.

I told myself it was simply the concern for his wellbeing that kept him in my thoughts. The horrible way we parted wouldn't let me rest until I knew that he was okay. The sooner I learned his fate, the easier it would be for me to leave Ivarr in the past.

Even if he was free and well by now, we were never meant to be—I knew it all along. After all, he was a sex demon. The magical night I spent with him might have been just one of many to him.

For all I knew, he probably didn't even remember my name anymore. By now, I could very well have become just another nameless, faceless *source* he'd fed off.

All I could do was to hope that my memories of him would finally fade with time.

IVARR

He lay on the narrow bed at the Base. Grey and dreadful, this place sucked the life out of him. He could almost feel the energy seeping out of his body and into the concrete walls around him, draining him of light.

Her light.

It was Katherine's energy that had been deserting him in a slow but steady stream, day after day, letting pain gradually take over. Afraid to move a muscle, he tried not to groan from it, not even to frown, to preserve every single drop of her he still had left inside him.

For as long as he could, he refused to feed, declining all solutions presented by the Council. He knew that sooner or later he'd have to accept whatever nourishment they offered or risk falling into Deep Sleep again, losing Katherine for good this way.

Not the pain from his healing bones, not even the torture of increasing hunger could overpower the agony of losing her.

Don't leave me, Katherine.

Night after night he pleaded with her in his mind, waiting for her call in a desperate hope that she did not forget about him.

Dream about me, my queen.

Chapter 30

ONE NIGHT IN NOVEMBER, a few weeks after I returned to work, I stood in front of my bedroom mirror again. This time, I didn't scrutinize my appearance. I admired it.

At lunch that day, I spotted a silk chemise in a shop window. It wasn't red, but the delicate feminine luxury of it reminded me of the night I spent with Ivarr, making me feel bold and beautiful once again. Unable to resist the urge to wear something so gorgeous, I bought it.

Blush pink, it had silver lace accents in the front and a small satin bow between the breasts. The colour lent a fresh glow to my skin. And when I ran my hands down the modest curves of my hips the sensation of gliding silk under my palms brought back memories of Ivarr's hands on me.

For once, I didn't fight it. Instead, I closed my eyes, recalling the feeling.

Arching my back, I cupped my breasts through the lace, remembering him doing the same. Yearning to have him near took over, along with a desperate ache for his touch.

With a sudden sob, I jerked my hands away and climbed under the covers.

It was not the same. Touching myself could never compare to his caress.

Nothing could.

The truth of this realization ran through me in a cold shiver of dread. Every lover I ever had from now on would forever be compared to *him* in my mind. And I already feared none of them would measure up.

I tossed and turned. The silk of the nightgown slithered between my legs, caressing my inner thighs. The lace rubbed softly against my hardened nipples, sending a rush of heat to my lower stomach.

Suddenly too hot under the covers, I tossed them off, and with a groan buried my face in the pillow.

My daily struggle to have a *normal* life was exhausting at times. Striving to appear strong—as if my encounter with the world of demons had never happened and didn't affect me in any way—I tried to act as I always did, before my abduction.

I tried to show everyone that I was just fine—coping, dealing and moving on.

And maybe it was true. Maybe I was mostly okay. But tonight, I felt crushed by the effort to be *normal* when, in fact, so much in me was no longer the same.

Things that I was too scared to admit, even to myself, floated to the surface. I missed the sensuality of a demon's touch. I wanted someone to make love to me as thoroughly and completely as only an Incubus could.

I desperately missed having him in my life.

Just once, I didn't want to pretend to be stronger than I really was. I wished I could allow myself to be weak for a moment, to curl against his hard chest and have his arms enclose me in a world of safety and protection.

And if I fell apart, I wanted to know there was someone to help me pick up all the pieces and take care of me without judgment or any set expectations, just the way he did during the brief time we spent together.

Tonight, I didn't want to be reminded of the long list of differences between Ivarr and I. I didn't care if it was wrong—I wanted to relish the things that united us, completing us both.

Loneliness swelled tight in my throat, and I wrapped my arms around myself, wishing he were here, with me.

'No matter what, I'll find you.'

I was sure he referred to finding me down the road somewhere if I drove away that night. But right now, I imagined he'd somehow find me here. In the darkness of the night, even the impossible seemed at least probable.

"Ivarr," I whispered, drifting into what I already knew would be a fitful sleep.

'Eligor. Remember it. Dream about me.'

His eyes, his voice, his touch.

Come to me. Even if just as a memory of a dream. I need it.

"Eligor."

I need you.

I WAS RUNNING THROUGH narrow streets filled with strangers. Their wide, grey backs closed in on me, forcing me to push my way through, shoving at them left and right.

None paid any attention to me. No one even so much as glanced my way.

A panicky feeling of being lost in this cobblestone web of streets vibrated through me. I opened my mouth to call for help, but there was only one word bouncing in my brain.

"Eligor!" I called out, shoving yet another broad back out of my way with force.

"I'm here," came a low reply, and a pair of strong arms caught me as soon as the back of the stranger disappeared. "God, I've waited for your call," his voice rasped in my ear.

And for one impossibly brief moment that seemed to last a lifetime it was just *him*—his hands on me, his warm spicy scent enveloping me, his mouth peppering my face with frantic kisses.

"Ivarr . . ." I breathed out, melting into him. "You found me." I tangled my fingers in his hair, reveling in his closeness.

My very soul seemed to have found peace in his arms, fear and worries dissolving into thin air, now that he was here.

"Finally." I pressed myself to his chest, running my hands along the wide planes of his shoulder blades. He was shirtless, wearing a pair of gloves and jeans. And I caressed his skin, savoring the sensation of its smooth warmth under my palms.

"I missed you, Ivarr. So, so much . . ."

"Come here, sweetheart," he murmured, lifting me with his hands under my backside. I wrapped my legs around his waist, hiding my face in his shoulder.

He carried me somewhere, away from the narrow, crowded streets, then placed me down—my back onto a warm, hard surface.

I heard the calming sound of running water and glanced around to find myself on the back of a stone lion at the edge of a marble fountain on a cobblestone plaza.

"Where is everyone?"

"There is no one here. Just you and I, my queen."

"You and I, my Viking," I echoed, taking his face between my hands. My gaze sliding along his familiar features, I smiled. "You're too beautiful to be truly a Viking. You need some scars or some Nordic tattoos to make you look rough."

"All wounds heal without scars on me." He grinned. "Including tattoos."

I had a bizarre feeling that we already had this conversation—somewhere in another time and place, infinitely long ago. Then it passed, as everything beyond this moment dissolved into nothing.

I stroked his cheekbones with my thumbs, feeling the prickling of his short beard.

"Don't shave this off then," I murmured. "I like it."

"As you wish."

The sunny expression in his eyes directed at me left me basking in his obvious affection.

"What do you see?" I asked, knowing that he saw more than I could.

"Everything." He turned his head to kiss my hand. "All the gorgeous colours and magnificent lights that I missed so much. They are all there."

There was the familiar intensity in his stare, but something was missing.

"Where are the blue sparkles then? You're not hungry today?"

"I'm always hungry, Katherine." He shook his head. "And with you, I'm simply insatiable. But I can't take any of it here."

"Why not?"

"I need to be next to you to skim or take any of your emotions."

"But you *are* next to me. Right here." I raked my hands through his hair, the tickle of silky strands between my fingers as real as ever.

He didn't answer. With a sad smile on his lips, he took my hand and kissed my wrist.

"I can't feed off you here." He leaned back and sat upright, straddling the statue, with my legs still wound around his waist. "But I can feel and taste all of you."

He tore his gloves off, tossing them into the fountain, then leaned over me again, covering my mouth with his.

This time, the kiss was slow, unhurried, as if he were taking his time to enjoy every moment of it, every sensation of his lips sliding against mine and of his tongue dancing with mine.

He gently ran his hand down my neck and along my shoulder. Catching the strap of my chemise with one finger, he dragged it down until my breast bounced free into the fresh, misty air of the fountain surrounding us.

"Every. Single. Inch of you," he whispered against my mouth, trailing kisses down the side of my neck to my naked breast.

I moaned from the exquisite sensation of his lips tugging at my nipple. Right before he sucked it in, rolling it with his tongue, tiny prickles of his beard against my breast.

The wave of heat that had been simmering just beneath my skin rushed over me, released by his caress. I sank my fingers into his hair, pressing him closer, and arched my back.

He slid his hand lower and dipped between my thighs. With a gasp, I let my knees drop away from his sides, opening wider for him. Gently, he glided his fingers through my folds then drew languid circles, spreading the slick moisture that seeped out of me.

Waves of arousal rippled through me with his touch, setting every nerve on fire.

"More," I whispered, lifting my hips to follow his fingers.

With his hands around my thighs, he slid lower along my body and hiked my nightgown up to my waist. He lowered his head between my legs and put his mouth on me.

Hot shivers ran up my thighs, with the first swipe of his tongue between my folds. Liquid heat pooled inside me, ready to burst, as he circled the sensitive bud. Again and again.

Slow at first, the sweet ache inside me built higher and stronger under the skillful glide of his tongue, until orgasm exploded in what felt like a million fireworks bursting though me in waves.

He nuzzled every last blissful shudder out of me then placed a few tender kisses on the inside of my thigh.

"God, I missed this," he said softly, pressing the side of his face to my leg. "You have no idea how much I need you."

"You said you can't feed here," I panted, catching my breath, as frantic heat inside me slowly dissolved into languid warmth.

He slid up to cover my body with his, and I marveled at the satisfied expression in his clear blue eyes, not a hint of red in them.

"Oh, I'd love to have taken all of this energy churning around you right now. But there is so much more about being with you." He searched my face with his gaze, as if taking it in. "The feel of you." He cupped my naked breast, massaging it gently. A small pinch of his fingers on my nipple sent a wave of tingles along my skin again, and I whimpered softly. "Your taste." He lowered his head to my neck, nibbling on my skin. "I want it all."

I cradled him between my raised knees and rocked my hips against the solid bulge in his jeans. The hot wave of desire flashed through me again, washing away the dreamy contentment of afterglow.

"I want you, too, Ivarr," I whispered and found the button of his jeans then yanked his zipper down, freeing his rock-hard erection.

He groaned into my neck when I circled his length and lifted my hips urgently, desperate to have him inside me.

"I'll have you any way I can, Katherine," he gritted though his teeth, slowly easing in, with a gentle thrust. "Anywhere."

I wiggled under him, in an attempt to take him deeper. Long and thick, he stretched me impossibly tight around him. The delicious sensation of complete fullness made me lightheaded as he began to move.

My arms around his shoulders, fingers digging into the hard muscles of his back, I moved with him, meeting him thrust for thrust in a slow sensual dance to the trickling sound of the water in the fountain.

"Then have me, Ivarr," I whispered, the anticipation of another approaching orgasm already coiling through me. "Right here, right now."

He circled his hips, rubbing just the right way against me and setting another explosion off inside me the very same moment his own release surged out of his body.

Panting, he collapsed over me, his chest to mine, his face at my neck, our lower bodies fused together. My arms tight around him, I basked in his closeness, ready to stay like this forever.

But he rose over me, separating us way too soon.

"You have to ask me questions, my queen." His eyes searched mine, imploring me with an unnerving sense of urgency.

"I have none." I clung to his shoulders, refusing to let go. "Now that you're here, there is nothing I miss."

"Oh, Katherine." The regret on his face puzzled me. Then a dark cloud of dread extinguished my happiness with the sudden realization that I was about to lose him.

"Don't leave." I flexed my fingers, digging them deeper, as the reality of the plaza with the fountain thinned around me and the sound of trickling water was slowly being replaced by the eerily familiar muffled noise of traffic.

Ivarr!

Panic overwhelmed me, and I opened my mouth in a scream of despair, but no sound came out. Instead, a silent gasp tore through my chest, as my eyes opened and the white ceiling of my bedroom came into view.

I lay in my bed, covers on the floor, my hands fisted in the sheet. The panicky sense of loss still rang though my chest, swishing in my ears with the blood pumped fast by my racing heart.

Panting, I closed my eyes again, willing the wonderful delusion to return, even as I knew it was useless to hope it would.

It was a dream, as vivid and as realistic as it seemed, none of it was real.

With a frustrated sigh, I rolled over on the mattress. The delicious ache of satisfaction rocked through my body as I stretched head to toe.

Dream or not, the feeling of having been thoroughly loved followed me into this world.

Chapter 31

FOR DAYS AFTER, THE dream wouldn't let me be.

At work, everything was back to normal. By working long hours and taking on any extra projects that came my way, I tried really hard to prove that my "amnesia" did not affect my performance in any way.

Losing myself in work helped me focus on things that had nothing to do with the demon of my dreams through the day. At night, however, the thoughts of him barraged my mind and the memories of his touch tormented my body.

Lying in bed, staring into the dark, I wondered at the vivid clarity of the dream.

That I definitely orgasmed in my sleep felt incredible to me, that and the distinct feeling of having been filled—I could have sworn he had been inside me. His touch lingered on my skin long after I awoke.

Incubus—a demon who came to women in their sleep. That was the general knowledge about Incubi. So, how much of the dream was actually a dream?

Despite my close encounter with Incubi, I knew very little about that aspect of their demonic nature. I hadn't had a chance to discuss it with Ivarr, and Delilah never mentioned anything about it.

I turned to the Internet for answers. Of course, none of the information I was able to find could be considered factual or in any way scientific, but almost all sources I came upon confirmed Incubi's ability to appear in a person's dreams. The reasons for them doing so and the consequences of such visits mentioned were what got me confused and even disturbed.

One of the earlier sources mentioning Incubi was a long analysis, recorded by monks centuries ago. It speculated on how the sex demons would steal semen from dead bodies to impregnate unsuspecting women by assaulting them in their sleep.

Other claimed that prolonged sexual relations with an Incubus resulted in deteriorating physical and mental health and eventually led to death.

The mentioning of *cambions*, the hideously deformed offspring of demon-human unions, made me shut off the computer, killing the desire in me to read any further. I might not have to worry about having children with an Incubus—and all of this could be just fiction, anyway—but the fact that speculations like that even existed left me feeling uneasy.

For centuries, it seemed the existence of Incubi had been blamed by people caught having wet dreams and self-pleasuring. Sex demons had also been accused of impregnating unmarried women who never left home without a chaperone. The allegations in these cases most likely were invented to cover up domestic sexual abuse and explain unwanted pregnancies.

Obviously, people's sexual desire and even human crimes were often blamed on demons.

That didn't help me to understand exactly what was happening with me.

Could my dream be a result of Ivarr actually visiting me while I slept? Or did I miss him more than I realized for my subconscious to conjure the unusually vivid dream?

The alternative was to accept that the ancient sources were right and my mental health actually was deteriorating as a result of fornicating with a demon. I was literally beginning to lose my mind.

Real or not, the dream did nothing in helping me let go. On the contrary, the longing for him flared up every time my thoughts drifted to him.

Worry over him still gnawed at me daily. As I waited for Delilah to tell me anything about his condition, I kept recalling the images of him from my dream, searching for any possible clues to his wellbeing and whereabouts.

In the dream, he appeared to be well, but I believed the shadows of hunger on his face were actually more prominent than before.

I kicked myself for not thinking about it and for not asking him any questions even when he prompted me.

But then and there, despite the visual and sensual clarity of the events and surroundings, my mind still seemed to be wrapped in the usual haze of a dream where the logic was flawed and the focus was narrow.

The utter joy of having Ivarr near me had cleared any concerns from my brain, as if he were to remain with me forever. I hadn't even considered that he'd leave me, until it happened and I woke up.

I didn't know how I made it through the days that followed until—finally—Delilah called with news of him.

Ivarr was being held at the Base, his injuries healed. A decision had been made not to send him to Inferno. Instead, the Council somehow made him agree to feed within the current norms.

I wondered how they made him comply so quickly after centuries of rebellion but forced myself not to dwell on the actual way he'd be fed while at the Base.

According to Delilah, with all captured women being released, Incubi were allowed to feed from willing sources only. How exactly that was being accomplished, Delilah couldn't tell me, as the changes were still being developed and as a non-member, she wasn't privy to that information.

She let me know that she wouldn't be able to get any more updates for me. Now that I knew Ivarr was doing fine, I should focus all my energy on moving on.

I'd hoped that learning Ivarr was well—not tortured by Deep Sleep or burning in Inferno—would release me from his constant presence in my mind.

Distressingly, it did nothing of the sort. On the contrary, knowing that he was here, in my world—not banned to another dimension—seemed to only bring him closer.

Instead of disappearing, the worry about him shifted in another direction. Now, I wondered if he was suffering from debilitating hunger. At the same time, the notion of him finding a *willing source* to feed from simply destroyed me emotionally.

None of it was made easier by the idea that Ivarr may have already forgotten about me. If the dream was just a dream, then I was simply obsessing over a figment of my imagination.

Calling on all the common sense I could muster, I managed to resist whispering his name before falling asleep for over a couple of weeks. As another week started though, the pain of not having him near became unbearable.

I was too far gone. Now, that I'd discovered a way to "see" Ivarr, I no longer could deny it to myself.

He'd become my weakness, my addiction, and just like a person craving a fix, I kept lying to myself.

No one needs to know.

Just this once, I can stop after that.

Sure, the sexual desire for him burned hot through me like always, but it was the simple need for his arms to hug me tight that made me finally cave in and call his name again.

Lying in bed, wearing my beautiful pink nightgown, I recalled the feeling of peace I had when he held me, the silk tendrils of his hair tickling my face, the scent of his skin surrounding me. I had to feel it again, needing him more than my next breath.

Still, in the last attempt to resist, I didn't call the name he gave me.

"Ivarr," I whispered the name I used to call him when I knew him. "Where are you?"

Ivarr. . .

MY EYES CLOSED, I STRETCHED head to toe on the bed. A light breeze, warm and refreshing all at once, stroked my body through the pink silk.

I lifted my face to its caress and opened my eyes to sheer white curtains billowing in the wind around the four posts of my bed, a bright blue sky above me instead of a canopy.

Sunshine slid along my face, making me squint. I smiled in its warmth.

A light, airy feeling of delight and excitement reigned inside me, with not a speck of worry or apprehension.

"Ivarr," I murmured, thinking that I would love to share these amazing emotions with him.

"I'm here," immediately came his reply. The mattress dipped at the opposite side, as he climbed in, and with a happy giggle I rolled into his arms.

"There you are." My palms splayed flat on the hard planes of his naked chest, I kept smiling as he covered my face with kisses. "I didn't use the word, how did you still come?"

"My Mistress." He rolled onto his back, dragging me on top of him. I rose on my elbows propped against his chest and moved his blond strands from his face. "Unlike other humans, you can summon me to your dreams by any name you know me by."

I ran my fingers through his hair and spread it on the pillow, carefully arranging it in a golden halo around his face, strand by strand.

"Am I your Mistress, then?"

"I chose you." He placed a quick kiss on my wrist when I moved it close enough to his lips while playing with his hair. "I felt you were my everything, Katherine, long before we parted, but I gave you my demon name, too, just in case."

"How long have you been Ivarr, Eligor?"

"Since I first came to Norway."

"Was I right? Were you a real Viking?"

"No." He laughed. "I came to Norway a couple of centuries after the Age of Vikings, the Norwegian Empire had already been established by then."

"You're still my Viking," I murmured, kissing the ridge of his strong jawline, my lips sinking into his beard, fuller this time. "You didn't shave it off?" I placed another kiss higher, on his cheekbone.

"You told me to let it grow." I sensed the warmth of a smile in his voice.

"Is it because of that *Mistress* rule? Will you have to do everything I tell you now?" I kept kissing up to his temple.

"Not because I have to, but because I want to, Katherine. I want you happy, and I'll do everything for that." He ran his hands up my sides and shifted me to better see my face. "You have to keep asking me questions, only then can I tell you things."

"Why wouldn't you just say what you want to say?"

"Because it's *your* dream, Mistress. You *need* to ask the questions."

"It's not a dream." I shook my head. "You're real. I can touch you." I cupped his face then slid my hand down the thick cords of his neck to his chest and circled his nipple with the tip of my fingers. He groaned softly, tensing under me. "I can kiss you." I slid down his body, straddling his hips, and leaned in to trace the ridge of his pectoral with my lips.

"Katherine." His voice came from deep inside his throat. His large body arched under me, but he threw his arms aside fisting his gloved hands in the satin of the bedding as if to stop himself from touching me. "Where are we?"

"In my bed, silly." I darted my tongue out to taste the warm saltiness of his skin, slowly moving down his stomach over the hard landscape of his abs.

"Look around," he rasped.

I glanced to the side quickly, not wanting to pause for too long in my exploration of his body.

The curtains swayed in the breeze blowing around the top of the mountain ridge where the large bed with the dark ornate frame stood.

"If you don't ask, I will. Does it look like your bedroom?"

"I'm not sure. . ." For some reason, I couldn't tell for certain what my bedroom looked like, but I *knew* this was where I lived. "This is home." I nodded and reached for the button of his dark pants, determined to avoid any further interruptions.

Right now, I needed him as close as a man could be with a woman. And I knew this was what he wanted, too. His insistence of talking was puzzling, the delays created by it irritating.

Yet he wouldn't stop.

"Where do you work?"

"In the office," I replied quickly, using both hands to rip the fly of his jeans open, to free his bulging erection.

"What is the name of the firm you work for? Do you know it?"

"Of course I do." Thinking about my work brought an image of a desk and a computer, but not a building, a logo or the name. "Um . . ." Any effort to remember the name only annoyed me further, distancing me from this moment where I wanted to remain. "It doesn't matter." I slid my fingers up and down his straining length, making him bare his teeth and roll his eyes into his head. "Nothing matters when you're with me, Ivarr."

He sat up in bed abruptly and grabbed me in his arms, shifting my hips to his. I rocked against him, making his hardness rub between my slick folds.

"Just remember," he whispered against my mouth, between his hungry kisses. "You'll have to ask me where I go when I leave." Quickly ripping his gloves off, he tossed them aside then found my breast with his bare hand. Freeing it from the lacy cup of the chemise, he rolled my nipple under his thumb.

"Don't leave." I wrapped my arms around his neck, vowing to hold on to him with everything I had. "Don't go." I lifted my hips to let him align us perfectly then slowly sank down, taking him in. "Never." I flexed my legs to slide up and down his shaft.

Any confusion brought by his questions disappeared, as I slowly lost myself in the exquisite sensation of him being inside me once again.

"Katherine," he exhaled my name, as if finally surrendering to the moment with me. Tightening his arms around me, he held me close, seemingly also lost in the rhythm created by our bodies moving together.

I angled my hips to make sure the most sensitive part of my body was rubbing just the right way against him.

Our joint climax exploded, my nails digging into his back, his head at my shoulder. Then sudden fear moved in before we had a chance to relax into each other.

"Stay!" I ordered, circling my legs around his middle, and tightened my arms around him. The panicky sense of helplessness to prevent what was happening fractured me from the inside.

Then I felt the graze of his teeth at my shoulder, before he jerked his head to the side.

"Remember." His whisper came with the wind from a distance. He was no longer in my arms.

Chapter 32

"NO!" I SOBBED, CURLING into myself, feeling acutely the void in my arms and in my chest.

Even before I opened my eyes, I knew I was back in my bedroom—in my actual bed—painfully aware that *he* was no longer with me.

The agony of loss seemed even sharper this time, making my first impulse to try forcing myself to go back to sleep again.

Ridiculous! I can't spend the rest of my life asleep.

But was it possible? To fall asleep for years? I actually considered this—a lifelong coma in the sunny happiness of an endless dream with the illusion of Ivarr in it.

You're pathetic, Kitty.

I groaned and shoved from the mattress to roll myself into a sitting position on the edge of the bed, my feet dangling just above the floor.

What was I supposed to do? Was it time to come clean to Doctor Yung about Ivarr's nighttime visits? So far, I had been completely open with her about my time in Incubi captivity. Together, we worked through my emotions about being held and pleasured against my will.

However, anything that had to do with Ivarr felt too private to discuss even with my therapist. I reasoned that since he had no part in my incarceration, I could keep the memories of him to myself.

Doubts gnawed at me again, though. What if the unusually vivid dreams were simply some kind of aftereffect of too many intense events happening in a relatively short time in my life. Was this some weird way my mind chose to process the stress of severe emotions? Then I would need professional help with it, wouldn't I?

I hopped to the floor and raked my fingers through my hair.

A slight movement against my skin made me jump with a cry of surprise. I swatted with both hands at my arm and shoulder, convinced there was a spider crawling over me.

The lacey cup of my camisole fell away from my breast, the fresh air of the room puckering my exposed nipple.

Quickly, I turned on the light on my night table.

The delicate shoulder strap was ripped in two. The ends frayed and a little moist.

'Remember,' Ivarr said when he must have bit through it. Making sure I had a proof when the dream was gone?

Stunned, I fingered the ruined strap, considering everything for a minute. It appeared it wasn't Doctor Yung I should be calling after all, but Doctor Neri. Despite her strong aversion to all things Incubi, Delilah was the only one capable of giving me any answers.

I grabbed my phone from the night table and searched for her phone number.

"KITTY, DO YOU UNDERSTAND that this obsession with one of them is unhealthy. Did you discuss this with Doctor Yung?"

"It's not an obsession." I mumbled stubbornly, dismayed that our conversation once again resulted in an argument.

I realized Delilah had solid reasons to be wary of Incubi. Unfortunately, I didn't have any other source of information about them but her.

I had many reasons to be wary of the demons, too. However, it wasn't Incubi as a whole I was concerned about. All I wanted was to know more about them to better understand just one Incubus, whom I couldn't stop thinking about, and who now haunted my dreams.

"A relationship with him would be toxic, Kitty," Delilah stated grimly.

"I'm not talking about having any kind of a relationship here. I just want to know exactly what Incubi can do. Can they really invade people's dreams?"

"Yes. They can manipulate human dreams. The goal is to turn you on and feed off your sexual energy while you're asleep. However, they need to be physically near the sleeping person to feed. I can guarantee you that Ivarr is not in Seattle, in which case, it makes no sense for him to visit you in your sleep. If he can't feed, why would he bother?"

Because he misses me.

Because he wants me in other ways than just feeding.

Because he chose *me.*

Because if the dream was not just a product of my imagination then he really said everything I heard him say in it.

My heart sped up and my stomach fluttered with nerves. What if Ivarr really cared more about me than my mind allowed me to hope. What we had was supposed to be a one-time experience. However, it had been proving significantly more for me already.

What if it meant more for him, too?

"Kitty." Delilah's voice rang with a soothing note. "I believe you had a dream about him. Your mind must be still processing everything that has happened, and it would be perfectly normal to dream about him. You've been doing a great job adjusting back to your life. And with enough time the dreams will stop, too.

I realized with a hefty share of panic that I didn't want them to stop. The dreams were all I had left of him.

Delilah went on, "I would never encourage anyone, especially someone who like you has just escaped their captivity, to enter into a relationship with one of them."

"He wasn't part of it . . ."

"What would his motivations be to pursue you in any way? Feeding off you. Using you as a ticket to the ultimate forgiveness."

"You said there is a successful human-demon relationship out there now . . ." I wasn't sure why I held on to this piece of information I'd received from Delilah and why I mentioned it now. Could there be any hope for me to even consider a relationship with Ivarr?

"I said there was a confirmed case of pregnancy. I haven't met the woman to speak to her wellbeing or accurately assess how successful their relationship is."

"Wouldn't The Priory know—"

A heavy sigh on the other end of the line stopped me from finishing the sentence.

"Kitty. You need to focus on your own wellbeing and recovery. You got a second chance at life. So much is ahead of you. I can tell you from my professional experience that finding a suitable life partner is not always easy.

"My own personal belief has been that it's best to be with someone close to you in aspirations, convictions, and principles. What can you possibly have in common with a hundreds-year-old demon? I'm afraid you're setting yourself up for heartbreak by nursing hope."

"I'm not nursing anything . . ."

Obviously, there was no point discussing this with Delilah. Especially, since I hadn't even made it clear to myself what it was that I hoped for now.

"Good," Delilah conceded, effectively closing the discussion. "Are you happy with Doctor Yung?"

"Yes."

During the past session we had talked about my guilt over enjoying the things done to me by Incubi.

Interestingly enough, any animosity I had was directed towards the ones I held responsible for my kidnapping and incarceration—the Council and even The Priory. I did not feel much resentment towards the individual demons.

I hardly held anything against Garrett or whoever was there before him who had the role of my Handler, as I sensed they were mostly mindless executioners of someone else's will.

Neither, did I blame Ivarr for the crimes of his kind.

This seemed to be one big difference between Delilah and I—whereas I saw the demons as individuals, she judged them en mass.

Chapter 33

FOR THE DAYS THAT FOLLOWED, I did all I could to avoid calling his name before falling asleep. I needed some time to sort through everything I'd learned as well as my own feelings and hopes.

If what Ivarr said in my dreams was true—if he truly cared about me—was there a real chance for us to be together?

I didn't care that much about The Priory's or the Council's opinion on this, not even about the fact that Ivarr and I were thousands of miles apart, with no easy way to meet again, since there was obviously not much hope of Delilah's assistance. As long as both of us wanted it to happen, I was confident we'd find a way.

Nothing had changed, though, from the time we parted. My feelings for him might have grown, but our situation remained the same.

He was an immortal demon. What was the best either of us could hope for? We might have a few happy years—maybe even decades—together, just like what he had with Margreta. Ultimately, however, we'd need to part. There'd never be growing old together for us.

More importantly, I'd kept a very essential part about myself a secret from Ivarr. If demons really got a chance for forgiveness and salvation by finding the right woman and becoming a father, I could never give him that.

If the forgiveness was what he was ultimately after, wouldn't it be extremely selfish on my part to hope for any kind of a future with Ivarr at all?

ONE FRIDAY EVENING, Pam, my best friend at work, dragged me out for drinks. It was December already, just days before Christmas. Streets were lit bright with festive lights. The small bar across the road from our office building was packed with people, buzzing with merry mood.

This time of year had always been bitter sweet for me. I'd celebrated by accepting every invitation to dinner that came my way, avoiding going home to my empty apartment as much as I could.

This year, it was somehow especially hard to get into the holiday spirit. The feeling of loneliness cut through me more painful than ever.

"What happened to you is insane, Kitty. Absolutely crazy," Pam started, sliding a glass of red wine my way along the table. "But I wonder if that's really what's dragging you down."

"Nothing is dragging me down, Pam." I took a huge swig from the glass, thinking that at this rate I might as well get the whole bottle.

"It's still about this guy, isn't it?"

An arrow of surprise shot through me. What did Pam know about *him*?

"Ever since he broke up with you, you've not been yourself."

Finally, I realized she was talking about Derek.

"Oh God, Pam," I exhaled. "I really don't care about him. Not in *that* way, I mean. We're just friends now."

"Honestly, I don't understand how people can remain friends after what he did. Kitty, remember, I was there picking up the pieces the day after he left you. You were a mess."

"Derek and I are fine now. We talked—"

"Yeah? And what did he say?"

"It's not that. It's about how I feel over our past relationship, our breakup, and myself. Derek and I were never meant to be. We may be good friends, but we suck as a couple. I'm absolutely fine with it." I took another sip of my wine and leaned back in my seat. "You should be, too."

"Oh, I am glad he is out of the picture now. I'm not even voting for him whenever he runs for public office."

"That's your political right to choose whom to vote for." I shook my head, smiling.

"But there is still something off with you." She narrowed her eyes at me.

"I'm fine. I'm doing great at work."

"Way too great," she muttered, swirling the wine in her glass. "All those long hours you put in."

"I'm in accounting. Everyone works long hours at month end."

"With you, it's all month long, it seems. Whenever I come in, you're already there. And when I leave, you're still up to your ears in work. Do you even go home to sleep or do you just pass out at your desk?"

"Of course I go home."

I had wondered if it would make it harder for Ivarr to find me in my dreams, if I slept somewhere other than home.

"What I'm saying, Kitty, is that life is all about balance. And yours doesn't seem to have any."

It wasn't just my life. Everything—my mind, my feelings, my emotions—were severely out of balance.

"Oh, Kitty." Pam leaned across the table and covered my hand with hers. "We need to do something fun. Do you want to go out dancing tonight? I know you don't like the club scene that much and dancing is not your thing," she added quickly before I managed to reply. "But you don't even have to dance. We'll take it easy—have some drinks, mingle with people a little. You know. Have some fun."

"Um . . . I'm—"

"Or we could go out of town." Pam wouldn't give up. "You, me and Coco. Remember that time we went to Vegas to see that hot magician perform, and you were too much of a prude to even—" She stopped herself, her expression lit up with an idea I was afraid I might find terrifying. "Oh. My. God." Pam said slowly, reaching for her cellphone. "Did you get Mindy's email?"

"Who?"

"Mindy, one of Coco's friends from high school?"

"No. I didn't get any emails from her. And I'm pretty sure she doesn't know me because I don't think I know her."

"It doesn't matter." Pam waved me off. "They're going to Vegas. Like two weeks from now, after the holidays. We should go. I've already said no, because, really, I don't like Mindy very much. The feeling is mutual, too. But I'll go if you go."

"I didn't get invited, remember?" Surprisingly, however, the idea of a trip didn't seem too bad. Deep inside, I longed for some carefree fun with my friends. Despite what Pam said, I wanted to dance again.

"Pfft! Just say the word if you want to come. I'll call Coco, and she'll make it happen." Pam grabbed her phone, punching energetically at the screen. "Oh, my God!" She bounced in her seat. Her auburn hair, cut in a stylish bob, swung around her face. "Can you believe it, we're going to see this."

She shoved the phone in my face, and I had to lean all the way back for my eyes to focus on the picture she wanted me to see.

A row of topless men, backlit by brilliant stage lights that left their faces in the shadows, lined the dark stage. Multicoloured lights glistened off their massive shoulders, well-defined abs, and thick biceps. Their muscled arms crossed in front of their wide chests.

Demon Army was written in glowing blood-red letters across the picture.

"These guys are great! It's a new show. And it's getting rave reviews. Apparently, it's sold out for months in advance now, but

Mindy's boyfriend scored some tickets through someone he knows . . ." Pam started frantically typing on the phone. "I'll just have to let Coco know ASAP that we're coming, to hold the tickets for us."

"Can I see the picture again, please," I asked quietly.

"You like it, huh?" Pam gave me a knowing smile. "I knew you would. How can anyone not like this?" She gave me the phone again. "They're dancers, not strippers—this is as much skin as you're going to see at the show—which is a shame if you ask me. Still, no one seems to complain. Apparently, they are amazing. Super talented. Their show has this fantasy, supernatural, paranormal theme. See?" She leaned across the table, hovering over the phone in my hand, and scrolled to more pictures.

Artful shots of perfectly built men in dramatic poses against stunning backgrounds.

Some wore fantasy armor, wielding swords and holding shields, their faces obscured by ornate golden helmets.

Some of them were draped in long fur capes or black cloaks.

And others wore long coats, akin to vampires, princes of darkness or . . . demons.

"They are so freaking perfect—they don't even seem real," Pam gushed.

"They don't," I agreed, my gaze going to the one thing that was common in all the pictures—leather gloves worn by every single man on stage. Dark grey, they looked just like the ones worn at the Incubi Base.

"Here you go, Pam." I gave her the phone back, hating to see my hand shake.

"Holy cow, Kitty," she gasped, ducking to search my face. "Are you okay? You're white as a sheet. She grabbed both of my hands in hers. "I swear I really hate that ex of yours. Whatever did he do to you that you can't even see good-looking topless guys now without nearly passing out?"

Chapter 34

I GOT OFF THE BUS TWO stops before my place. The air inside suffocated me, and I needed to walk as fast as my legs would carry me in a futile attempt to outrun the thoughts rushing through my brain.

Demon Army.

The gloves.

'They are so freaking perfect . . .'

What were the chances of them actually being demons? The gloomy memory of my basement cell came to mind, bringing the air of cold and despair. Could my captors end up doing something as harmless and peaceful as . . . dancing? Why would they?

All of it must be just some odd coincidence.

The group's name alone was not indisputable proof. Anyone could have come up with the idea of having a paranormal themed male dance show.

And the fact that they wore gloves . . . Well, it was a cool look.

Everything about the dancers in the pictures was cool. Amazing. Perfect. Too perfect. And every demon I ever met wore gloves.

Except for Raim. He didn't.

Would the Grand Master even allow something like that? Dancing on the stage in the centre of hundreds of female fans, I imagined, would be breaking a whole bunch of his precious rules.

On the other hand, Delilah had mentioned that all Incubi were going to feed off *willing sources* only. With all kidnapped victims now released, I imagined, it wouldn't be easy for the Council to find women willing to be hauled up on the cross to feed the demons nightly.

The energy coming from spectators of the show might not be the orgasmic emotions my captors had elicited in me to feed the Council, but it should still be strong and positive—nourishing enough for the demons to stay awake and function.

If so, could Ivarr be in the show?

Oh, I had no doubt he could dance well enough to amaze any audience. I'd had the chance to find this out for myself.

Racing along the sidewalk, my arms wrapped tight around me from the cold winter air, I swayed on my feet, remembering that night again and nearly tripped over my heels on the pavement.

The last time he appeared in my dream, he was dressed like the faceless men on the promo pictures—wearing nothing but dark pants and gloves. I couldn't be certain, but I believed the shadows of hunger on his face had eased, as well.

Delilah said he agreed to follow the rules when feeding now. He must have been offered an acceptable way to stay awake this time, and he conceded.

If he was awake, why wouldn't he come to see me in person?

Would he want to be with me?

He'd had a relationship with a woman before. That was a starting point, I supposed. But if he really had any feelings for me, would they change once he found out that he could never have children with me?

Would he take a few decades out of his quest for forgiveness to be with me? Would I want him to be my life partner, knowing that I'd be the only one aging?

I tried to imagine what it would be like to spend the rest of my life with a sex demon, and I couldn't. Honestly, it proved impossible for me to envision even a week of a regular domestic life with someone like Ivarr. But I realized I wanted to find out what it would be like to have him in my life.

By the time I reached my building, there seemed to be only one way to get any answers for all these questions—Ivarr and I needed to have a real conversation.

It seemed to me, the only way *'to find my balance'* was to lay everything in the open with him. Then, we either find a way to be together for as long as my limited lifespan would allow us, or part for good.

NO LONGER COUNTING on Delilah to get information for me, I had to turn to Ivarr himself for his whereabouts.

That night, I went to bed with the firm intention of summoning my demon.

'You need to ask me questions,' he'd told me.

The trouble was that in my dream no problems existed. I remembered feeling joyful, excited to be with him. I questioned absolutely nothing and loved every moment near him—until I woke up and he was no longer there.

Uncertain if it was even possible to keep a grip on reality while I slept, I went to bed determined to try.

Summoning Ivarr was easy.

Keeping thoughts and memories of him out of my head was more difficult than allowing them in. They flooded all my senses as soon as I stopped holding them back.

The straining to remember to ask him questions brought with it tension and anxiety. Still the excitement of seeing him again made me fall asleep with a smile on my lips.

I FLOATED IN A POOL of warm water. The gentle stream carried me along without any effort on my part to stay afloat. White, fluffy clouds passed in the sky above me. I splashed my hands in the water, squinting from the droplets hitting my face.

I must be on vacation.

But why was I alone? Wasn't someone else supposed to be here with me right now? Someone I couldn't wait to see.

"Ivarr," I called up to the sky.

"I'm here," came immediately after, just like it always did whenever I wanted him.

His familiar arms found me in the water, and he pressed me to his chest. I slid my hand behind his neck right away. "I need you."

"I know." He kissed my temple.

His simple caress ignited sparks of desire, and I melted into him, finding his mouth with mine.

But it wasn't all I needed him for, was it? The urgency to do something nagged at me, dulling my arousal with anxiety.

The clouds in the sky turned grey and gathered together, shrouding us in semi-darkness. The warm pool chilled. And the lazy stream sped up to a treacherous torrent.

"What is it, Katherine? What is bothering you?" Worry vibrated through Ivarr's voice.

I clung to his shoulders, as the strong current carried us through churning rapids, fear colder than the water around us spread through me.

"What is going to happen to us, Ivarr?"

"Anything you want, sweetheart." He brushed my lips with his and smoothed my hair, seemingly unconcerned about the dangerous waters around us. "You are my Mistress in both worlds, here and there. You have the power to make it all happen, my queen."

"You're going to leave me." The certainty of this realization increased my anxiety. "That's what always happens, doesn't it?" Panic rose in me, as I already sensed the power that was ripping Ivarr out of my arms. "Don't go!" I grasped for him, but instead of his shoulders my hands gripped a cold, hard rock sticking from the torrent.

"Ivarr!" My scream, caught by the wind, was lost in the roar of the raging water.

"Ask me the question." His voice came from the distance, and I glimpsed him being hurled over the edge and down the vertical drop of a waterfall.

"No!" I let go of the rock just to be immediately swept into the current after him.

Question. Question. Question . . .

The word bounced inside my head as I went over the rocky edge as well and now floated in free fall surrounded by water and mist.

"Where do you go when you leave me?" I whispered, just as I was yanked out of danger and into the safety of a familiar place—my bedroom.

'Vegas,' echoed in my brain, less as a spoken word and more as a transmitted thought.

Vegas.

The awakening was brutal in its swiftness. The terror of free fall disappeared instantly, along with the cold water and . . . Ivarr.

The feeling of loss crushed me, hollowing my insides. I stifled a sob and curled in bed, tucking my forehead into my knees.

"I can't," I whispered, clutching the bed sheets in my fists. "Please."

This couldn't go on. The rollercoaster of the hazy bliss of the dream—even when it turned into a nightmare—replaced by the acute feeling of loneliness in reality was emotionally devastating. The craving to have him near was crushing.

"I need you here, Ivarr. With me."

Vegas.

I had a specific location and the means to be there in two weeks. I needed to find out for sure if there was something strong and lasting between us.

And if I couldn't have him, he had to let me be. Even if I called him in the moment of weakness, he had to leave me alone in my dreams. There was no other way.

Chapter 35

"OH, KI-ITTY, YOU'RE so pre-etty!" Pam sang, giggling. Leaning against the wall of the hotel bathroom where I was brushing my hair, she gave me another appraising look. "Love this dress."

"You do? Thank you." I put the hairbrush on the counter and smoothed my palms over the silk of my flared skirt.

The vivid colour of burnt orange, the flirty skirt, and the off-shoulder cut were a daring step out of my usual style of understated elegance, but I absolutely loved the way this dress made me feel when I put it on.

Pretty, just like Pam said.

My Aunt Sue used to say, *'Pretty is not a look but a feeling.'* And I never understood her more than right now.

I needed to feel this sunny, giddy confidence inside of me to deal with the nervous anticipation that buzzed though me ever since I boarded our flight to Vegas that morning.

Tonight was the night of the show. If my assumptions were right, I might see Ivarr again. And this time it wouldn't be a dream.

It'd be real.

"WHO DID MINDY'S BOYFRIEND have to sleep with to get these tickets?" Pam gasped under her breath when we took our seats at the table next to the stage.

My heart sped up even faster, threatening to jump out of my throat.

Too close.

I would prefer to sit at the back, somewhere in the shadows. But then it would be too easy to chicken out and sneak away at the first sight of Ivarr. I couldn't afford to miss a chance to talk to him. If he was truly on stage tonight, he needed to see me to know I was here.

With a deep breath, I took my seat.

From the moment the lights dimmed, and the first beat of epic music filled the room, I was drawn into the show.

A group of men dressed in golden armour over their bare torsos entered the stage. Enthralled, I stared at their hard bodies awash in a kaleidoscope of pulsing lights as they moved to the music. Then several more joined, these wore a pair of white feather wings each.

The more I watched the dancers' flawless execution of the complex mix of dance and athletic choreography, the more I became convinced they were not humans.

Pam's words *so freaking perfect* came to mind again.

Next, a group dressed as fantasy archers were replaced by a lone figure in black standing with his back to us as he appeared to emerge from the silvery mist spreading over the stage.

Slowly, he turned around. The ends of his open black coat swept the ankles of his boots. Light slid along his bare chest and hard abs as he sauntered to the edge of the stage. Seductive music lured me and undoubtedly anyone else in the audience to him.

Tossing the ends of his coat back, he jumped off the stage and stalked along the first row of tables, scanning the women in their seats.

His ink-black hair was neatly cut and the stylish facial hair trimmed to perfection. Certain I'd never met the man before, I couldn't take my eyes off him, entranced by the penetrating stare of his dark eyes.

The lights turned to deep shades of red and purple. Dancing along the pale skin of his face and chest, they gave an even more enticingly dangerous air to his appearance.

Silent, he stopped at our table, and I heard a choked gasp from Pam when he offered his gloved hand to her.

"Oh my God. Oh my God," she kept repeating in a startled whisper on a loop, even as she accepted his hand and rose from her seat. "Me?"

Still without saying a word, he bowed to her and briefly pressed her hand to his lips.

In the ever-changing show of flashing multi-coloured lights, it would've been easy to miss the tiny blue sparks rushing through his eyes at that moment, had I not been that close to him and had I not expected them to appear.

I went to grab Pam's arm, but with a reassuring smile flashed my way, the demon led her away from our table.

Her eyes wide, Pam's face froze in an expression of wonder. She didn't protest when he grabbed her around her waist and easily lifted her onto the stage. The way she gazed at him at that moment, I suspected she would've let him take her to the Moon without questioning it.

The music increased in intensity. A powerful instrumental stream joined the sensual tones of the violin, as the demon turned Pam to face the audience and took a spot behind her.

Slowly, he traced the tips of his gloved fingers up her arms, making her tremble. With one hand running along her throat, he gently tipped her head to the side and bared his teeth, licking his lips.

His vampire fangs glistening in the dark violet light might have been fake, however, the feral hunger that raged in his eyes seemed absolutely real.

Pam's chest heaved when the demon lowered his mouth to the side of her neck. Her gaze glossed over, and she swayed under the kisses he trailed along the side of her neck, from her ear to her collarbone.

At first, he gripped her upper arms to hold her in place. But as her eyes fluttered closed, and her knees buckled, he wrapped her in his arms, pressing her back to his chest.

The music broke into a passionate crescendo. The lights turned to blood red, masking the scarlet glow in his eyes. The demon spun Pam in his embrace, turning her to face him then led her to the music, in a slow dance along the stage.

With a loud moan, barely masked by the music, Pam dropped her head on his shoulder and wrapped her arms around his neck, bringing her body flush with his.

Without skipping a step, the demon continued to devour her neck, her collarbone, and her bare shoulder in a trail of sensual kisses.

Afraid to breathe, I pressed my clasped hands to my chest. Deep in my mind, I knew that Pam was safe. This was not the first time it must have happened. I knew Incubi could learn to control themselves around humans. After all, the demon wouldn't be wearing gloves if his intentions were to harm her.

Yet the eerie atmosphere created by the lights, the music, and the thin wisps of mist trailing through the air all around us filled me with excitement and dread as I sat on the edge of my seat.

The Incubus took Pam through a few more steps of his sensual dance as the music slowed, gradually fading into the background. He made an attempt to release her from his arms, but visibly boneless, her legs refused to support her right away, and he swept her into his arms instead.

Pressing her to his chest, he jumped off the stage with ease and headed our way.

The mist cleared as if by magic, the lights brightened as another demon took the stage. I didn't spare a glance for him at first, all my attention on Pam being returned to her seat.

The Incubus gently lowered her into the chair then kneeled in front of her, kissing her hand again. She swayed after him when he got up to leave then slumped back in her chair when he moved away.

"Zander," MC announced, as Pam's Incubus took a bow before exiting the room.

"Holy cow," Pam exhaled. Her hand pressed to her chest, she followed Zander with her gaze.

"Are you okay?"

"How was it?" Coco and Mindy leaned in across the table. "That looked . . . intense."

"It was . . ." Pam blinked, as if still coming back from being put into trance. "Fuuuck," she suddenly hissed in a loud whisper. "It's crazy. Another minute of that." She tipped her head at the stage. "And I swear I would've come. Just from a neck kiss! Really?" She huffed a deep breath. "How am I supposed to go on living my life now? Tell me," she demanded, sweeping all of us with a glare. "I'm ruined for all the men who ever come after him."

With another heavy sigh, she leaned back in her seat again.

". . . it is his last performance today." The MC's announcement brought all our attention back to the stage. "Ladies and gentlemen, a round of applause for Lucius please."

The demon, who took the stage after Zander, dipped his head in a bow.

His luminous gold hair that curled past his shoulders reminded me of Ivarr. However, he was leaner. The armour he was wearing had a kind of barbarian flair—crudely ornamental and trimmed with fur. He held a helmet under his arm as he stepped to the front of the stage to give everyone a wave.

"Baby, you're the best!" A girly voice shouted from a table across the room from us. Everyone, including myself turned to see where the voice came from.

A young woman with skin the colour of dark caramel rose in her seat, blowing kisses towards Lucius with her both hands.

'Love you,' she mouthed between the kisses, jumping to her feet and bouncing with joy.

The corners of his mouth twitched up when Lucius gave a small discreet wave in her direction. A moment later, seemingly unable to hold back, he beamed at her with a wide smile and blew a kiss in return.

"Awww," the crowd crooned as one. I myself smiled so wide, my mouth hurt.

The music grew louder again, slowly filling the room with a raw, powerful beat. Lucius put his helmet on quickly, as more demons joined him on the stage.

There were at least a dozen of them, taking a wide stance in two rows. And my attention was immediately drawn to the tall figure in the back.

Like all of them, he wore dark pants and boots in addition to the uniform gloves. Two wide, golden armlets circled his biceps, and a fur-trimmed belt sat low on his hips.

He sported a full beard. The helmet concealed the upper part of his face, but I still would've recognized him anywhere.

This time, I was only half-aware of the actual choreography of the number performed. I knew it was just as breathtaking as the rest of the show, with its ever-changing lights, fine clouds of mist and epic music.

The mix of graceful dance moves and fluid athletic jumps, handstands and flips that defied the laws of physics was mind-blowing. However, all my focus narrowed on Ivarr.

During the whole time he was on stage, he did not make any eye contact with me, leaving me fairly certain that he hadn't spotted me. However, as soon as the music slowed down to a more lyrical melody, he immediately turned my way and headed to me.

My heart jumped to my throat. The whole world fell apart, as he held me pinned to my chair with his vivid blue gaze.

He offered his hand to me as he approached our table.

"Kitty!" Pam hissed in a sharp half-whisper and nudged me with an elbow.

From the corner of my eye, I noticed the other demons jumping off the stage too and inviting women from the audience. Some couples where already swaying in a slow dance on the stage and in the space around the tables.

"Kitty doesn't dance," Coco offered helpfully, as I froze in place and silence.

With both hands, Ivarr took his helmet off and set it on the table, giving his golden mane a shake.

"But *Katherine* does," he replied confidently in a low, raspy voice then extended his arm my way again.

The past couple of months disappeared as if they never happened—I was in the hotel restaurant again, with Ivarr asking me for a dance.

Excitement bloomed inside me as I took his hand.

And just like that, it was only he and I again.

No one else existed.

Hands on my waist, he spun me around then lifted me onto the stage, jumping effortlessly after me.

This time, he didn't attempt any spins or fancy steps. Holding me in his arms, he slowly led me in a wide circle along the stage.

I spotted the familiar blue-white twinkle in his eyes a moment before he closed them and inhaled deeply.

"God, I missed you," he whispered so softly, I could barely hear him, his arms tightened around my waist.

I slid my hands up his bare chest. Glistening faintly with a thin sheen of sweat from the performance he'd just gave, his skin was warm and smooth just the way I remembered it, with little give over the hard muscles underneath. I leaned in closer, unable to stop myself from inhaling a lungful of the spice of his skin.

It was just like my dream and so, so much better than any dream could ever be. All sensations were sharper, the images clearer—real. His presence took over my senses—the scent of him, the sensation of his naked skin under my palms, the feeling of safety and comfort brought on by his large body next to me.

Clinging to him, I followed his lead and hoped that my feet could continue to move on their own somehow since my brain couldn't focus on anything but Ivarr at the moment.

I felt the small icy prickle under my palms on his chest—he never claimed to have good self-control. My impatient demon was greedily skimming every drop of my emotions off me, dipping in a little too deep. The sensation was not lasting. It didn't alarm me—I knew he would never harm me. The frosty nibbles disappeared as soon as they started, melting like snowflakes under sunrays.

The music softened to a background volume. The lights grew brighter. I blinked, realizing that this signaled the end of the show.

Everyone rose from their seats around the tables, cheering and clapping as the demons returned their dance partners to their seats. Soon, it was just the two of us left on the stage.

"Don't leave." He flexed his arms around me, holding me in a firm grip.

"That's my line." I smiled, referring to my begging him at the end of each dream.

"Wait for me in the lobby," he whispered hurriedly as more Incubi entered the stage from behind the curtains.

Dressed in whatever costumes they performed in last, the demons carried armfuls of bright red roses that they began to hand out to departing women. With a gracious bow and sometimes with a kiss on a woman's hand, each Incubus moved through the receding crowd, saying goodbyes and giving out roses.

"Kitty!" Coco waved our way. And I noted blushing Pam, who accepted a rose from the pale demon who kissed her neck as a stage vampire, Zander.

"Wait for me, please," Ivarr begged, helping me off the stage.

I nodded, not trusting my voice at this moment, and reluctantly let go of his hand.

"Oh, my God," Pam sighed and pressed the rose to her chest, seemingly oblivious to the prickly stem. "He is so dreamy."

"They all are," giggled Coco, taking a rose from an Incubus dressed like an angel with golden wings.

"Dreamy," I echoed. "More than you know . . ."

Someone handed me a rose, too, just before Mindy ushered us all to the exit. Moving along with the noisy crowd, I craned my neck, straining to catch another glimpse of my Viking, but all performers seemed to have been directed backstage at this point. As hard as I tried, I could no longer see him.

Chapter 36

IT WAS NOT AN EASY feat to convince Pam and Coco that I was fine being left behind in the lobby on my own. In the end, I had to confess that I met Ivarr once before and trusted him. I also promised to call Pam in an hour to prove I was still alive, before they finally agreed to leave me there.

After the three of them left and most of the show spectators had departed the lobby, a male employee approached me as I leaned against one of the several wide stone pillars in the venue.

"Are you Katherine?"

"Yes." I nodded, nervously clutching my ridiculously tiny evening purse to my chest.

"Follow me, please."

Without questioning, I did as he said, following him along a wide hallway behind a set of double doors and then along a corridor that seemed to be backstage.

"Where are we going?" I finally decided to ask.

"You got an invitation to one of the dressing rooms." He stopped in front of a plain white door and knocked briefly before opening it wide for me. "Here you go." He gestured for me to enter, staying in the hallway himself.

Carefully, I took a step in, and he closed the door behind me without saying another word.

The room appeared empty—white, with a rolling clothing rack against one wall. A large mirror, framed with lights, and a long countertop under it made it look exactly what I imagined a Vegas dressing room would be. Except that the counter was completely bare of any makeup boxes, wigs or fake eyelashes. No feather boas hang from the backs of the four chairs neatly pushed under the counter, either.

The faint sound of running water directed my attention to a door across from the mirror. The door opened, and Ivarr came in wiping his face and neck with a towel. He must have splashed some water on his bare torso, too, as the droplets of it glistened on his shoulders with a few running down his chest.

I swallowed hard, torn by so many emotions at the sight of him. Then the fierce desire to simply hold him in my arms pierced my heart, overpowering all the others.

"There you are," he exhaled gruffly, tossing the towel to the counter across the room and closing the distance between us in a few long strides.

The sheer force of his advancement made me step back, my shoulder blades flush to the door behind me.

His hands above my head, he leaned over me, surrounding me once again.

"Night after night I lay in my bed, waiting for you to summon me. Now, I can hardly believe that you are really here. In the flesh." He lowered his head, brushing his cheek against my hair, breathing me in. "You found me, my queen."

He slid his hands down and lifted me into his arms.

"Ivarr . . ." I whimpered and instantly wrapped my arms and legs around him, wishing I never had to let go. "What are you doing to me?"

"I'm taking you," he growled low, kissing the side of my face, my neck, my shoulder. "Right here, right now."

"No control . . ." I moaned, tilting my head to give him a better access to my neck and feeling my own control quickly evaporate under his kisses. He was here, and nothing else mattered.

"None," he agreed, his voice raspy and thick. "With you, I have none at all."

Sliding the zipper of my dress open, he tugged the fabric down to expose my breast then took the nipple between his lips, rolling it with his tongue.

A hot wave of need for him that I'd held in check until now finally burst through my defences, rolling over me in a powerful swell. I rocked against him and buried my fingers in his hair, relishing his touch.

Ivarr . . .

Hooking his thumbs in the thin elastic of my underwear, he yanked it down. I shook them off then and reached for the buckles of his massive fur-trimmed belt.

He helped me click the belt open, and it fell to the floor with a loud thud. I went immediately for the zipper of his pants.

My fingers trembled, as heat of arousal raged through me. I desperately wanted him closer to me, inside me, sooner, as if I still had to prove to myself that it was real.

His hands under my bare ass, he shifted me up and pressed my back to the door then gently cupped my breast, plucking my nipple with his fingers and increasing the electrifying heat spreading between my legs.

"I want you inside me, Ivarr," I whispered in his ear and wiggled my hips impatiently, rubbing myself against him, hot and slick.

Inside. As close as I could have him, without the haziness of a dream or hundreds of miles separating us.

"Give me a second, darling." He nuzzled my hair, letting go off my breast, and lowered his hand between us. "I don't want to hurt you, sweetheart." I felt his fingers part my folds and rocked my hips against his touch, seeking relief for the achy pressure between my legs.

"Soon," he gritted through his teeth, his jaw tensed with restraint as he forced himself to hold back while circling my opening, stretching me for him. "Soon, my sweet."

I curled my fingers into the silk of his hair at the back of his head, and buried my face in his neck, riding the waves of intense pleasure from his skillful touch.

More of him. I needed all of him at the moment, wishing I could feel him with all my senses at once. Parting my lips, I nibbled on his skin and gathered whatever droplets of water were still left on his shoulder with my tongue. I savored the faint salty spice of his taste along with the warm sensation of his skin under my palms and his scent in my nostrils, taking him in.

"I can't get enough of you," I breathed out. The pure joy of being here with him rippled through me. This was so much better than any dream could ever be.

"Katherine." He shifted me in his arms and took my mouth in a scorching kiss, then rocked his hips into me, finally sliding inside me. Inch by delightful inch.

I flexed my legs around him, desperate to hold on as he moved deliciously slowly at first. The sweet pressure between my thighs built up with every thrust of his body into mine.

He steadily increased his pace until he finally was driving into me with abandon, fast and hard.

I dug my fingers into the hard muscles of his shoulders, as a powerful swell of pleasure rolled through me, with the explosion of an orgasm. The heady force of it blinded me for a moment. Ivarr's low growl filtered through the thick cloud of bliss floating in my brain, as he pumped his release into me. A series of amazing ripples rushed me with every frantic spasm of his hips against mine.

My arms and legs locked around him in a death grip, I held on to him as our bodies rode the aftershock of our climax.

He leaned his forehead to mine.

"You are my breath of fresh air, my queen." The fire in his eyes cast a red glow on the tanned skin of his cheekbones. "Without you, every day is a struggle, like trying to breathe under water."

I cupped his face tenderly. My heart still raced against his chest and my legs felt as if filled with warm honey, but I willed my thoughts to get organized.

"We . . ." I said softly. "Can we talk?"

That was what we should have started with—a talk. I came here to have a conversation and ended up having frantic sex against the door before we managed to barely say a word to each other.

At the very least, I should let go of him now, yet my arms and legs refused to obey, wrapped around him as if fused together.

"Anything you want." He kissed my temple, gliding his hands all over my body in a caressing dance again—along my sides, up my arms to my throat, from my knee up to my hip . . .

A sudden loud knock on the door made me jump in his arms, and he cradled me to his chest before stepping away from the door.

"Ivarr?" someone called.

"Later," he bit out, but zipped up my dress and straightened my skirt.

"Now." The voice behind the door was not loud, but firm and commanding.

"Who is it?" I whispered.

"Grand Master." Ivarr frowned.

I immediately leaped off him, picked up my panties from the floor, and put them on quickly. I had no desire to see Raim whatsoever. However, if I had to face him, it was best to be fully clothed.

"Everyone is in the party room." The voice behind the door held a definite authority but lacked the steely note of arrogance I remembered in Raim's.

Besides, Ivarr's frown appeared to be one of mild annoyance. Not the expression I would expect him to have when facing the demon, who ordered his bones broken.

Unhurriedly, Ivarr zipped up his pants and picked up the belt off the floor then opened the door.

The man who entered the room was undoubtedly an Incubus, but it wasn't Raim.

His skin tone was deeper than Ivarr's tan, a rich shade of brown. Tall and handsome, he wore his dark mahogany hair tied back. Instead of white silk that Raim seemed to prefer, the newcomer's strong, solid frame was draped in a worn grey robe that had seen better times, possibly a century or so ago.

He didn't seem to be overly surprised to see me.

"Are you Ivarr's Mistress?" He tilted his head, an inquisitive glint in his eyes the colour of dark whiskey.

His attention on me, the demon reached back and produced a pair of grey leather gloves from the rope tied around his waist.

"She is," Ivarr replied for me, his voice gruff but not hostile. He put his arm around my shoulders and pressed me to his side. "Katherine, this is Andras, our new Grand Master."

"What happened to Raim?" I'd only just met Andras, but I definitely liked him more than the previous Grand Master. The glimmer of warmth in his eyes on me was vastly different from Raim's icy glare.

"Nice to meet you." With a courteous bow of his head, Andras offered me his gloved hand, and I shook it. "Raim renounced his position and left the Council."

"Just like that?" I furrowed my brow in disbelief. As little as I knew Raim, he gave the impression that he was rather fond of his position and the power it provided. As far as Raim could be fond of anything, of course. "When?"

"Last week," Ivarr replied.

I turned to him.

"He left the Council voluntarily? Why? Where did he go?"

Ivarr moved his gaze from my face to Andras's, as if deferring my questions to him.

"Ivarr told me you ran away from the Council?" Andras asked me, effectively putting an end to any further discussion about Raim.

Even though I didn't believe Raim had a solid reason to wish me harm, a feeling of unease rose inside me at the idea of him roaming the world freely.

"She didn't *run* from the base, she was abducted, I told you," Ivarr responded for me again, bringing me back from my worries about Raim.

"I'd like to hear the story from you, Katherine," Andras retorted coolly, without taking his attention from me.

"Now? I thought you ordered me to the party room." Ivarr leveled a heavy glare on Andras.

The Grand Master's gaze flickered his way. He exhaled in visible displeasure but conceded.

"I can wait. Would you join us for the after party, Katherine?"

"I..." I hesitated. "I probably should be going soon." I felt Ivarr's arm tighten around me. "I was just hoping to talk to Ivarr before I went."

"You're not leaving." Ivarr turned to face me, both hands on my shoulders. His features hardened as he searched my face.

I closed my eyes to hide from the intensity in his.

"Well, maybe you could spare a few minutes?" Andras insisted politely. "Just long enough to meet everyone? Ever since Ivarr told us about you last week, we have all been waiting anxiously to meet you."

"Is that why you've been lurking at my door?" Ivarr muttered under his breath.

"You knew I was coming?" I asked Andras incredulously.

"No. That was indeed a lucky coincidence. For the past few days, we've been researching ways to get in touch with you, without jeopardizing the fragile new status quo we have achieved with humans recently." He narrowed his eyes at Ivarr. "I'm afraid I had to uphold the threat of Inferno that Raim placed on Ivarr to prevent him from rushing to search for you, potentially derailing our progress."

"Raim threatened to send you to Inferno if you came to see me?"

"For a hundred years." He nodded. "To make sure you'd be dead by the time I was released."

That was how they'd forced the rebel in him to obey, using me as the bargaining chip.

"That is low, even for him." I turned to Andras again. "Why would Raim want to keep us apart, though? And why exactly would you, the new Grand Master, try to get in touch with me? Just to make it clear here, I'm not going back to the basement." Deep inside, I didn't believe that was the purpose of Andras being here but added the last sentence just in case.

"Of course not, Katherine. We are trying to move away from all that, as you can see." He gestured at Ivarr's stage costume—the armlets and the belt in his hand. "We're searching for harmless ways to obtain our nourishment."

"Why did it take you this long?" The question came out rather gruffly. Personally, I had survived my incarceration, and I'd been working successfully on putting any lingering aftereffects of it behind me. But I never forgot about the many women who weren't as lucky.

Andras's chest rose with a sigh, a gloomy expression settled over his face.

"There are many reasons why that order of things prevailed for this long. Some of them seem to be tied with Raim, but the connections are still unclear. I will gladly explain what we have discovered so far if you care to stay in the city a little longer to have this conversation." He tilted his head, giving me a chance to reply, but I remained quiet, unable to give him any promises at the moment.

Ivarr had stepped aside to pick up a white t-shirt draped over the clothing rack. Tossing the t-shirt over his shoulder, he walked back to us, unbuckling the wide armlets from around his biceps.

"You can't leave, Katherine. And if you do, I'll go with you. Whatever it is that causes that dark twister of worries churning inside you . . ." He circled his finger in the air, illustrating the way my emotions apparently moved within me, "is not going to stop me. We'll work it out," he promised, reaching for me.

Ignoring Andras, Ivarr drew me in for a kiss. I leaned into him, really wishing to believe that everything could be worked out somehow.

"Well?" Andras waited patiently until the end of our kiss before clearing his throat. "The party then. Shall we?" He opened the door and ushered us out even as Ivarr was still pulling his t-shirt over his head. "My wife is eager to meet you."

"Your wife?" I stared at Andras, flabbergasted, certain that I must have heard him wrong.

He just smiled and proceeded down the corridor, leading the way.

Chapter 37

THE AFTER PARTY WAS held in a large conference room in the hotel connected to the venue. I'd never been to a party after a show. Some of them might be loud and vibrant, I imagined. However, the atmosphere in the room where Andras took us was far from it.

With the dimmed lights, the candles on the several round tables supplied a warm glow to the space. Several couches and armchairs were casually arranged into sitting areas. And soft music played in the background.

A few dozen men, some of them I recognized from the show, sat on the couches and around the tables. I noted with curiosity a handful of women among them. A few hors d'oeuvre and dessert platters stood on the tables along with sparkling water and bottles of wine. Some men held a glass in their hands. However, the women were the only ones who nibbled on food.

A man rose from the couch and headed our way as soon as we entered. I recognized him as the performer who took Pam to the stage. He still had his long, black coat on, but he had put a black t-shirt underneath it now.

"Zander." He stretched his hand my way as soon as he approached us.

Ivarr's grip on my hand tightened and he stepped forward, shielding me with his shoulder from the demon in front of us.

With a quick glance at the offered hand to make sure his gloves were on, I snuck my arm around Ivarr to accept Zander's handshake.

"Kitty. Nice to meet you," I said, since Ivarr remained silent, with only a glare for a greeting.

As courteous as other men seemed to be to me, the Incubi didn't appear to have good manners with each other.

"Will your friend be joining us, too?" Zander bent forward in a bow, lifting my hand to his lips for a kiss.

"No." Quicker than lightning, Ivarr covered my hand with his, way before Zander's lips had a chance to touch my skin.

"My apologies if I offended you, Kitty," Zander addressed me, without sparing a glance for Ivarr. "I was simply being polite—I can see you've been claimed." He straightened, letting go of my hand. "My only intention was to enquire about your friend."

"Pam? She won't be coming tonight."

"That's a shame," Zander said softly.

His expression of crushed disappointment prompted me to ask, "Did you hope to see her again?"

"No. I had no hope until I saw you. Perhaps . . ." His eyes of dark agate met mine. "Perhaps, you could pass a message to her from me? If you deem it appropriate, of course."

I found the formal way he expressed himself rather endearing. It gave him, and our whole conversation, a slightly old-fashioned air, making me fight the urge to dip into a curtsy or do something equally archaic.

"If you share your intentions in regard to Pam," I started cautiously, "I would definitely consider passing your message."

His gaze slid off my face for a moment, as he seemed to focus intently.

"I may not be able to fully explain it. But I sensed some longing in her, beyond the usual . . . um, arousal in reaction to my kisses. I found the taste of it extremely intriguing. Alluring." His dark eyes flashed in the candlelight of the room when he returned his gaze to mine and added in a low voice, "I want more."

The blatant directness of his request blew away any sense of politeness, baring his intense hunger for my friend—the poor unsuspecting Pam.

Should I subject her to the temptation and hidden danger of the world of demons by connecting her with Zander? Did I have the right to stand in their way by refusing to do it?

After all, the same hungry expression in Ivarr's gaze directed at me didn't scare but excited me. What if there was a future for Zander and Pam?

"I'll think about it," I promised the dark-eyed demon, who stared at me expectantly. At my words, he exhaled with a visible relief.

"Thank you." He bowed his head. "*Pam*," he said slowly, as if savoring the name on his tongue, and glanced my way before departing. "Is it short for Pamela?"

I nodded.

"Beautiful," he murmured, going back to his seat.

"What do you think?" I turned to Ivarr.

"Bizarre." He shook his head.

"What? Why?"

"I've never seen Zander express interest in anyone. And this is the most I've ever heard him say."

Yet something in Pam's emotions had sparked Zander's interest.

What makes a woman special for an Incubus? What was that longing Zander mentioned?

I had more questions to ask, but others had noticed our arrival by now. Several people waved in greeting in our direction. Andras, who had stepped away during my conversation with Zander, was now standing next to one of the tables in the middle of the room.

"Come, I want you to meet someone." Ivarr tugged at my hand, leading me in that direction.

Three of the five women present in the room sat at the table in the company of two Incubi. Both demons rose from their seats as we approached and bowed their heads in greeting.

"Good evening, Kitty," one of them called my name before anyone had a chance to introduce me.

My eyes snapped wide open with a stab of surprise at the sound of his voice. Although the tone had much more life in it now, I still recognized its even cadence.

"Garrett!"

A wide smile spread across his face, lighting his coffee-bean-coloured eyes with humour. It was because of those eyes that I'd always imagined him dark-haired under his helmet. However, his hair turned out to be flaxen blond. In the fashion, seemed to be preferred by many Incubi, Garrett wore it long.

"You've met?" Ivarr tilted his head.

I wondered how potentially awkward it would've been, had Garrett actually got a chance to perform his duties as a Handler during my incarceration.

However, Incubi seemed to count a true connection as a sign of intimacy, not whatever mindless stimulation was performed on me during the Council's nightly feedings. Since I failed to form any connection with either one of my Handlers, my time on the cross didn't seem to count as being intimate at all.

That was exactly the way I preferred to look at it myself.

"You know her?" Ivarr directed his question to Garrett this time.

"I had the honour to be Kitty's Handler at the base." Garrett leaned across the table to shake my hand.

"Then you were there when she swas drugged and abducted?"

"I was in the building that night, yes." Garrett's expression darkened. "I'm so sorry, Kitty, I have no idea what happened or who took you. I spent the night by Simone's door." He gestured at the petit, dark-skinned woman who sat at the table at his right.

"Simone?" I'd only seen her from the back before. The image of the tiny figure curled up on the mattress on the floor came to mind.

"Nice to meet you, Kitty." She flicked the mass of glossy ebony braids behind her shoulder and offered me her hand.

"Allow me to introduce everyone else here." Andras moved to my side. "This is my wife, Natasha." He gestured at a tall woman with strawberry blond hair gathered in a bun.

"Hello." I shook her hand, staring at the woman who was married to a demon, the Grand Master. How did it work? I was dying to know but held back my questions—my ogling her could be considered rude enough.

Natasha smiled.

"I am very happy to meet you," she said with a strong accent. "Ivarr told us about you a few days ago. He said you woke him up. A very dangerous thing to do. I am so glad everything turned out okay and you are well."

I nodded, but Andras moved around the table continuing the introductions before I could reply.

"This is Alyssa." He pointed at the woman with a light-blonde braid. Her sitting at the table didn't disguise the fact that she was heavily pregnant. "Alyssa came to the base two days after you were taken."

"As a Source?" I asked, remembering that the kidnappings were supposedly stopped by then already.

"No," she replied with a rueful smile. "Not *that* time."

"Alyssa used to be a Source, less than a year ago, but she escaped."

"You did?" I spent so much time figuring out a way to get out of there myself, wondering if it was possible at all. Apparently, someone had actually done it.

"Well, Sytrius rescued me." She took the hand of the Incubus standing next to her as her expression melted into that of utter adoration.

"Sytrius?" My gaze moved between him and Ivarr, gauging the reaction of both.

"Finally, I get to meet the woman who helped to keep Ivarr put." Sytrius said brightly, shaking my hand, his blue eyes sparkled with humour behind a strand of sandy-blond hair that fell across his forehead. "I spent centuries chasing him all over the globe. But the threat of never seeing you again kept him firmly in place for the last few months."

This took away any doubts I might have had—it was the same Sytrius who arrested Ivarr, more than once. And now here they were, sitting at the same table with no hard feelings apparently. I wondered if living lives as long as theirs made holding grudges useless.

"I—I'm so sorry we took your truck," I blurted out the first thing that came to my mind as the reply.

"Well." Sytrius laughed. "I took his car first. And I honestly have no idea where it is right now."

"Please join us." Alyssa gestured at the two empty seats at the table.

Ivarr moved a chair back for me then sat between Simone and I.

I glanced around the room again. Besides the three women I'd just met, there were only two more present at the party.

One of them I recognized from the show. She was the one who blew kisses at Lucius on stage. Now she sat in his lap on the couch, animatedly talking to another young woman sitting next to them.

Then two men on the couch across from them caught my attention.

One of them had all the characteristics of an Incubus. Tall and muscular, he had a soulful expression on his beautiful face. The other, however, seemed human. Even though he was young and definitely attractive, he just didn't have that out-of-this-world appeal that I came to expect from Incubi.

"Is he from The Priory?" I leaned into Ivarr.

"Who?" He followed my gaze. "Braden? No. He is with Radimir. They met about two months ago, when Braden came to see the show, and they have been inseparable ever since."

Only now I noticed their hands clasped together between them.

"They're planning on getting married this summer," Sytrius added casually from his seat at my right.

"So marriages between humans and Incubi are allowed now?"

Andras called Natasha his wife. And the ring I spotted on Alyssa's finger, combined with her pregnant belly, led me to believe that she and Sytrius must have been married too.

"Well, marriage with a demon is more of an afterthought, really." Alyssa laughed. "The true connection happens first. And once it does, there is no going back. With the union already formed, it's up to couples whether or not they want to go ahead with a ceremony."

Natasha stirred in her seat.

"Andras simply asked me one fine morning if I wanted to be with him for the rest of our lives. When I said yes, he put the ring on my finger, and told me I am his." With a wide smile, she showed me the gold wedding band on her right ring finger. "I am from Belarus," she added. "We wear the wedding ring on the right hand."

"Can I get you some wine?" Ivarr whispered in my ear.

"Please." I nodded, feeling a little overwhelmed at finding myself in the company of happily mated demons all of a sudden.

My phone rang the moment Ivarr left for the small bar in the corner of the room. I glanced at Pam's number on the screen and excused myself from the table to take her call.

"It's been over an hour!" She yelled in my ear accusingly the moment I picked it up. "Please tell me you're still alive."

"I'm still alive."

"Thank God! Why aren't you calling me? You promised!"

"I'm so sorry, Pam. I was just invited to the after party, and there are so many people here, I got a little distracted. I was going to call you—"

"The after party?"

"Yes. Kind of. It's rather quiet here. Casual—"

"Are all those guys there?" A note of curiosity cut through her voice. "I mean the dancers."

"Um. Not sure about *all*, but many are."

"Okay."

She paused, and I could almost hear the wheels turning inside her head.

Still unsure if it was at all responsible of me to involve Pam in this world, I glanced back to the table. The sight of the women glowing with happiness at their demons' side was reassuring.

"Zander is here," I said.

"Really?" Pam exclaimed, her voice breathless. "You got to meet him?"

"I did."

"How is he? In real life, I mean."

"Charmingly old-fashioned and . . ." I sighed. "Very hungry."

"Hungry?"

"Pam, we need to have a long talk when I get back."

"What do you mean? Did he say anything about me? Do you think you could, maybe, ask for his number for me? Please? Or give him mine?"

"He wants more than your number."

"He does?"

"Yes. He pretty much said so."

"Oh, my God." The excited squeak at the end of her statement clued me in that Pam would not have minded more herself. Except that she couldn't truly comprehend what *more* meant for Zander.

"I'll really have to talk to you about all of this."

"Oh, my God," she repeated.

"Pam?"

"Yeah. I'm still here. When are you coming back?"

I caught a glance of Ivarr walking back to the table, a glass of wine for me and one with whiskey for him. I still needed to talk to him too.

"Um, not sure. Later tonight. In any case, Pam, you don't need to worry," I assured her with an absolute certainty. "I'm safe."

Chapter 38

ONE GLASS OF WINE LATER, I sat at the table, leaning into Ivarr. Somehow during the time it took me to finish the wine, our chairs ended up flush with each other, and his arm draped casually around me, my head on his bicep.

"One more?" He tipped his chin at my empty glass, his eyes twinkling bright blue.

"You just want to get the buzz from my drinking." I giggled. He'd explained earlier that the only way for an Incubus to get intoxicated was to consume a significant amount of emotions from a drunken human.

"I already have all the buzz I need from your simply being here. I'll get you some more." He kissed my hair and got up, heading to the bar.

"I don't believe I heard him say a word in the weeks I've known him." Simone leaned my way. "It's amazing how happy he looks with you around."

I followed Ivarr with my gaze, hating to see him depart even for a minute.

She shifted in her chair, and only now I noted the small bump of her belly.

"You're expecting, too?" My gaze moved to Garrett's beaming face.

"We are," they both said in unison then laughed at each other, impossibly adorable together like this.

"You have a good eye. I'm only three months and just started to show anything at all." She patted her stomach with obvious pride.

"Congratulations," I offered sincerely.

"Thank you. The doctor assures me all is going well, but I'll never stop worrying until I hold a healthy happy baby in my arms." A dark cloud moved over her face next. "I, um, I've lost a child once. Stillbirth."

"I'm so sorry," I gasped.

She nodded, acknowledging my condolences.

"It was the worst experience of my life. By far."

Garrett hugged her shoulders and kissed her temple. By the way her expression settled to that of calmness I wondered if he had taken some of the pain from her at that moment.

"The grief is forever with you." Simone sighed. "But the fear of another loss doesn't stop my hope." She glanced at Garrett with a warm smile. "In any case, I know that Garrett will be at my side, no matter what. This knowledge gives me strength." Her gaze shifted back to me. "The father of my first baby left me a week after we had the stillbirth."

"He did?"

"We had problems in our marriage, even before I got pregnant, but that was the last nail in the coffin of our relationship."

I winced inside. Granted, I didn't know Simone well, but the loss of both the baby and the husband within a week couldn't be easy on anyone. "How did you manage?"

"Not very well." She fiddled with a napkin in her lap for a few moments. "Really, I had no idea how to go on. I just gave up. Got fired for not showing up for work. Then just stayed in bed, all day every day."

"When did they abduct you?"

"Honestly, I'm not even sure. I don't think my kidnapping even registered with me for a while. Everything from that time is just one long, foggy nightmare in my memories. First the hospital. Then my empty apartment. The cell in the basement. Then the white room with a cross . . ."

She swallowed hard and took a sip of water from her glass.

"After a while, though, I started noticing Garrett. His touch during the Feeding was the only thing that made me *feel*. Good or bad, it didn't even matter at that time. What was important was that I felt something beyond the crushing agony of loss and loneliness. And I began viewing the Feedings as a reprieve, a break in the dark clouds constantly hanging over my head otherwise.

"When they told me I was free to go. I had no idea where. It was really sad and somewhat pathetic that out of everywhere in the world, I felt most at home in that prison cell in the basement. I realized only much later why it felt that way. It was because I knew that Garrett was nearby."

She covered his gloved hand with hers.

I was certain neither of the married demons at our table performed in the show tonight. Still, all of them wore gloves. Assuming they all could control their touch with their wives, just like Ivarr did with me, I suspected they wore the gloves out of respect for the women of other demons.

The way Ivarr reacted when Zander almost kissed my hand clued me in that touching another demon's woman skin-to-skin must be considered offensive to her or to her partner or both.

"He told me you wouldn't see him."

"No," Simone agreed with a tiny smile. "I even asked for someone else to bring me meals. I believe I detested my perceived growing dependency on his presence. But he didn't really leave. Every night I lay in bed, waiting for the echo of his footsteps down the corridor outside of my cell, then for the sound of his back sliding down my door as he took his seat on the floor. Only then I could fall asleep, knowing that he was there to guard me. Then one night, I wished he were closer. I didn't know he could walk through walls then, so I requested to leave my door open after dinner that night. When Garrett came, I asked him to hold me while I slept."

Simone gazed up at her demon, her eyes glistening from reliving the emotions of her story.

"He's been doing it ever since." She smiled at him. "Every night, he holds me in his arms while I fall asleep."

"What made you know Simone was the one?" I asked Garrett.

But he just shook his head.

"I'm not sure," he finally replied. "I knew she needed *me,* no one else. Despite the armour suit, the recognition sparked inside her every time she saw me. I loved seeing that spark. Still do. Only now it's no longer just a spark, more like a raging storm of fire." He gazed upon his woman with an expression of pride and satisfaction. "My Simone's fierce love for me."

"Is that what ignites a demon's interest in any particular woman? Recognition?"

Silent, Garrett kneaded his forehead, as if pondering my question.

"Recognition, affection, gratitude, sympathy," Alyssa replied instead of him, joining our conversation. "For each couple it's different. But I've been noticing that any positive emotion can trigger interest in an Incubus, as long as the woman who experiences it feels it specifically for him. She needs to glimpse the man in the sex demon, the real person behind his enticing appearance." She waved her hand in front of Sytrius's handsome face to illustrate the *enticing appearance* she was talking about.

He just chuckled in response.

Ivarr returned, putting a glass of wine in front of me along with a plate piled high with cheese, fruit, and desserts.

"Sexual desire in humans is a normal reaction to Incubi," Ivarr joined the conversation, taking his place at my side again. "We want it, we crave it, we feed off it. Human lust is our bread and butter. But it's that special flavour of personal affection that makes someone irresistible."

He drew me to him and placed a tender kiss on my lips, in front of everyone, generous with his own affection for me.

Breathless from his kiss, I blinked and quickly took a sip of wine, hiding my heated face. The women at the table might have guessed the way Ivarr made me feel, but I was certain their men would see clearly the flare of arousal his kiss ignited in me.

Ivarr brushed his bare hand across mine, and the sensation of a slight dusting of frost calmed both my nerves and my hormones at once.

"Incubi are eager to learn," Alyssa stated with firm belief in her voice. "They have been feeding on human emotions for centuries, absorbing the very essence of our minds and hearts. They've learned from what they've taken. There is no other explanation for the humanity I've found in so many of them. Turned out they can learn to love, too." With a smile, she leaned into Sytrius.

"Is a human-demon bond forever?" I asked her. "You said once it forms, there is no going back..."

"To my knowledge, there is no magical mating bond that binds us together," she replied. "But I don't want to through life without Sytrius, and I see no way to separate us. We are one. I am a part of him just as much as he is a part of me now. And I wouldn't want it to change. Ever."

I nibbled on the grapes and cheese from the plate that Ivarr brought, contemplating what I learned from everyone tonight.

Meanwhile, the conversation turned to a different topic, flowing casually around me. Surprisingly comfortable among the couples that united two worlds. I almost felt like I belonged here.

Almost.

"Should we go?" Ivarr stroked my bare shoulder after a while.

"Um, where?" I snapped from my thoughts.

"You said you needed to talk. And I really hope it has something to do with that recurring cloud of worries that keeps gathering inside you. I don't want to see it any longer. Tell me what it is, and I'll make it go away."

Could it really be that simple?

"Where can we talk?" I turned around. The crowd didn't seem to get any smaller, since we came. If anything, it only got livelier and more excited as the time passed. People and demons moved around the room, talking and laughing.

"My place." Ivarr got up and tugged at my hand, urging me to follow.

IT TOOK US A FEW MINUTES to say our goodbyes.

"I would like to ask you a few questions in regard to your abduction from the base, Kitty," Andras said to me before we left. He seemed to have switched to calling me *Kitty*, like everyone else, leaving *Katherine* for Ivarr's exclusive use. "I'll stop by Ivarr's suite after breakfast tomorrow morning if you don't mind."

"Um. I'm not sure I'll stay until then," I mumbled, feeling my cheeks flare up at his assumption that I would spend the night.

Ivarr's hand squeezed mine tighter.

"Do you have to be anywhere else tomorrow morning?" he asked.

My flight back to Seattle didn't leave until late afternoon, but that was not the point here, was it?

"No, but—"

"Then you are staying," he replied, his voice as firm as his grip on my hand. He turned to Andras. "See you then."

Andras moved his gaze from Ivarr to me.

"See you tomorrow, Kitty. And thank you very much for coming out here tonight. It was wonderful to meet the woman who captured Ivarr's unruly heart."

Chapter 39

"YOU DON'T STAY IN THE same hotel?" I asked, hurrying next to Ivarr across the road to a hotel nearby.

"No. I need my space." He shook his head. "The chances of someone knocking on my door for some stupid reason are lower when they know they'd need to cross the road to do so. This city is pretty crowded as it is. I don't need the aggravation of living in a hotel full of demons."

"Do you miss living on a farm?" I rubbed my arm with the hand not held by him. Nights in Vegas turned out to be rather chilly in January, especially for me in my silk sleeveless dress.

"I never really *lived* there when awake." He let go of my hand and wrapped his arm around my shoulders instead, drawing me into his side for warmth. The cold didn't seem to bother him much even though he wore only a t-shirt. Grateful, I leaned into him. "I needed to live among people to feed. The farmhouse was isolated enough for me not to be disturbed during Deep Sleep. Well, in theory, anyway." He smiled, glancing my way.

I grinned back at him. Waking him up nearly took my life and ended up costing me my heart. Yet, I was certain I'd do it all over again.

"If you prefer to live in a big city, we should find a house somewhere outside downtown to avoid the crowds," he announced as we entered the lobby.

"Ivarr . . ."

"Okay fine. A penthouse at least? With its own elevator?" He glowered at the small crowd that rushed the open elevator doors.

With his arm still around my shoulder, he literally carried me inside the elevator, parting the crowd with his broad chest, then out of it in the same manner when we stopped on his floor.

"Alright, what is it, Katherine?" He spun me by my shoulders to face him as soon as we entered his suite. "The more I talk about us living together, the darker your emotions become. I can see you love me—"

"What?" I croaked, choking on the word.

"You may not recognize your own emotions for what they are yet, but I know how love looks. For years I fed on a woman's love for another man. And this right here—what you have inside you—is all my own. I'm not giving you up."

"You—you don't even know me that well. We hardly had any time together."

"I *see* all of you, remember?"

He took a step back and searched my eyes.

"Katherine, to me, it's obvious, but do *you* need more time to sort it all out? What bothers you? Tell me, and I'll get rid of it."

The only light in the room came from outside the window and from a small desk lamp in the living area. With my back to the front door, his figure was backlit, and his face remained in the shadow. I couldn't see his expression clearly, but I sensed the sincere conviction and passion in his words.

"How important is for an Incubus . . . No. For *you*, personally, to become one of the Forgiven?" I finally managed to ask.

"Forgiveness is everything. For me, it would mean freedom from pain and hunger and a chance to live a meaningful life side by side with the woman I care about. You."

His grip on my shoulders relaxed, and he stroked my skin with his thumbs.

"What if you never got the forgiveness?" I swallowed hard, as my throat tightened.

"That would simply mean I needed to learn to love you more," he said softly. "Since I know for sure you love me already, failing to earn forgiveness would be my own fault. In which case," he stepped closer to me and brushed his lips along my temple. "I'll need to spend more time one on one with you. In real life, not in a dream." Lowering his head, he placed another kiss, this time right behind my ear. "I'll have to study all your emotions carefully. Taste them." He nibbled on the skin of my neck. "Savor every moment, every ounce of you to learn how to love you the best I ever could." He leaned back, a happy glimmer in his eyes. "I'm looking forward to it."

Struggling against the longing his words and kisses evoked in me, I closed my eyes, as if it would make it hurt less.

"I can't give you what you need, Ivarr." My biggest fear was not that he would reject me—the passion with which he spoke left no doubts about his commitment already.

I feared that in order to do the right thing, I would have to find a way to leave him myself, and I was afraid I didn't have it in me.

"Whatever do you mean, Katherine?" His voice sounded hollow.

"The accident that took my parents . . . I was in the car, too." I drew in some air, completely running out of oxygen with every word I said. "A steel rod speared my stomach . . ."

Silent, he slid his hands behind me, enclosing me in a hug.

"I can't get pregnant, Ivarr. It's not a hormonal imbalance or anything like that . . . I simply don't have the parts needed to carry a baby. There is no chance. Absolutely none."

With my last words the gates that held the sorrow in check inside me opened, and the black, icy tide swallowed me whole. I trembled in his arms, my chest swelled with tears, but they couldn't find their way out yet.

"Katherine." He swayed with me in his arms, rocking us side to side. His large body enveloped me like a cocoon, shielding me from the rest of the world. But even his embrace was powerless to protect me from the pain this time.

"The right thing would be for you to let me go now." I closed my eyes tightly, my forehead pressed to his chest, and forced the words out. "And for me to leave."

"No," he dismissed in a tone disallowing any doubts, then lifted me in his arms.

"They say there is no bond. There is not one woman destined for each Incubus." I called on whatever reason and cold logic I still possessed. "Now that you're allowed to socialize more openly, you'll have a chance to find someone else . . ."

"There is no one else, my queen," he replied firmly. "Only you."

He carried me into the bathroom, turned the water on in the tub then sat on the edge, holding me in his lap.

"I don't care what they say, never did. And unless it's with you, I don't care about the forgiveness, either."

"How would it work then?" The images of pregnant bellies in the party room rose in my mind. "How can we be together?"

"Tell me how we can be apart, Katherine?" His voice rose. "Now that I finally have you here, how am I supposed to let you go?"

I inhaled a shaky breath. In my mind I knew he had the right to have it all, even what I couldn't give him. Instead of watching me age and die for the next few decades, he should be out there searching for the right woman for him.

But if he expected me to talk him out of being with me now, I couldn't. My confession took all I had. With no more strength left, I had no willpower to pry my arms from around him on my own. I did what I could to do the right thing. Now someone needed to physically tear me away from him.

"You'll never earn your forgiveness with me," was all I said in a quiet whisper, barely audible behind the sound of the running water.

"As long as I can be with you, I don't care about anything else." He cupped my face, shifting me in his lap to see my eyes. "Katherine, sweetheart. There are some differences from couple to couple, but a pregnancy seems to be a consequence of the forgiveness, not a reason for it. Only a mortal can father a child. So, I believe an Incubus can impregnate his woman only *after* he has earned his mortality. A woman's love must be what grants him the forgiveness in the first place. That and his ability to love her back."

"Are you sure?" I searched through my memories for everything I'd heard about it and remembered the information about pregnancy came from Delilah. She seemed to have a solid knowledge about Incubi despite her biased opinion about them. Still, could she have been mistaken here, especially if his woman's pregnancy was the first physical sign of a demon's forgiveness, the most obvious one, too.

"So, without a pregnancy, how would one even know he's been forgiven?" I asked quietly, afraid to believe anything yet.

He shrugged and shook his head.

"I'm not sure. When his woman stops aging?"

"That may take years to become apparent."

"Then all I'd have to do is to be careful not to die during those years." A hint of humour twinkled in his eyes. "Maybe, be a little more cautious in a fight, just in case I've become mortal already."

"Or stay out of a fight altogether?" I offered, my voice still raw with unshed tears, but a spark of hope already shredded the overwhelming darkness inside me to pieces.

"Staying entirely out of trouble may not be possible right away. Century-old habits are not easily broken."

His tone was lighter now, but his eyes flickered between mine intently. Peering deep inside me, he was watching my emotions closely.

"Katherine, what you told me tonight is heart-breaking. I'm so sorry you had to go through it." He smoothed the hair out of my face and brushed his lips against mine in a light, tender kiss, like the flutter of butterfly wings. "But it's not the end of life, and it's definitely not the end of us."

"You'll never be a father."

"There are many ways to be a parent, without actually giving birth to a child." He pressed me to his chest again, stroking my back gently. "I'm sure your aunt would agree with me on this one."

"She would," I whispered. "I was the daughter she never had."

My lips trembled, and the first tear finally slipped down my cheek.

"We'll figure it all out in time, my queen," he said softly, unzipping my dress. "Together." He rubbed the bare skin of my back soothingly. "But right now, I'm going to give you a bath. This conversation has wrecked you." He wiped the stray tear from my cheek then slid the dress down my shoulders.

I cupped the side of his face, sinking my fingers in his beard.

"My dear Viking." I blinked another tear out of my eye, as a sense of deep gratitude for him filled my heart along with another, much stronger emotion. "I love you, Ivarr."

"I know. And I'll never get enough of it." He leaned in to kiss my face, my neck, my shoulder then brushed his lips along the scar on my right arm. "I'm forever grateful to whatever fate led you to that desolate house of mine that day."

HE GAVE ME A BATH. Gently washing my hair and scrubbing every inch of my body, he cleansed every single dark stain from my soul, filling me with light again.

Afterwards, he wrapped me in a fluffy, white towel and carried me to bed. Then he held me in his arms while I fell asleep. And he was there when I woke up the next morning.

"I could get used to this," I murmured, pressing my nose to the t-shirt stretched over his chest.

"Good," he chuckled. "Because that's how I intend to spend every night from now on."

"No more disappearing when I wake up?" I smiled.

"Never." He found my mouth with his.

I melted into his kiss, which turned more urgent the longer it lasted. He slipped his tongue between my lips, and I greeted him eagerly sliding mine along it.

My hardened nipples brushed against his chest, making me aware of my complete nudity. A series of electrifying ripples ran along my skin.

"I need to get you breakfast," he rasped, letting go of my mouth for a moment. A rim of red already edged the brilliant blue of his irises.

"No," I protested, wrapping my leg around his thigh. "You're getting *your* breakfast first."

Without saying another word, he kissed me again then cupped my backside, bringing our lower bodies together.

Needing to feel him against me, I tore at the bottom of his shirt, tugging it up to yank it over his head.

"Come here." I wrapped my arms around him.

With a low rumble deep in his throat, he rolled us over and leaned over me. I felt his bare hand on my breast, his fingers rolling my nipple. A shot of intense heat dashed through me, and I lifted my hips to him.

"I need you, Ivarr."

"I know, sweetheart."

Unbuckling his belt with one hand, he trailed short, hot kisses down my neck to my chest. Squeezing my breast gently, he sucked the nipple into his mouth, grazing it with his teeth.

"Oh . . . God," I panted as the need pooled between my legs, building up quickly. "Now, please," I begged, shoving his pants down his hips with the heel of my foot.

"Just one taste," he pleaded, sliding down my body. He peppered soft kisses along the sensitive skin of my inner thigh. Then I felt the heat of his tongue glide over my folds.

With a moan ripped through my chest, I bucked my hips, as his lips moved along my sensitive flesh, sucking, tugging and driving me mad with lust.

"Now," he murmured against my skin, then positioned himself over me again.

I felt his hard length slide inside me, inch by delicious inch, slowly stretching me until I took it all.

The side of his face pressed to my temple, one arm propped on the pillow next to me, another hand kneading my breast as the speed of his thrusts inside me increased, taking me higher and higher with him.

"I love you," he breathed out the moment the rolling waves of pleasure collided inside me in a mind-blowing climax. "I *know* I do, my queen." He groaned with his own release as his body shuddered against mine.

A faint echo of past panic prompted me to tighten my arms around him and flex my thigh muscles, trapping his hips, "Don't leave."

"Never." He collapsed at my side and buried his face in my hair. "I'm all yours now. In soul *and* body."

Chapter 40

REALITY FELT MORE LIKE a dream that morning. Except that my demon didn't disappear.

This was a dream I would never have to wake up from.

I was perfectly happy to spend the rest of the morning and the rest of my life with Ivarr in bed, but the ring of the hotel phone eventually put an end to that for now.

With one last kiss on my lips, Ivarr cursed under his breath and got out of bed.

"Must be Andras." He took the phone, stretching to his full impressive height, which gave me the chance to admire him in all his naked glory backlit by the morning sun from the window.

Finally, tearing my gaze away from him, I used the moment while he talked on the phone to text Pam. At this point, I was fairly certain I would need to postpone my afternoon flight back to Seattle, but I had to get together with her beforehand to explain as much as I could about Ivarr and I.

"He is on his way up," Ivarr announced, getting dressed. "He can be rather annoying in his persistence."

"Um," I searched around for my dress. "Where did my clothes go?

"I left your dress out for dry-cleaning last night. Here . . ." He walked over to his closet and took out a gorgeous mid-length gown in a delicate shade of lavender. "I've waited to see you in this."

"What is it?" I gasped at the beauty of the colour.

"A dress." He shrugged, laying it out on the bed next to me.

"No, I mean . . ." I fingered the rich silk. "You have expensive tastes."

"I like exquisite things." He kissed the top of my head. "I saw it in the window of a shop and thought how it would bring the purple and lavender in your eyes."

"I don't think I have any lavender in my eyes. They're grey with some green, mostly."

"Sure you do." He propped himself with a knee on the mattress next to me. "Lavender, magenta, turquoise, sea foam, ginger, auburn and coral . . . I see all the colours of the world in there."

He stared into my eyes, and I realized he was describing every happy emotion I felt inside me.

A wide smile spread on my face as my insides melted into a soft-butter puddle.

He kissed the tip of my nose. "I see them all and love all of them. But red is still my favourite." He winked at me with a wicked smile that heated my face.

"Get dressed," he ordered, as the knock on the door came. "Let's not give Andras to see more than he should."

ANDRAS DIDN'T COME alone. Sytrius came with him.

"Come in," I invited them into the room as soon as Ivarr opened the door. The heart-shaped amulet around my neck would not have let them enter otherwise. I had it in my pocket for the show last night, but put it back on shortly after.

"For you, Kitty." With a friendly wink, Sytrius handed me a bag and a paper cup of coffee. "I wasn't sure if Ivarr would have the time to get breakfast for you."

"Thank you." I accepted his offering with a quick glance at Ivarr, who just rolled his eyes and shook his head. "Would you like anything?" I felt obligated to ask, even as I had no idea what the suite's kitchenette had to offer.

"Nothing for me, thank you." Andras moved a chair from the table and gestured for me to sit down. Ivarr stepped to my right.

"I'll just get some water." Sytrius moved to the sink in the kitchenette and grabbed a glass from the cabinet.

"Sytrius and I were a team in the Army. Long ago," Andras explained, taking a seat across from me.

I remembered Ivarr mentioning something about it once.

"Are all of you split in teams?"

"Most of us were back then. Ever since we came to Earth, Incubi moved in pairs whenever there was a chance of encountering humans."

"Like the Retrieval Teams still do now?"

"Right." Sytrius took a seat at the table, too, placing his glass of water in front of him. "For the simple reason to watch out for each other. If one of the team lost control, the other one could always intervene and possibly prevent a murder."

"So, killing humans was not desirable back then?"

"It never has been." Andras joined in. "We don't know for sure how this rule and many others came to be, but I have my theories. Even though Incubi were created with a raging hunger for human energy, difficult to control, there seems to be a protective streak in all of us. Deep inside, no one wants humans dead. On the contrary, human fragility entreats us to protect them from harm. I believe this quality is left from the times we were angels, before we fell to become demons. Severe starvation deprives us of any rational thinking and even hinders our basic instincts. However, the more we remember, the stronger this trait becomes."

"How about Raim, then? I understand he is responsible for most, if not for all the murders at the Western Council Base, isn't he? He's been the Grand Master forever."

"This is what we've been trying to solve here." Andras rubbed his forehead. "When starved, neither one of us were a match for Raim. Only now, we are able to attempt untangling his way of thinking to understand his actions."

"Why is he not like the rest of you? What happened to his *protective instincts*?" I didn't even try to keep the sarcasm out of my voice.

"He left before we had a chance to ask him any questions," Sytrius replied, regret thick in his voice. "Andras had a chance to stop him—"

"Raim renounced his power, fair and square," Andras argued. "His only request was to be left alone when he walked off the base. I had no right to detain him—we have no case against him."

"He should have answered for his crimes," Sytrius muttered under his breath. The way he said it led me believe that it must not be the first time they'd had this argument.

"Technically, Raim committed no crime," Andras pointed out. "Whatever he did, he always strictly adhered to the rules—"

"Yes, to the ones that he himself created," Sytrius interrupted.

"Not true. Every point of the treaty came from humans and was signed by them."

"How can you know for sure?"

"I've talked to every single Incubus who served on the Council then. They all negotiated the terms of the treaty, together."

"But they weren't there when the treaty was signed. No one was, except for Raim."

"Sytrius, it's irrelevant. If the treaty was laid out already and every point of it agreed upon, what difference does it make who signed it?"

"Then why would he go in alone?"

With an exasperated sigh, Andras dropped his shoulders, as it became apparent the argument had come full circle.

An observation I made while watching them arguing prompted me to ask, "Has Raim ever fought in the Army? Who was his partner? The other part of the team I mean."

There seemed to be a comfortable understanding between Andras and Sytrius. Despite them having an argument—or maybe the way they led it—it was obvious how easily they could read each other. I wondered if this camaraderie stemmed from all the time they had spent together, fighting side by side.

"If Raim had a partner, could you talk to him? He might be able to give you a better understanding of Raim's past. Right?"

"Raim's partner has been dead for over two centuries," Andras replied grimly.

"Dead?" I frowned, for it made no sense. "An immortal demon?"

"His name was Gremory. And he was the first known Forgiven, Kitty."

"What the hell?" The power in Ivarr's exclamation startled me. "There was another Forgiven? Before him?" He tipped his chin Sytrius's way. "And no one ever heard of him?"

"I have seen the records of him but only had a vague recollection of it and no name until very recently. With the return of my memories, I remembered his name and more of his story."

"Did you know him in person, Andras?" I asked.

"Yes, I met him a few times. Gremory was his demon name. Back then not many of us took human ones. Only when more people learned how to summon us, we started to hide behind human monikers, keeping our true ones a secret. Some of us do a better job concealing it than others." He shot a mocking glance at Sytrius, who leaned back and crossed his arms over his chest with a challenge in his expression.

Unexpectedly, Ivarr burst into hearty laughter, and I moved my curious gaze from one demon to another, feeling like I hadn't been let in on some inside joke.

"Adding two letters to your name, hides nothing, you doofus," Ivarr roared in laughter as Andras sat there with a wide smile on his face.

Not dignifying either one of them with an answer, Sytrius turned to me.

"My demon name is Sytry. I trust you not to use it against me, Kitty." His calm, friendly expression told me he didn't consider me a threat in earnest, still I shook my head energetically.

"Of course not."

"I added the two letters over a millennium ago, to make it sound more human," he explained. "It's a miracle I came up with anything at all, considering the foggy state of mind I was in back then."

"And now?" Ivarr tilted his head.

"Now, this is the name *she* calls me. And that's the one I'll keep," Sytrius replied firmly, putting a stop to their teasing.

"To be fair, the use of human names has become rather unnecessary," Andras conceded. "Hardly anyone knows the proper ritual to summon a demon nowadays. There hasn't been any true attempts for over a hundred years."

"Well, obviously, Raim hasn't considered it a threat at all," I pointed out. "Since he's never changed his name, has he?"

"Another thing I'm working to understand," Andras muttered.

"What happened to Gremory?" I reminded.

"Right." He returned to his story. "Back in the tenth century, there was just one Incubi Council, in the territory of what is now called the Middle East. But the Incubi were spread much more than they are now. With all of us awake and with no treaty to restrict us, we moved around freely, spreading into Europe, Africa and Asia.

"Raim and Gremory left together, but months later only Raim returned, just in time for an election process for the position of the Grand Master. It was before I served on the Council. Back then I worked at the base, taking care of the archives. Raim had been a long-term Council member, but this was the first time he put in his candidacy for the Grand Master and won. When asked about Gremory, he claimed they had been separated.

"A few months later, Raim left the base in search of Gremory. When he came back, we added to the archives what he told us about him. Raim said that Gremory lived in a relationship with a human woman. Even though it was still hundreds of years before the treaty, pairing up with humans in a long-term relationship was not allowed. It is always potentially dangerous for a human to be one on one with a hungry Incubus. Some women ended up being drained in the early times. That's what set up our wars and prosecutions in the first place.

"Gremory was deemed to have broken the unwritten rules and ordered to be brought in for punishment. However, no one could find him. Over the centuries, Raim himself went searching for him several times, but always returned empty handed. He even moved the Council to Minsk, the place where he saw Gremory last, but no one saw or heard of him again.

"It was impossible for an Incubus to vanish without a trace like this. Normally, his impulsive feedings would cause a commotion in human settlements, leaving a path for a search party to follow. The stories of a demon with red eyes or reports of women having *impure* dreams would be the signs of an Incubus on the loose. But, as far as Gremory's disappearance went, we had nothing.

"Until about two hundred years ago, when Raim returned from one of his solo expeditions with the news of Gremory's death. Raim claimed to have witnessed his execution with his own eyes. Gremory and the woman he had lived with were burnt at the stake for sorcery by a group of overzealous humans. That's when we knew that Gremory had been forgiven and lost his immortality."

Andras leaned back in his chair.

"So, all reports about Gremory came from Raim. How do you know he was telling the truth?" I wondered out loud.

"We don't," Sytrius agreed. "Except that honesty would be the first impulse in any Incubus. I wouldn't put it past Raim to lie if it were in his interests to do so. All we have to go by here are his words. However, judging by what we know now, what he told us about being a Forgiven turned out to be true."

"Did he say anything about Gremory and his wife having any children?" I asked.

"No. We always knew that only mortals could father children. And Gremory was obviously a mortal. So, there may be some descendants out there."

"You didn't get a chance to question Raim about any of this before he left." I couldn't stop feeling regret about it. What Andras just told us only brought more questions, and with Raim gone, there didn't seem to be any way to find the answers now.

"He did say something before he left, though." Andras straightened up in his seat. "A warning."

I lifted my gaze to him in question.

"*Beware of the Priory. They are the ones with real power.*"

"But they're just humans," I exclaimed. "What gives them all this power?"

"I don't know, but I'll find out." Andras' voice held a firm promise. "Sooner or later I swear I will figure it out. This leads me to my questions for you, Kitty. What happened the night you were taken from the base?"

"Ivarr and I have figured it out—it was humans who abducted me that time." The seed of doubt about it planted by Delilah prompted me to add, "Although, I was later told that those might still be Incubi who'd wanted to frame humans. Confusing. I know."

"Can you just tell me the order of events? The way you remember them, please?"

I paused for a moment, thinking back to that night to give him as detailed an answer as possible.

"I only got a glimpse of one of them when I got back to my cell, but there were others. At least one more, maybe two. One held me from behind. Someone gave the order to give me the shot."

"The shot?"

"They drugged me." Mechanically, I lifted my hand to my neck. The marks from the injections had long gone, just the memory of them lingered. "Repeatedly over time, to keep me under while they transported me, I believe. That's why I figure they were humans. Demons would've just touched my skin, right?"

"You said they wore our uniforms."

"The one I saw in my cell did. The two who had me in the car wore suits. No masks, but I didn't see their faces, only the back of their heads. And their suits . . . They were regular, every-day suits. Similar to the one worn by Keller—"

I cut myself short, thinking back to the voice hissing the order, *'Give her the shot.'*

"It was him, ordering the other person to drug me," I said slowly as the certainty of this realization spread through my mind. "Steffen Keller."

"The monk?" Andras frowned.

"He said he held an official position with The Priory. Is he a monk, too?"

"The organization has religious roots. All members of The Priory of Grimien used to be monks. Some still call themselves that. Are you sure Steffen Keller was in your cell on the night of your abduction?"

I nodded, as conviction settled firmly in my heart.

"Yes. He whispered, so it was hard for me to recognize him right away, but now that I think about it, the intonations and the accent were undeniably his."

Andras leaned back in his chair and folded his arms across his chest.

"Was Keller one of the two men who were in the car with you when you came to?"

"No. I only saw them from the back, but I heard them clearly. Neither of them was Keller."

"What did they say?"

"I don't know. They spoke German and were of a smaller build than you guys."

He nodded with an expression of concern and deep concentration.

"Delilah assured me I was in no danger from returning back home and living my life now. She told me The Priory would protect me."

"Who told you that?"

"Delilah Neri. She was the one who drove me home after Raim and the others caught up with us. She said she doesn't work for The Priory but she wanted to help them in their efforts to control the Incubi."

"I've heard about her from Alyssa," Sytrius interjected. "She's been a part of the effort to help the freed women to recover."

"Have you met her?"

"No. Alyssa hasn't, either. Apparently, Delilah never came to the base."

"She never would," I said. "Delilah doesn't trust Incubi. She shared some family history with me—she believes that Incubi abducted her baby brother years ago."

"That makes no sense." Sytrius shook his head, a frown of disbelief crossing his handsome features.

"In all of our history, Incubi have never preyed on children," Andras stated firmly.

"Delilah thinks it was done to influence her father, who held a high-power position with The Priory before his death."

"I have a hard time believing this." Andras's frown deepened. "In all my time at the Eastern Council Base I never saw or heard of children being held there. Have you?" He turned to Sytrius.

"No. Never," he replied with conviction.

"My time at the base was rather brief whenever I happened to be there," Ivarr added. "But I never heard of anything like that, either."

"Delilah, um . . ." My hand still at my neck, I slid my finger along the silk cord of my pendant. "She has an amulet, made from the same stone like mine."

"*Soros* stone?" Andras asked quickly.

"Are you sure?" Ivarr's eyebrows lifted in obvious surprise.

I nodded.

"I saw it light up when she came close to Raim. She said her brother had one, too. They both got it from their father."

"The one, who was the member of The Priory." Sytrius exchanged a look with Andras.

"I'll add it to my list of things to investigate," Andras moved his gaze from me to Ivarr. "Meanwhile, I would advise you both to stay close to Vegas, whatever you do."

"Um . . ." I stared at him. Ivarr and I never got a chance to discuss the future yet. "I have a job in Seattle."

"We'll talk about it, sweetheart." Ivarr put his arm around my waist and drew me into his side, kissing my hair. "There is no reason why you can't keep your job if that's what you want."

Well, not if he intended to continue his dancing career in Vegas. Did he want to continue with that? I had no idea.

He was right, we needed to talk.

Andras got up from his seat.

"Well, thank you for answering my questions, Kitty." He shook my hand.

"I hope it helped. Sorry, it wasn't much." I then shook Sytrius's hand, too. Thank you for breakfast."

My phone buzzed at that moment.

Pam.

I quickly excused myself and walked into the bedroom to take her call, leaving the door slightly ajar.

"Ivarr." I heard from the living room before I had a chance to accept Pam's call. Something in Andras's voice when he said Ivarr's name made me pause and hit '*decline*' on my phone instead.

"Don't move out of Vegas yet."

"Well that's up to Katherine and I to decide, isn't it?" Ivarr's tone remained light, but the somberness in Andras's voice made my heart skip.

"It wasn't all Raim said when he left. His full statement was '*Beware of The Priory. They are the ones with real power. No one with Incubi blood in them is safe.*' I want all of us to stay together for now. The European tour of *Demon Army* has been cancelled, and I'm meeting with Vadim to see if the Eastern Council can combine their base with ours until we find out everything there is about this."

"Like I said. It's up to Katherine and I to decide." Ivarr's voice was quiet, but the note of defiance still rang through it. "I'm not afraid of anything Raim had to say."

"Don't you understand? None of us would be that worried if the threat was meant for Incubi alone. The real concern here is what it means for our women. If Kitty gets pregnant, she'll carry a baby of Incubi blood, which puts her in danger, too—not just you."

The phone buzzed in my hand again, and I quickly typed a message for Pam that I'd call her later then sat on the bed, the phone clutched to my chest.

Of course, Ivarr wouldn't be afraid for me in this case. With no chance of me getting pregnant, I was in no danger here.

But how about him?

"THERE IS NO POINT IN living in fear, Katherine," Ivarr replied to my worried questions when the two men left, and it was just the two of us in his suite again. He stood in the doorway of the bedroom as I sat on the bed. "You have a job you love in Seattle. And you can keep it if that's what you want. I don't care where we live, as long as we're together."

"Well, I'm good at my job. Doesn't mean I love it that much. Definitely not enough to risk your life over it. Besides, how about your job here?"

"The show? It's just a means to feed, not a job in the traditional sense of the word. Now that I have you, I don't intend to go back."

"Is that why Lucius quit, too?"

"Lucius? Yes, he's met Shanayah. There is no point for mated Incubi to continue with the show, and there are more than enough unmated ones to keep it running."

"How do you support yourselves if you're not working?"

"Katherine." He smiled. "I have enough money to last us a lifetime, no matter how long our lives will be. All Incubi have enough wealth accumulated to never worry about working for money. The show is only for feeding, nothing else. Any revenue money that's left after paying the production cost goes to various charities. We keep nothing for ourselves."

He came over and sank to his knees in front of me, bringing his face level with mine.

"You and I, we can go anywhere, live in any place you want, do whatever you wish. You're my queen. Just say the word."

"I don't want to be a queen without a king." I smiled and dipped my fingers into his beard to cup his face. "What Andras said really scared me. Let's stay here for a little while. At least until things get sorted out. If we leave, I'll be forever worried about you."

Not that I wouldn't worry about him here. But being close to other Incubi felt a little more comforting right now. I believed that it would be easier to get any updates from Andras if I got to see him on regular basis.

"Besides," I added. "I'd like to get to know all the demons' wives better. Now that I'm going to be one of them."

A bright expression of delight spread on Ivarr's handsome face.

"Can I call you *my wife* now?" He circled my waist with his arms, shifting me closer.

"If you ask me to be one." I smiled, a giddy feeling of happiness dousing all my worries for the time being.

"Will you be my wife, Katherine? In sickness and in health? For as long as we both might live? May it be a few centuries or longer."

"Yes, Ivarr." I slid my hands to the back of his head, bringing his face even closer, his lips just a whisper away from my kiss. "I'll be delighted to be your wife, my Viking."

EPILOGUE

HE SWEPT THE NEIGHBOURHOOD with a quick glance, making sure there was no one watching him. Although the house he and Katherine chose was at the end of a very quiet street, well hidden behind a curve of the road, the old habit of always watching over his shoulder for prying eyes kicked in before he lifted the double-door fridge and effortlessly carried it inside the house.

The fridge came with free delivery. But after watching the two humans who delivered it huff and puff, straining themselves to un-load it from the truck, he gave them their tip and sent them on their way.

It made little sense to watch them struggle with that thing all the way up the front porch steps and then across the main floor to the kitchen in the back, possibly dropping it on the way or damaging the walls in the process. He could do it himself in a fraction of the time and with much less effort.

"Hi, honey," Katherine greeted him the kitchen, her lovely face flushed from the heat of the oven she had open.

"The fridge is here," he announced, carefully setting it near its spot at the wall.

"I see that, my Hercules." She smiled, blowing a strand of hair from her face. "If you've kicked the delivery guys out already, you'll have to connect it all by yourself now, too."

"Piece of cake." He got a couple of tools he kept in the kitchen drawer out and sat on the floor next to the fridge, ripping the plastic and Styrofoam packaging from it. "Speaking of cakes. It smells nice in here."

"I'm trying one of Andras's recipes." She took the cake dish from the oven and sat it on the countertop of the kitchen island. "Again," she sighed.

"Don't you try to compete with that demon," Ivarr chuckled. "He has centuries of experience."

"According to you, I now have centuries ahead of me, too. And I'm intending to use at least some of this time to beat him." She laughed.

He had nothing to prove to her that he was one of the Forgiven now. Physically, he didn't feel any different, except that the constant gnawing of torturous hunger had completely gone.

Other than that, he still was inordinately strong, could walk through walls and locked doors, and entered her dreams freely. Now that she was near him, he delighted enjoying her in every way, in dreams as much as in reality.

It would take years before her lasting youth would confirm it, but he felt certain of his forgiveness even without that confirmation. The powerful love he felt for her with all of his being gave him the absolute certainty. For centuries, he knew its taste and its appearance. He longed to have a woman experience it for him, and he never even dared to hope he'd feel it himself one day.

Until her. His Katherine.

The strength of his love for her thrilled and astounded him, giving him the absolute certainty that no other feeling could ever be as powerful.

"Well," she said slowly, critically eyeing the cake on the counter. "This looks good. Definitely better than the last time." She huffed another sigh. "Let's just hope it tastes as good as his. Honestly, if I didn't know Andras better, I'd swear he intentionally left out some important part of the recipe, just to mess with me."

"It smells amazing, sweetheart." He didn't care for the cake, or for any human food for that matter, but the small blush of pleasure at his words inside her immediately looked enticing.

Holding up the tool he had just used to connect the water line to the fridge, he paused, giving her an appreciative once over.

Katherine wore her usual simple clothes, a pair of denim shorts and a loose grey t-shirt. The bright splash of colour came from her frilly apron, printed with large, red strawberries. He smiled to himself, thinking about all the things he'd do to her, to make that shy little blush inside of her turn the same scarlet colour of raging passion as the berries on her apron.

She intercepted his hungry stare.

"Don't you look at me like that, mister." She waved her hand at him. "I still need to ice this cake. And you have to put that fridge in place."

Without taking his eyes off her, he plugged the fridge into the outlet and dropped the tools back into the kitchen drawer on his way up from the floor. "Done." He gave the fridge a small shove with his foot, sliding it in its spot between the cabinets, then sauntered over to her.

"Really, Ivarr . . ." She leaned with her back to the island, hands pressed to the counter on each side of her hips. "I have to make sure this cake is good. I want to bake it for dessert for dinner on Sunday. Pam is really looking forward to coming over for a visit."

There was no way of knowing if Pam had allowed Zander to enter her dreams yet. But everyone knew that they talked on the phone daily for last several weeks since the show. This was Pam's first visit to Vegas since then, and it was obvious Zander was beside himself with anticipation and excitement at finally seeing her again.

"I'm looking forward to Pam's visit, too," he huffed a laugh. "Maybe then she'd take Zander out of his misery. He's getting rather irritating in his pining after her."

As much as Ivarr was ready to move anywhere with Katherine, he had to admit he was happy staying in Vegas with her for now.

Somehow, over the centuries, he realized that Sytrius had become a close friend to him and living in proximity with other demons was as close to an extended family as he could ever give to Katherine. Seeing her building friendships with Alyssa and the other women filled his heart with gratitude and sense of belonging.

This month was the due date for Alyssa's baby. And as much as everyone was excited, there was a definite worry about having a human-Incubus child brought into the world.

Cambion was what humans used to call offspring that a demon-human union might produce. Although all prenatal tests came back fine, the concern about what the baby would actually be was clearly there.

Right this very moment, though, Ivarr didn't want to think about any of this. His focus was firmly on that tiny little spark of blush inside his Katherine.

His hands firmly planted on the counter on each side of her, he leaned over, inhaling her sweet scent mixed with the warm smell of her baking.

"I really need to ice this cake," she whispered, even as the spark inside her flared into a bright tendril of anticipation.

"Don't you need to let the cake cool off first?" He slid the tip of his finger up her arm, watching the bright orange and pink wisps of her pleasure curl in its wake.

"I guess so . . ." She tilted back her head, and he noted her pulse flutter under the delicate skin on her neck.

Whatever control he had left him that very second, as often happened with her around. A low growl rumbled in his throat as he lifted her onto the counter, shoving the cake aside.

"Show me all the mesmerizing colours you can feel, my Mistress."

Grand Master

CHAPTER 1

(Warning: Unedited and subject to change)

Clutching the window curtain in my sweaty hand, I stared at the dark street outside. The sole streetlight in front of my apartment building was broken. Again. And the only illumination came from some distant storefronts and from other lit windows around.

All lights in my apartment were off on purpose. It's not like *they* could see me here, on the seventh floor, hiding behind the curtain. I was fairly sure, they wouldn't even look up, expecting me to be ready and downstairs within minutes as soon as their black car with tinted window pulled over at the entrance of my building. Still, standing openly in front of a brightly lit window would make me feel too exposed and even more vulnerable than I already did.

Nobody is forcing you to go ahead with this.

I inhaled, attempting to calm my nerves that tied my stomach into a quivering mess.

It was true. No one made me stand here, wearing a tight black dress and a pair of hooker heels, waiting for a black vehicle to arrive and take me some place unknown to entertain a group of men I'd never met.

No one was forcing me, except for my insatiable appetite for adventure that my mom lamented would be responsible for my untimely demise one day.

Maybe this was the day she so often talked about?

As the youngest of five children and the only girl, I grew up spoiled, I admit it. But having four older brothers made me want to keep up with them in everything or die trying. Whatever sports any one of them played, I had to play too. And I needed to excel in them, no matter what it took—from scraped knees to broken bones.

Always chasing another adrenaline rush as I teenager, I'd tried every extreme I could—skydiving, bungee jumping, swimming with sharks, and surfing off the coast of Australia. I grew up fearless.

Dreaming of becoming a spy one day, I diligently learned Russian language from middle school and all the way through university. Never in a million years would I have guessed that by the age of thirty, I would end up having an ordinary office job in an international communication company.

Granted, my position was with their office in Minsk, Belarus—still far and fairly exotic for someone born and raised in a small town in Australia. And even though no actual spying was expected from me, my duties as a Communications Manager included organizing local events and socializing with people of many backgrounds from pop stars to government officials and local business moguls.

During one of such events—a party at a nightclub with a number of clients and politicians—I stepped outside to get some fresh air.

The mentality of Belorussian officials on sexual harassment was not quiet on the same level as that of the western world. I often found that I had to educate them on the proper work-place etiquette on case-by-case basis. *The education* was even more necessary at the parties like this, where alcohol was involved.

After batting off the advances of yet another middle-aged asshole in power, I simply needed a break, and leaned against the restaurant's wall outside a few feet away from a young woman smoking a cigarette.

Everyone seemed to smoke in this country—that wasn't what brought my attention to her. Neither was it her outfit of short skirt and mile-high heels or the way she glanced up and down the street, scanning every single passing car. She looked and acted like a prostitute waiting for a client, which wasn't unusual for this place or time.

What made me watch her with more than curiosity was the obvious signs of extreme nervousness. Her trembling fingers all but crushed the cigarette with every long inhale she took.

Despite the mild spring evening, she rubbed her upper arms through her cheap pleather jacket as if chasing the chills away, and her knees shook every time she shifted from foot to foot. I didn't think she was drunk or stoned, but she swayed in her stiletto boots, as if she was about to pass out any minute.

"*S vami vse v poryadke?*/ Is everything okay with you?" I asked her in Russian, fully expecting to get no response beyond maybe a suspicious glare.

She didn't appear to be in a mood for a friendly chat. Besides, I've learned early on that people preferred to keep to themselves in this part of the world, not being particularly keen on conversations with strangers.

She swore under her breath and indeed threw a glare my way at first. Then as if thinking of something, she turned my way.

"Listen. I'm really scared here." She threw the unfinished cigarette down and crushed it with her foot, only to get another one from her purse immediately after.

"Do you need a ride home? I can get you a cab," I offered.

She shook her head so energetically, it appeared to be in danger to fall off.

"No fucking way. I could never say *no* to the kind of money they're paying."

"Is it enough to risk you life over it?" I didn't need to know the details to guess that whatever she was up to might be rather dangerous.

She attempted to light the cigarette and failed—her fingers shook too much and her body vibrated with a sad nervous laugh.

"My life isn't worth much."

Without thinking, I reached over to move a strand of bleached blonde hair away from the lighter, lest she set herself on fire. She jerked her head away from my touch. Her eyes narrowed at me.

"Who are you? Are you a tourist, you speak with an accent."

"My name is Jade." I decided against getting into too many details about myself. "I'm here with the party." I tipped my head towards the restaurant door behind us.

"Are you from England?"

"No. Australia." I changed the subject back to her. "I'll pay for the cab to take you home."

She shook her head again and tossed the unlit cigarette back in her clutch purse then pulled the cellphone out of it instead.

"Can I get your phone number?" She asked out of the blue.

"What for?" I frowned, taken aback from her unexpected request.

"Here," she shoved the phone with the picture of a somber teenager in my face. "This is my sister. Her name is Sveta. If I don't call you tomorrow morning, could you let her know that I won't be coming home?"

The harsh realty of life was often more brutal in some parts of the world than in others. There was no solution, no one quick way to change it. The grim determination with which this girl seemed to have accepted the fact that she might not make it through the night was soul-crushing. Yet, I knew that if I were able to talk her into going home right now, she'd be out here again the very next night.

"Should I call *the militsya* instead maybe?" I asked.

"What's the point? They'd do nothing."

Sadly, there was a good chance she might be correct on that one. The local law enforcement seemed to be rather selective in their response. Besides, she sounded as someone who spoke from experience.

"So, you didn't tell your sister were you went?"

"No. She is thirteen. The less she knows the better. Besides, she wouldn't have let me go if she knew." She stepped from foot to foot and anxiously glanced down the street again. "They're here." Her eyes widened at the sight of the black car turning from around the corner. "Copy her number."

Hurriedly, she shoved her phone my way again, and I quickly punched in the numbers from her screen into my phone as the car approached.

"So, what's *your* phone number, Jade?" She asked, stuffing her phone back inside her shiny clutch.

I told her just as the car pulled over in front of us and the back door opened as if on its own.

Hesitantly, she took a few steps towards it. Her shoulders hunched, she ventured a nervous peek inside the darkness of the open door then threw a quick glance over her shoulder at me.

"My name is Tanya," she said quietly before getting inside the car.

The door closed almost immediately, and the vehicle drove off into the night.

My phone still in my hand, I quickly took a picture of its licence plate. I desperately hoped for Tanya's call the next morning. But no matter what was about to happen to her, I vowed she would get justice, even if she didn't believe that her life was worth it.

COMING SPRING/SUMMER 2019

More By Marina Simcoe

<u>*Demons Series*</u>
Demon Mine
The Forgotten
Grand Master – 2019

<u>*Standalones Set in Demons Universe*</u>
The Real Thing
To Love A Monster

<u>*Valos of Sonhadra*</u>
Enduring

About the Author

MARINA SIMCOE LIKES to write larger-than-life love stories with characters, who may or may not be entirely human, because she firmly believes that our contemporary world could always use a little bit of the extraordinary.

She has lots of fun exploring how her out-of-this-world characters with their own beliefs, values, and aspirations fit into our everyday life.

She lives in Canada with her very own sexy demon, their three little angels and a cat, who might be The Lucifer himself.

For more illustrations of all of her books please visit Marina Simcoe Author page on Facebook or www.marinasimcoe.com.

Please Stay in Touch

Newsletter signup: http://eepurl.com/c__RGn
www.marinasimcoe.com
www.facebook.com/MarinaSimcoeAuthor/
www.amazon.com/author/marinasimcoe
www.bookbub.com/profile/marina-simcoe
www.goodreads.com/MarinaSimcoe